CU⟮...⟯

A

PSYCHO

Cupid's a Psycho
By J.M. Gale

© J.M. Gale

ISBN: 9781912092185

First published in 2022
by Arkbound Foundation (Publishers)

Arkbound is a social enterprise that aims to promote social inclusion, community development and artistic talent. It sponsors publications by disadvantaged authors and covers issues that engage wider social concerns. Arkbound fully embraces sustainability and environmental protection. It endeavours to use material that is renewable, recyclable or sourced from sustainable forest.

Arkbound
Rogart Street Campus
4 Rogart Street
Glasgow, G40 2AA

www.arkbound.com

CUPID'S

A

PSYCHO

J. M. GALE

ACKNOWLEDGEMENTS

With thanks to the venerable Valerie Lynch who read the earliest scraps – and laughed at the rude bits. Thanks to Isabel Arjona Peña who read the whole damn thing when it desperately needed a polish. A final thank you to Victoria Hazael for the encouragement that softened her wise criticism.

And of course to Jamie, Elsie and Rosie at Arkbound.

CHAPTER 1

Classes converged across the hall. Fully grown in full school uniform, the pupils were unaware of moving as one. Neither were they aware of the extent to which they thought as one; after almost five years at secondary school, the future beyond was looming. There was a collective wistfulness for a time beyond worry, when the doubters had been proved wrong and success had been achieved. There was also the quiet fear that this might never happen.

The soundscape filtered through the swing doors, taking with it the squeak of shoes against linoleum. Blithe stood alone at the centre of a long corridor. Slack-jawed and sluggish, she had been the last to emerge. Her narrowed eyes, defined with black, powdery eyeliner, watched the vanishing figures, as though she knew them too well. She was pleased that she was watching them, rather than the other way round.

The voices and footsteps continued elsewhere; banging and echoing through the building. Blithe let her school bag slip from one shoulder and swung it round to her front. Her bag was faux leather in dyed patches of primary colour, a little too small for her needs. She fished around at the bottom until she produced a tiny tangerine. Her thin lips tightened. She punctured the skin with an angry jab from her index finger and peeled the skin away to reveal chalky shrivelled fruit. She sighed, looked up and down the corridor, and made her way to the bin by the stairwell. She passed a window and stopped to lean against its narrow frame while her brown eyes scanned the grounds below.

She watched from the second floor as pupils made their way to the canteen for their morning break. She noticed that a boy in her year, Robbie Mazani, had been stopped by a third year. Though Robbie was two years older, he was smaller. As he smiled resignedly and pushed past, the boy smacked him across the head. Robbie turned.

Blithe extended her arm through the window's narrow opening and lobbed the tangerine as hard as she could. Not taking precise aim, she didn't expect it to hit its target. Her hand was firmly over her mouth as the tangerine bounced off the third year's head. She retreated from the window for a second, ducking her head and grinning with childish glee. She saw no reason to hide and slammed herself right back against the window, laughing loudly. The third year tried to lock eyes with her, but this only made her laugh harder. Gradually, she slipped from view, sliding down the glass.

Robbie looked up at her with a steady gaze, which her moving eyes met just before she disappeared from sight. He smiled. Robbie was a wholesome looking boy with olive skin and wavy black hair, whose fading puppy fat made him look about twelve. He was almost seventeen.

The following day, he sought Blithe out to say thank you. Her eyes lit up and, though she tried to sound dismissive, her joy was apparent. He'd not tried to interact with her before. Until then she seemed always to stare stubbornly through sympathy and enquiry and, what little she did say, came out in a nasal mutter. For the first time he heard her voice clearly, without it sounding as though she had a cold.

A week later, as she tried to scurry through the school gates, Robbie tapped her casually on the shoulder. She was a little agitated at being stopped on her way home, but he persevered. "Do you want to go out... some time?"

Blithe looked around her, hesitated for a beat or two, and

simply responded, "Aye. Sure."

After they had exchanged numbers, she hurried away with a sinking feeling. This feeling returned days later, as she walked, hand in hand with Robbie, to his house after school. The spring in his step tugged at her arm.

"Do you think Trump will be president?" he asked at last.

She shook her head.

"I'm starting to think he might." Robbie continued. "He's the confirmed Republican nominee now."

She wrinkled up her nose. "Doesnae mean he'll get in."

"No. Weird though?"

This was familiar and pointless small talk, she sighed. "It'll just be the same shite coming from a pickled bawbag."

Robbie grinned. "No, he's worse. He's the Death Star of the pickled ballbags."

"I'm sure he is..."

"Misogynist too," he added earnestly.

"Aye but...it's probably nothing that I don't hear every day."

"Okay but leaders shouldn't come out with the stuff that he comes out with."

"Misogyny's not that shocking." She looked at him mischievously and smiled. "I'm not saying it's okay. I just don't trust politicians."

"Well, that's fine, but world leaders need to watch what they say." He squeezed her hand.

"May as well be honest." Blithe said. "These days everyone can tell when you're lying, so you may as well say what you think."

"But if the stakes were high..."

"See, that's exactly why I don't trust politicians."

Robbie smiled. "Very clever."

Blithe smiled back, but regretted accepting such patronising praise.

He led her to his house through the back alley. He revealed the hidden gate in his back garden, after nimbly scaling the fence and letting her in with a ceremonial flourish, as though its existence was a great secret now shared.

Robbie's home was a narrow, slightly gothic old house that smelt of ginger and polish. She was led into a boxy hallway that contained a bookshelf protruding too far into the available space. She didn't want to meet his parents but, moving through the house, she had the unsettling sense that their presence might be sprung on her.

The lounge was as dark as the hall. Beyond the two small windows, overgrown shrubs tackled what limited light would otherwise have come in from outside, matched by huge pot plants that deflected light from within. Bookshelves stood against every other wall; colourful rugs overlapped colourful rugs. The pristine TV was mounted high on the wall facing the sofa.

In the silence Robbie sat down beside her, put his arm around her shoulder and pulled her towards him. She wriggled free, looked up at him and once again could only smile awkwardly. As she tilted her face upward, he kissed her and, though she was unprepared, she closed her eyes as though it was what she wanted.

She smiled as she pulled away, feeling dampened to pulp as he stared at her with nothing to say, sure that her reticence was as sweet as his. Not at all; she wanted to shake the feeling off – it was constricting not knowing what to say or do. She took a deep breath and looked at him closely. He waited for affection to come back to him. It would not. Nice is nice but not enough.

He video called her at home after dinner. The connection on her laptop often cut out but he managed to make a few suggestions for their next date. She didn't want him to visit her in the tower block, and she didn't want to head into the centre of Glasgow, and so, a few days later she found herself, once again, making her way to his house. As she walked, it occurred to her that she was in no real hurry to reach her destination. Nerves had gathered and they contained an element of dread.

She wanted the nerves to go, she wanted to like him but once again, his embraces felt awkward and uncomfortable.

Later, on the pretext of making sure that she was safely home, Robbie Skyped her again. His cheerful round face beamed from the screen and Blithe relaxed. Safe from his touch, she found she liked him more.

"How's yer mum?" he asked.

"Aye, she's better, I think. We were out at the weekend and the battery on her scooter died. Halfway up the hill, loaded with bags and bags, she was stuck, like a fat duck brimming out of a pothole."

Robbie scoffed and then stopped himself before Blithe continued.

"So she gets out and starts pushing but in no time, she's getting looks. She's bent over, sweating, red, huffing and gnashing."

Blithe couldn't resist recreating the noise until Robbie, laughing, stopped her.

"That sounds like a dug humping!"

"Aye! Exactly! I couldnae let her go on making an arse of herself! I took over and I tell you, no wonder she was making that noise. It's fucking heavy! I was vowing to charge it up the drive and through the window of the guy that gave it to her – he's got a new one, the batteries last longer on the new ones. So, anyway, my mum was teetering on her wee feet, swaying around like a bowling pin, about to roll down the hill. Took us over an hour to get home."

"Bet that was embarrassing." Robbie added.

"Aye well. It is what it is."

Robbie was surprised by her stoicism but not necessarily impressed by it. If she had been embarrassed, he'd have known how to respond, but laughing at her mum, as she seemed to be inviting him to do, seemed disrespectful. Pity was worse.

Meanwhile, Blithe liked the girl she saw on screen. She liked the effect she had on Robbie and the confidence and natural ease with which she had made him laugh. As freeing as the video calls were, they did not make seeing him in the flesh any less awkward.

A month later, having never been able to relax in his arms, she dumped him.

Robbie hardly shone in the school hierarchy, but he was nonetheless acceptable as a boyfriend. Blithe, on the other hand, should have counted herself lucky just to have one. She was a surly nothing. Her dark eyes might sometimes divert from the ground, but whatever could be seen through the black hair barrier did not welcome attention, though she had no reason to hide her face. She had expressive dark eyes and a small mouth, often controlling a wry smile and pearlescent, slightly greasy skin. Her clothes were bobbly and her blacks washed away to grey. Her school slip-ons could barely cushion concrete and the thin soles frayed like damp cardboard. At school, the perception that she'd been punching above her weight was made abundantly clear as she was repeatedly asked, "*You* dumped *him*?"

No matter how many times she confirmed the truth, no matter how often she explained that she didn't want to talk about it, her hearers struggled to believe any of it.

Although dumping Robbie had been painful, in a few years, she might barely have recalled it. Instead, it became something that would haunt her.

CHAPTER 2

Blithe sat on her bed, reading from her broken laptop. Months ago, stumbling out of bed, she had trodden on the screen. The crack formed a bleeding cobweb of emerald lines, obscuring the top left of her screen. Most people would have thrown the laptop away. She had adapted to it.

Blithe suddenly squinted. In the bottom right of her screen a message popped up from Madeline Stephenson.

Maddie: Are you getting back together with Robbie?

She had never received anything from Maddie before, who had no business reaching out now. Though she had been at primary school with her, she did not know her well. They may as well have been magnetically repelled for seven years. She had noticed, even as a smallish child, that when Maddie fucked up, the class laughed with her. When Blithe fucked up, the class enjoyed it without her.

Blithe was mystified, but she was of a mind to be reached out to, appreciating that it took effort.

Though staring at a broken screen could induce migraines, it was the only way she could talk to friends online. Her phone was just a phone, a clumpy old thing that took blurry photos. Since her peers embraced smartphones and superior means of communication, she rarely received text messages.

Blithe: No.

Maddie: Do you want to?

Blithe: No.

Maddie: Why did you dump him?

Blithe: Really fucking clingy. He's a nice guy though.

Maddie: Was he wanting to get married like?

Blithe: Probably. I dunno. Disnae matter.

There was a knock on her bedroom door. Blithe scowled and did not reply. The door opened a fraction and a dark eye peered into the room. Once opened fully, Blithe's older brother Donnie stepped inside. He wore baggy blue tracksuit bottoms and a plain blue t-shirt, several sizes too big. His short black hair was a mixture of grease and residual gel. Blithe ignored him and watched the icon that indicated that Maddie was typing.

Maddie: Did he no take it well?

Blithe: Fuck No!

Maddie: Did you do it face to face?

Blithe: Skype. I watched it back. I was quick and brutal. He was right state though. Wasnae easy.

Maddie: Wee shame.

Donnie said her name. Blithe looked up from the screen, "What?"

"When's mum back?" He asked.

Blithe glanced up for a second, let her mouth hang open and shrugged.

Like Blithe, Donnie's eyebrows were like long black brushstrokes over his almond eyes. On Blithe, the effect was penetrating; on Donnie it was shifty.

"5.30 or 6," Blithe muttered, staring fixedly at her laptop screen and the messages coming through.

Maddie: You recorded it?

Blithe: Aye.

Maddie: Why?

Blithe: Because I could. No for revenge, it's like keeping a letter.

She glanced up at Donnie and narrowed her eyes. He didn't notice, too busy nipping at the loose skin around his nails. She did not trust him. Money went missing too often. When asked directly, he became defensive and protested that bit too much. Their mum's tablet had vanished and Blithe suspected, deep down that Donnie had either sold it or broken it; either way, she did not want him poking around in her room.

"I cannae find my stuff for work," he said. "I've no got a shirt ready."

"Go and see if she put it in ma wardrobe," Blithe mumbled.

Donnie stomped inside and looked with distaste at the school blazer that was once his, hanging over the wardrobe door. He yanked it open to a clatter of mainly empty hangers and heaps of fallen clothes dropped down into jumble. The room was cluttered, and a damp smell wafted from below the window. He hadn't been in there for a few days and noticed her new zombie poster, displaying a tower of bodies massed in a tangle like barbed wire. Blithe had requested the poster from a shop, knowing it was about to be chucked out. She wasn't afraid to go into shops and just ask, 'Can I have this?" Donnie had encouraged her to do that, 'You don't ask, you don't get'. Now that he was twenty, it didn't feel right to expect anything for free.

"Yer no borrowing anything of mine," she muttered.

Donnie tutted and left her room. Blithe pushed back the laptop screen as responses pinged in.

Maddie: Is Robbie okay now?

Blithe: Maybe. I hope so. He was properly sobbing, wanting to fix it. He wanted to talk about it, like we were married and had to hold it together.

Maddie: So how did you end it? Did ye just hang up?

Blithe: Tell you what, you watch it, maybe you'll want to go out with him.

Maddie: Are you really going to let me see it?

Blithe: It's big. Can you really be bothered?

Maddie: Aye.

Blithe: Can I be bothered?

Maddie: Do you not trust me?

Blithe: Because we've just had this conversation, obviously, I trust you. I widnae give it to you if I didn't.

Maddie: Awesome. Soz Bli ma wee darling. My mum wants me. I'll see you tomorrow. Xxx

Blithe did not trust Maddie particularly, nor was she desperate for her approval. It wasn't friendship she wanted; she yearned to share. She was celebrating and sharing indisputable proof of the person she could and would be. Evidence that she could not resist launching into the light of day. Blithe delayed slightly and, while the file compressed, she considered that the clip showed her at her best; strong and unsentimental.

At school, she sat in the middle of the road coasting along. Even at the end of the school year, some teachers still struggled to remember her name, though she was the only Blithe they taught. Her dad always needed to be reminded of her un-demanding existence, almost understandable given that she was the fifth of his six children.

She clicked send.

The message gone; a chill cracked open from the pit of her stomach.

She closed her laptop abruptly and began to bite her nails. She noticed an odour and followed the smell to uncover a dirty plate under her bed. She sprayed her body spray around until the fumes made her cough, then removed the plate from under her bed and took it to the kitchen. The kitchen stank, and she refused to stay there long enough to do the washing up. A key turned in the door. Blithe retreated to her bedroom to nurse her worries.

* * *

Blithe had known what would happen when she went to school. The first she knew of it came as a message that evening:

Elaine: You legend.

Elaine, who sat in Blithe's maths class, was kind but had a tendency to overshare. Her response worried Blithe, but she hoped the clip was being contained within a group. She messaged Madeline, asking her not to share. She received no reply.

She knew it had spread far and wide when she received a message from an almost-friend who was not particularly friendly with Madeline,

Daisy: Do you record all your conversations? How would you feel if someone did that to you?

Then it was Blithe who didn't reply. She thought about warning Robbie, to show him that this wasn't what she had wanted. He would want to kill her, but she would have done something at least. She prepared a text, 'I'm sorry', but standing alone, the words didn't seem genuine. When she read back her own apology, she imagined how it would be received; Robbie would hear her voice communicating nothing but a taunt, a prelude to a bastard of a surprise.

When her alarm went off the following morning, she was stoic as she got ready for school. She slurped her tea and nipped at her biscuits, her face stiff, her movements heavy and mechanical. She appeared unperturbed, even as she approached the school gates but, the closer she got, the faster her heart beat. No one called out for her company, which was fortunate, as her throat had dried up entirely. Even if they had, she might not have heard them over the sound of her pulse thudding in her ears.

Walking through the school halls, nothing was said but eyes were on and off her from all directions.

In Chemistry, she felt exposed. There were six benches, three on either side of the room and all were full apart from one, where Blithe sat alone.

As her teacher gathered up equipment, the butt of a pen prodded Blithe in the back. A shrill voice asked;

"Why did you share that?"

The girls behind her were harmless but she wouldn't turn to face them.

"Shut up," she hissed.

The pen prodded harder and she heard giggles. "Why did you film that?"

Blithe moved quickly, she turned, grabbed the pencil, snapped it in two and dropped the pieces, letting them roll under the bench. There was silence for a bit and then the voice repeated,

"Why did you post that?"

The laughter increased. Blithe spun round on her stool to face a row of smirking faces.

"I-did-NOT, post anything to anyone in this room. If it was sent to you, it shouldnae have been and you shouldnae watch it and if you prod me in the back again, I'll slap you."

As Blithe turned back to her bench she heard:

"I'm not the one who recorded it, don't get crabbit with me."

At break, Blithe hovered outside the toilets, taking quick little sips of water.

A boy in the year above suddenly stopped in his tracks and turned to her.

"Hey!"

Blithe met his eye and in that moment he recognised her and pointed. He smiled and announced for all to hear,

"Cunt!"

With that he went on his way. Glances were exchanged, scoffs were heard. Blithe took a few sips of water and focused on her hand holding the bottle, not the faces beyond it. She heard one girl mutter,

"You're amazing."

Robbie had said those words just before she steered him to the inevitable.

When the bell rang, she lagged behind. The staircase was clearing as she made her way up and so she felt a little safer. Suddenly a plastic bottle hit the top of her head. It was half empty, but it had been hurled with some force and it hurt. Blithe looked up, but she couldn't see anyone or hear anything. Her hand went to the top of her head, but only for a second. She resisted the urge to sooth her head and feel for damage, knowing that it would only give the thrower satisfaction.

In Maths she sat next to Elaine, the slightly gormless girl who had, only the day before, called her a legend. Blithe, the last to arrive, slid into her seat and glared at Elaine.

"Who sent it to you?" Blithe demanded.

"I don't remember."

Blithe tutted. "How can you not remember? Check yer phone."

"I've deleted it. Forget about it."

Blithe edged an elbow onto Elaine's desk.

"Try and remember Elaine. Was it Maddie? Yes or no, was it Maddie?"

"No. It wasnae Maddie." Elaine murmured, staring straight ahead.

The room was hushed into silence. Blithe listened, without any comprehension. When it was time to put pen to paper, she hissed.

"Why did you say I was a legend?"

"I thought it was cool. Shut up. I'm trying to concentrate."

"I wish I'd never sent it, Elaine. The shit has hit the fan."

"I know. Shoosh."

Somehow it hurt to be shooshed by someone like Elaine.

Elaine wasn't the only one to feel deeply uncomfortable in Blithe's presence. No one who liked her knew what to say and she moved through crowds like a blast of cold air.

She walked the corridors, feeling less exposed in the windowless halls, marching over the rubbery lino that her flimsy shoes couldn't grip. It felt safer, a moving target was better than a fixed one. As she approached the entrance to the stairwell, she saw Maddie through the glass surrounding the doorway. The glass was broken, and it framed Maddie at the centre of a glass web. The doorway to the stairs presented a bottleneck, and a chance to block her way.

Blithe's fury mounted at the sight of that laughing face. Maddie stood so safely and firmly between friends Aleesha and Josie. The sound of their collective laughter cut through to Blithe. Her rage swelled.

She pushed her way through, ignoring the mutterings of 'bitch' until she and Maddie stood face to face.

"Who did you send it to?" she demanded.

Madeline tried to appear baffled and turned to Josie for support.

"Didn't I tell you not to send it to anyone?" Blithe demanded.

"No, you didn't."

Blithe couldn't recall what she had said, and she couldn't refer to her phone. She clenched her fists and jaw, keeping her blazing eyes firmly on Maddie.

"I told you it was personal!"

"I'm no the one who records and sends out stuff like that."

"Aye ye are, that's exactly what ye are."

"You sent it to me, though you don't know me all that well. I didn't pass it on."

"That's shite. You ken that's absolute shite!"

The corridor was packed, but Blithe's shout was clear and angry. Maddie's reply matched her;

"Don't you dare blame me!"

Blithe wanted to punch her, but she wouldn't hit her first, much as she wanted to. Maddie sensed this and pointed at her threateningly, keeping her at arm's length.

"If you're that stupid, that you send these things around and boast about dumping guys, then what do you expect!"

Maddie drove her finger into the bridge of Blithe's collar bone. Blithe slapped her hand away, inadvertently striking another girl, Codey Gallagher, who had pushed forward to intervene. Codey punched Blithe on the arm in irritation.

The appearance of a third defender was another burning

injustice. Shielding her bruised arm, Blithe stepped back, but she couldn't keep quiet and spat the venom out.

"Get tae fuck!"

Madeline shook her head and held Codey back by the shoulder; "Leave it! Ignore her."

As Maddie pushed past, Blithe managed to shout after her. "Yer full of shit!"

The crowd dispersed. She had the last word, but standing alone, it did not feel like success. She moved round the corner, towards the main entrance, wondering if she had a chance to sneak out. She stood with a clear view of the gates and considered keeping her head down and calmly walking through them. She was about to do this when she saw that Robbie was beating her to it.

He did not see her, he moved too fast and didn't look back. From the way he moved, with his head down, taking furious strides, it was clear that he knew what was circulating. She felt physically sick and watched him until he vanished around the corner.

At least she wouldn't bump into him. Now, alone and beyond the gates, he was safe.

Blithe made as though to follow, but suddenly turned towards the school office. Again, she tried to walk calmly, to hide her mission. A can struck her ankle – it didn't hurt. Blithe didn't look back, she could feel where its contents had sprayed up the back of her leg. By the time she walked into the office, her skin felt gummed where the substance had dried to syrup.

As she did not plant herself in front of the receptionist, she did not appear to be seeking attention. Blithe waited a few minutes and then reluctantly made eye contact from her side-line. She cleared her throat,

"Can you get me my guidance teacher?"

Blithe thought she was following procedure, but it seemed to startle the receptionist.

"Do you know who that is? What's it about?"

"It's, it's not... like, easy for me to say."

"Can it wait till this afternoon?"

"No."

"Can you tell me your name and your year?"

"Blithe Shearer. Fifth."

The receptionist moved with a knowing air. She asked Blithe to sit in the office while she made a few calls.

Sitting down, Blithe had nothing to do but bite her nails and nervously watch the main swing doors. She stood up and looked at the pupil's artwork on display, scanning names that meant nothing to her.

As she turned, the receptionist beckoned her over.

"Look, I know she's not your guidance teacher, but Mrs Logan is on her way down. Is that okay?"

Blithe knew and liked Mrs Logan. Taking a deep breath, she nodded and paced the office until her teacher appeared five minutes later. Mrs Logan was a young woman with elfin cropped hair. She tended to wear light colours and loose clothing, but what always struck Blithe about her, was her comfy black plimsolls, shoes that she didn't think teachers were allowed to wear.

"Hiya Blithe. Do you want to follow me this way?"

Blithe was relieved to be led in such a business-like way, down the corridor to the nurse's room. Mrs Logan opened the door, gestured to Blithe to go first and take a seat, while she went to the water cooler. She filled a plastic cup, offered it to Blithe and filled another for herself. It felt a little like an arrest; the large room contained only a desk, two cheap chairs and a filing cabinet.

Mrs Logan handed her a cup of water and pulled her chair round, positioning herself directly opposite. Blithe held her crinkly cup with both hands and looked searchingly at her teacher before her discomfort and guilt made her squirm inwardly.

"Would you like to tell me what's up?"

Blithe chewed her lower lip as she considered.

"There's a clip, that's being sent round the school. It's got me and a boy."

"A video?"

Blithe nodded.

"Did you know you were being filmed?"

"He, he didnae ken."

Mrs Logan sat back in her chair and stiffened before returning to a business-like impartiality.

"Was it... intimate?"

"No! We werenae even in the same room. It was a video call. I was dressed just, just like I am the now."

Mrs Logan frowned.

"And, to be clear, the same goes for him?"

"Aye. That's it. So it wasn't, like, humiliating for me... It is now but..."

"Is what?"

"Now it's being sent round, it's humiliating for me as well. I dumped him, and he was really upset."

"You recently broke up?"

"Aye well..." Blithe closed her eyes. "During. That's what the clips of. Me dumping him."

"Is it a boy at the school?"

Blithe, who had been avoiding eye contact, looked back and nodded.

"Can I ask who?"

"Robbie Mazani."

Mrs Logan the art teacher, vanished for a second.

"Oh, he's a nice boy!"

Blithe wondered what she meant by that, as though to have done this to a troublemaker would not have been such an issue. Of course, Robbie was a nice baby-faced boy. There were plenty of other boys who might have been able to isolate their emotional scars and be seen to carry on. Not Robbie. He allowed her to do her particular damage and send cracks running to every extremity.

"So", Mrs Logan continued, "If this has been circulated widely, Robbie must be aware of it."

"Aye. He's away home."

"You recorded him, without his knowledge, as you ended your relationship and then circulated the footage?"

"I didn't. I sent it to like, one girl."

"One girl or 'like' one girl?"

There was a note of anger in her voice.

"One girl. I sent it to Madeline Stephenson, she said she didn't send it on but she must have because it ended up out there."

"Why did you send it to her?"

Blithe kept herself to herself, theirs was not an obvious friendship and Mrs Logan knew it. She was not angry; she posed her question coaxingly. Other girls might have taken the opportunity to talk about their fears and vulnerabilities. Blithe would never do this, not even to a teacher she liked.

She took a deep breath, wanting only to bring the conversation to a close.

"She knew about it because I told her. She asked to see it. I said I would let her because I trusted her.... now it's all this..."

"Oh, you silly girl!"

Blithe said nothing. There was nothing to say.

"I have to escalate this. You realise that don't you?"

Blithe nodded, that was why she was there.

"And we need to contact his family."

Blithe widened her eyes.

"Is that not up to Robbie? Should he not say whether he wants them to know or not?"

Mrs Logan shook her head.

"No. If anyone receives the link, they should notify the school. If anyone circulates it, they should be punished. This will be made clear to all pupils. I won't say that you alerted us to it."

Mrs Logan widened her eyes in bafflement, exhaled slowly and took another gulp of water.

"We'll do our best to deal with it but, this won't be the end of it, for you."

"How d'ye mean?"

"There will be consequences for you."

"Me! Why me?"

"You sent it."

"But I'm telling you!"

"I know and, you did the right thing but look at it from his family's perspective."

"I huv!"

"Then you'll know why. If it had happened to you, would you want it to be dropped, just like that? Is there anything else to say?"

"No."

Blithe glared and Mrs Logan smiled sympathetically.

"You sure? Are you sure there's nothing you're not telling me? How's your brother?"

Blithe resented the question.

"He's okay. Actually Miss, can I get out one minute early today?"

"One minute?"

"Aye. I can get far in one minute."

"You can't leave the gates before the bell. You know that."

"That's why I said one-minute miss, I'll be at the gates when the bell rings."

Mrs Logan scrutinised Blithe's face silently. Blithe betrayed no emotion and waited passively for her answer.

"There are pupils you want to avoid? Yes, I can understand that. Who've you got last period?"

"Miss Payne."

"I'll talk to her but, can't promise. You just want a wee head start, I understand that. Feel free to hang around the office if it makes you feel safer, but you can't do this forever. If you're being bullied, I can help you."

Blithe didn't doubt that she was sincere, it was her ability that she questioned. A cheerful teacher like Mrs Logan probably imagined that any tale of bullying could be wound down to a heart-warming conclusion. What no one seemed to understand was that when you're alienated, everyone's a bully.

Blithe feared that the solution this sweet woman in plimsolls would dream up, would be something so messed up, it would sever her trust in one of the only teachers she liked.

God. She might engineer friendships with the hope that Blithe would finally be accepted into a big fold of girls. She would imagine the happy gang, doing makeovers and French plaits and Blithe taking her place among them. Fuck that.

CHAPTER 3

A tall skinny boy walked down the muddy alley between two rows of terraced houses. It was early spring, and pallets were haphazardly laid out as bridges over the drying mud. This was his route, always, even in the dark.

Fashion was difficult for Jamie, even the limited fashion of school uniform, as skinny jeans or tight trousers were impossible. His school trousers flapped around the pole-like legs and his blazer kept its shape only as much as it would on a scarecrow.

He did better for shoes as he was allowed to wear Vans for medical reasons, as long as they were black. He limped slightly, pressing weight on his right side. The limp became more noticeable when he sped up.

Today, even over mud, he managed to walk tall and proud. That was more a result of a few years of physiotherapy than conscious effort.

His brown hair fell across his eyes, down to the bridge of his long nose. He flicked his head when he needed to see something. He had gels, but not the time to apply them to his fine, straight hair.

Jamie saw, with relief, the familiar pallet crate leant up against the back fence. He tried the back gate. It was more of a hinge on a fence; unless you used it, you wouldn't know it was there. It was locked. He bent down and pulled the crate from the mud with a scowl and leant it against the fence. He rubbed his muddied hands against his trousers. He climbed up, using the crate as a ladder. The fence backed directly onto the garden shed but before he could transfer his weight, the pallet slid back to the muddy ground. As he landed, he looked right and left to ensure there was no one coming. Once again, he picked up the muddy pallet and repeated the procedure, moving quickly and hauling himself onto the shed roof before the pallet slipped back. Gripping the sandpaper layer of the shed roof, he clumsily swung his legs over.

Jamie normally had to wait for Robbie to do this for him. He'd hear the thump of a grassy landing and the fence would swing open. Now Jamie sat on the shed roof, he was not sure about jumping down. He didn't limp for nothing; he'd undergone several operations on his knee and had been warned against this sort of impact.

Today Robbie had left school hours early and Jamie was not even certain that he was at home. His mum might be. Jamie glanced at the kitchen window. It wasn't that she'd be angry at him for climbing on her shed, though she might be, he was more bothered by how badly the climb was executed.

At first glance it looked as though the house was empty. Even Robbie's room, directly above the kitchen looked dingy but – there! The bedroom curtains were raised from below.

"Can I come up?"

He expected Robbie to open the window, tell him to get the fuck off the roof and aye, come up. There was no answer.

"Ye ken I shouldnae jump! I'll shatter ma knee!"

The kitchen light came on and Robbie's mum Karen appeared at the window with her coat on.

She pushed the window open and called, "Come in and go on up!"

Jamie grinned and, moving as though he had a mad fear of heights, slowly levered himself down from the shed roof. Grazing his hands for as long as he could stand it, he allowed himself to drop the last few inches.

"But if that roof collapses I'll kick that skinny wee arse of yours!"

Jamie hobbled inside through the backdoor into the kitchen.

Karen faced him with a concerned frown. Only now did she think it strange that Robbie hadn't let his friend in and so perhaps she hadn't been wise to just send him up. It had also only just occurred to her that her son hadn't called out to her when she arrived home. She usually heard something from him.

Jamie gave an awkward smile before making his way through the kitchen and up the stairs. The house was cluttered and today, it smelled like cat.

Jamie stopped outside Robbie's door and heard nothing. His door was still covered with the residue of Star Wars stickers, that fingernails still picked at from time to time. Jamie nudged a flea comb towards the skirting board and into the fluff where it wouldn't get stamped on.

Then, he took a deep breath and knocked.

"Fuck sake, come in."

Feeling suddenly nervous, Jamie stuck his head round the door. Not only were the curtains still shut, Robbie hadn't turned on the lights and so he sat in what little light managed to permeate the thick fabric. It smelt like fresh Lynx; Robbie had probably sprayed it when he heard his mum let Jamie in.

"Ye alright?"

Robbie didn't reply. He was perched on the edge of his bed, with one hand gripping his knee. His posture suggested he was readying himself, but his face made it clear that he was not going to get very far. He seemed younger than ever, his dark eyes wild and bewildered, his black hair tousled. To see Robbie and Jamie stand side by side you would assume they were years rather than weeks apart in age.

"Okay?" Jamie repeated.

"No, I'm fucking not!"

Jamie looked down. There was nowhere for him to sit. Robbie sat in the middle of his bed, the spaces either side encroached on personal space.

"That...that's fair enough," he said.

Robbie fixed his eyes on Jamie and scowled. "Well?"

"Well what?"

Jamie did not want to lead on a difficult conversation and pulled an agonised expression. Robbie turned his head away and Jamie looked everywhere but at his friend.

"It's not your fault." Jamie said quietly. "She could just as easily have taped a phone call or shown off messages. I widnae have called you stupid then. You didn't know you were being recorded, did you?"

Robbie didn't look back.

Since being dumped, Robbie had been hard work; monosyllabic and slow, but he was starting to once again become his measured and too reasonable self. He was perking up, engaging in a world that didn't care about what had happened with Blithe. But that was to change. Earlier that day, as they made their way out of the cafeteria, a wheedling voice cried out.

"Can't we talk about this?"

Jamie turned to Robbie with a frown, waiting to understand. A look of horror dawned on Robbie's face. Jamie brought his face down to him with real concern.

"What is it?"

Robbie just shook his head.

Then the voice still mocking, called again from behind them, "What did I do?"

Jamie turned to face the caller; a big greasy guy called Lewis Moir.

"What are you on about?"

Lewis nodded towards Robbie and wiggled his eyebrows mischievously.

"That's not fucking funny!" Jamie spat back, assuming it referred only to being dumped.

"Aye it is. It's cringe but it's funny as fuck man."

"What is?" Jamie asked.

But when Jamie turned to Robbie, he saw the back of him, passing through the crowds to the double doors. Jamie didn't like to run, not when people were watching, and so Robbie successfully fled the scene. Had he turned around he would have seen Jamie stretching himself to full height with his arms raised, seeking an explanation.

He didn't reappear in the afternoon, but by then Jamie knew what had happened and couldn't blame him.

In no time, the clip was forwarded to Jamie by Lewis.

Jamie was tempted to watch it. He told himself that if he did, he might be able to think of something reassuring to say. To banish the temptation, he deleted it. Then it appeared again from someone else. Again, he deleted it.

During the second break Lewis handed Jamie his phone, and Jamie saw, for a second, his friend perched on his bed. He batted the phone away.

"Have some fucking respect!"

"You're just going to watch it when ye get home, you know you are. Everyone's seen it so it's not gonnae matter."

Jamie rested his eyes on the tense figure in the dark. He imagined himself in the same situation and could only feel very glad that he wasn't.

"Fuck'n bitch," Jamie spat, "What kind of evil cow forwards a thing like that? You know, it'll be worse for her. Least yer over her now eh? Bet ye widnae touch her now...?"

Robbie calmed, comforted at hearing just how angry Jamie was on his behalf.

"I can't go back now can I?" he muttered.

"Aye ye can. She's the bitch."

"Who's place would you rather be in? Hers or mine?"

Jamie opened his mouth and made a noise like a faint gargle. Robbie turned to him with something like a smile, sorrow temporarily distracted.

"See?"

"Well, people'll forget about it eventually."

"No."

"Oh, they will. Someone's sure to make a bigger fanny of themselves eventually."

"No. If I do anything, if I try to be anything it'll be as the guy who did that. That's what I am first, before I'm anything else."

Jamie couldn't honestly argue that Robbie wouldn't forever be associated with the clip. If Robbie hadn't been such a quiet presence at school, then there might have been other pieces to build on, bits that might have made the whole thing slightly forgettable. Robbie was no longer forgettable, he had one excruciating story and nothing else. Robbie took a deep breath.

"I want to die."

"Don't be stupid, it's no that bad!"

Robbie turned as though he was about to spring up and deal him a shove. Jamie took a small step back.

Robbie glowered. He knew he wanted to be angry and wished he hadn't said he wanted to die. It was too much to take back.

"People do kill themselves over this stuff, all the time."

"Well, here's a lot of drastic stuff you could try before you do that. Like changing schools, like seeing maybe, if there's a way we can destroy the clip. It's got to be illegal. And if that doesn't work, you could move."

Robbie shook his head.

"That's not fair on my mum and dad, making stupid demands."

Jamie frowned. "I'm sure your mum and dad would rather move than... not have a son."

He wished to soothe Robbie but heard only sarcasm and censure in his voice.

"Fuck sake Jamie. You'd just make it more valuable if you tried to destroy it. You're basically talking about exile. The damage is done. End of."

"You said you wanted to die. If you need to be drastic...fuck'n... be drastic but don't..."

As Jamie struggled, Robbie asked, in a smaller voice;

"Have ye seen it?"

"No. Cross my heart."

Robbie hadn't heard that expression in a while and in all innocence added:

"And hope to die?"

"Stick a kebab in my eye."

Jamie drew a cross over his heart and mimed a projectile hitting his eye.

"It'll follow me, it'll be stuck to me. I haven't turned on my computer, not looked at my phone, nothing. I think I'll type in my name and there it'll be..."

He trailed off; it was becoming too much. He stood up and walked towards the window, gripped the top of the radiator under the windowsill.

"I can never be famous now!"

Jamie smiled at the almost comical misery. He considered reassuring him that he was never going to be famous. Robbie now stood in a prayer-like silhouette by the window and Jamie felt bad for feeling the impulse to laugh at him.

"Well... It could help you get famous."

Robbie spluttered through the tears waiting in the wings. Hearing that splutter Jamie was at first relieved to hear something like laughter, then in the gloom he could hear only staggered breathing. Were he to go now, as he had been considering, Robbie would not know what to do. He would sit staring into his dark room in silence. It was unnatural, still it was his space and his choice. Robbie didn't move, his hand very slowly left the radiator and lightly tapped the space below his nose. It then returned to the radiator.

Jamie couldn't stand it anymore and took a step towards him

with his hand raised. He wondered if what he was about to do would be taken the wrong way, the hand heading to the shoulder hovered. It might be taken in the wrong way, that's the last thing the poor fucker needs.

He wondered who else could understand. Not Robbie's parents. He'll have to tell someone, he won't have a choice, when he does, he'll feel crushing humiliation all over again. Even then, they'll never understand what it feels like. This was something that Jamie could imagine all too well. His hand gripped Robbie's shoulder.

Robbie turned in towards Jamie. He grabbed him so quickly, as though to save himself from a crumbling ledge. Jamie was glad to be several inches taller, and laid his arms securely across Robbie's shoulders, holding him protectively. He could hear him swallow and wondered how long he would have to stand frozen like this. He sighed, accepting that what he was doing was only natural. What if someone were to see this? To film and distribute this embrace, what would the world think then? Why did the opinions of others matter? Jamie considered that he should not be judged by people who viewed without context or understanding. Sharing doesn't have the power to change a moment. This moment was no one else's fucking business.

Jamie spoke first.

"It doesn't matter for fucks sake."

Robbie loosened his grip and took a step back. His arms didn't immediately fall by his sides and, stayed up like pincers for a few seconds. His eyes were dry, but Jamie dusted down his school shirt for snot trails.

Robbie sat back down on his bed and gripped the sheets either side of him.

"It matters," he said quietly.

"Don't do anything drastic at least. What do you want to do?"

"I want to... not exist."

"Well look, don't do anything for a while. See what next

week's like and if it's shit then...then you're going to have to do something but just for now... Don't. Can I put some music on?"

Robbie nodded towards the desk, where Jamie could plug in his phone into the speakers.

"What are you going to put on?"

"Don't know..." Jamie began ponderously, "I'm trying to think of something without any emotional level... We should go up the town tomorrow. You're leaving this house – even if you just end up at mine. Try and get £30, message me when you wake up."

Robbie nodded. "Are ye staying here?"

Jamie saw a message back from his dad, telling him that tea was imminent.

"Sorry – no, that's my Da telling me to come back."

Robbie nodded as though it didn't matter but, he didn't want to be left alone again.

"Thank you."

That surprised Jamie.

"You wanting another cuddle?"

* * *

Jamie waited alone at the train station. The arrival of the Glasgow Central train was announced but Robbie, who should have boarded further up the line, hadn't yet confirmed that he'd done so. Jamie examined his phone, ready to act on Robbie's reply. The train emerged from the tunnel. Jamie had been standing for ten minutes and needed to sit down. He certainly didn't want to run up and down the platform looking to see whether Robbie was on the train. He was usually too self-conscious to run, running had earned him the nickname 'Quasi'.

He could have argued that he wasn't a hunchback, in fact his back was straight as a rod. When he ran, his leg wanted to stay straight, it was that that made his running ridiculous.

Everyone else slouched and would be hunched over sooner or later. He didn't point that out, he only thought it, knowing from bitter experience, the reactions that made a nickname stick.

As the train heaved to a halt, Jamie scanned the passing carriages. He couldn't see Robbie when the doors slid open in front of him. He quickly limped down the platform and then, three carriages up, he saw Robbie leaning out. Jamie hurried after him, fearing the doors would close. He loped along the platform, as fast as he could with his stupid, lopsided run, one leg dragged just a little by the other. His eyes held a panic that reminded Robbie of a dog fearing abandonment. He smiled and returned to his seat. Jamie staggered in as the doors closed and threw himself down in the seat opposite. He opened his mouth to speak but shut it as his phone pinged.

Robbie: Made it.

He wasn't sure if this message had been genuinely delayed or whether it was a joke. He decided to say nothing. Robbie knew he was angry and spoke defensively.

"Why didn't you just board where you were and walk down?"

"Sometimes the doors are locked." Jamie mumbled unconvincingly.

"How do the ticket collectors get down then?"

Jamie didn't reply. He had an aversion to being alone among strangers.

Robbie sat back and watched a familiar side of Glasgow zipping past. Jamie had amused him but that mirth quickly ebbed away, replaced with a greyness that crept over his skin as he stared vacantly out.

"So..." Jamie began.

Robbie rested his face against the glass but rolled his eyes in Jamie's direction.

"Ye alright?" Jamie asked.

Robbie looked out of the window again and murmured

vaguely. Jamie didn't catch it but still replied.

"She's the bitch man."

"Maybe..."

Jamie gave up and turned his attention to the city flying by. If Robbie wasn't going to even try to enjoy himself, he wondered why he'd agreed to come. Still staring out, Robbie murmured.

"The school called, got my mum on the phone."

"About you skiving?"

"Maybe. They called about the..." Robbie's voice trailed off. He sounded as though he'd had a rough night and was still too tired to clear his throat. 'They called about *that*."

"It didnae happen at school though...' Jamie began.

"But if people at school send it on and it's everywhere and being watched at school, they *think* they can do something. If anyone gets found with it, they'll get suspension, supposedly. So anyone who takes a wee bit of care, they can pretty much watch it easily. On Monday there's going to be an announcement or some shit. It's not going to mention any names, but I may as well wear it on a fucking t-shirt. They've got to be seen to be doing something."

"Crucify the cunt that posted it," Jamie suggested.

Robbie sat back in his seat, facing Jamie squarely for the first time.

"I heard that she told the school. Why would she do that?"

"To save her neck."

Robbie nodded to himself.

"No, she didn't want it to go viral. She's not stupid. Anyway, my mum knew I'd been filmed doing something, and that it was doing the rounds. You should have seen the way she was looking at me when she came upstairs. Ye see, she and my dad thought I'd been filmed having... sexy sexy time."

"Sexy sexy time? Shut the fuck up!" Jamie laughed.

"Or something like that..., that was the first thing they thought of. Like I would do that?"

"Do what? Come on; specifically, what did they think you'd been doing?"

Robbie shook his head. "I don't know, they weren't going to come up and tell me the kind of sick visions they had, you know the kind of thing."

Jamie nodded. "Filmed skipping about the place with your dick out?"

Robbie cringed and covered his eyes. He couldn't talk, his laughter was from embarrassment rather than amusement. It was still laughter.

"Sexy sexy time. Fuck sake Robbie, who says stuff like that? Middle aged men in like, revealing dressing gowns, eating salami, watching you through binoculars."

Robbie stopped laughing, wiped his eyes and took a deep breath.

"That's very specific."

"I know my paedophiles and how to spot them."

"At least ye know something."

Jamie conceded that with a nod before adding,

"So, I suppose you had to tell them that it was not, sexy sexy time."

"Can you just forget that I ever said that?"

Jamie didn't want to, but nodded.

"I was fucked off with them actually, I even...I actually shouted at my mum."

"I do that every week" Jamie said.

"Aye, but you're an arsehole."

Again, Jamie conceded and let Robbie go on.

"I shouted, 'what the fuck is wrong with you? I've not been pimping myself out!'"

"Those were your exact words?"

Robbie nodded. Jamie repeated those words in his head and began to giggle.

"I can't imagine you being like that."

Robbie raised his eyebrows; it wasn't a side of himself that he'd really heard before either.

"So I said, 'I was dressed, sitting right here. My girlfriend called me, she dumped me and...'"

Robbie spread out his hands to indicate closure, Jamie leant forward.

"And I wasn't happy about it."

Robbie looked out of the window again, as they slowed to a stop halfway across the Clyde. A silence hardened.

"My mum was so angry..." he said eventually, "She wanted to call the police, she wanted to go round there and drag Blithe's mum out...I wasn't having that..."

Jamie liked the image of Helen running up to the tower block, charging up and dragging a woman down several flights of stairs. Then he remembered.

"Didn't you say her mum used a mobility scooter?"

"Did for a bit, don't know if she still does. Usually, my mum keeps her distance but, I wasn't taking any chances. I shouted at her again."

Robbie turned away from Jamie and back to the window. He didn't want to describe what had happened and recalled how his mum angrily paced the room. She'd listed the crimes, as though they'd been committed against her. "'This was an assault, this was slanderous, this was a gross invasion of privacy. How could a girl stoop to this level? Something must be done. The girl's family needed to know.'"

On it went, until Robbie, by then crimson, shouted.

"This happened to me! It didn't happen to you! Fucking butt out!"

Robbie smiled. "I didn't shout at my dad because... honestly, he couldn't get his head around it. He was in the doorway, just trying to make up his mind while my mum was flipping out. My mum and Blithe, don't take this the wrong way but, they aren't all that different."

Jamie found the idea of having a girlfriend who resembled your mum strange, even a bit deviant. He frowned.

"Never mind," said Robbie. "My dad told me to calm down and leave my mum alone," he shrugged, "which I did."

His father had stepped into his room and commanded him in a loud, clear voice.

"Apologise! You will not use that language."

Robbie had muttered a sorry he barely felt. His father embraced him and, while it gave reassurance and security, it was also a dent on his independence. When Jamie had hugged him, he'd felt something a little like clarity. When his father hugged him, he felt smaller.

Jamie felt the money in his pocket and wondered again if the trip was a mistake.

Robbie stared out across the river below and the old ships, tied up at the docks and never to be collected. The train came to life again and pulled into Central Station.

The main shopping areas had never interested them, and they hurried their way through a packed Argyle Street. The Merchant City, with its spires and tower, asserted itself up ahead, from an almost fairy-tale history, cleaner than the present day. They turned off the main drag towards a bar and record shop. Throughout the walk, their conversations had circumvented what had happened. Silences often lingered. Robbie accepted these pauses as moments to take in his surroundings, stepping in and out of introversion at his own pace.

"You're walking faster now," Robbie remarked, recalling the same journey a year ago when he had to keep stopping.

They made their way to Kings Court, an open space containing a bar and some shopping units. They cut across the bar area and headed to the record shop at the very back. It didn't take Robbie long to browse, no more than ten minutes, but Jamie took his time over them. Robbie waited for him by the bar, behind the coffee machine, staring in through the partition, observing his friend flicking through neat wooden boxes of records. Light from the railway arch window poured in, reflecting off the white brickwork. Jamie couldn't hide in clutter but nonetheless, every so often he would pick something out, hunch his shoulders and then, keeping his phone close against his chest, he would photograph the album sleeve before replacing it. He'd been doing this for years. Robbie noticed that the staff regularly cast of glances of amusement and recognition in his direction. It might have been annoying were it someone else, a bratty kid or someone keen to sound off on what they knew nothing about. Jamie was fairly obviously a cash strapped seventeen-year-old. He would often, in a stuttering voice, dare to ask what was playing and on rarer occasions, he would quietly ask for a specific record to be played. He had the hesitancy of the well-intentioned and eyes that were quick to scare. He could be forgiven for almost anything.

When he finished browsing, Jamie shuffled out into the bar and sat down in a quiet corner by the wall while Robbie went to order chips. They would have their seat for as long as they could for the smallest possible amount of money. When Robbie returned, they turned to their phones while they waited. Every so often, Robbie glanced up at the subdued bundle of limbs whose presence seemed to help, more than anything else.

CHAPTER 4

When Monday came, Robbie prepared himself for the very worst. He'd conceived of many different responses to his return, all of them humiliating. Some of these were accurate, there was a lot of whispering and jostling at his expense. He had not anticipated sympathy.

"Ye alright?" seemed to follow him down the corridor. When he dragged his gaze from the floor, he saw sympathetic smiles, tuts and shakings of the head which all said; *we're on your side*.

The nicer they were, the more likely they were to have seen it and Robbie couldn't embrace friendliness that had such a disconcerting origin. It was almost as bad as the abuse.

His own recorded words followed him. Quotes were thrown out, such as "Can't we talk?", "What did I do?" and while laughter often followed, so too did defensive cries like, "Shut up yeh fanny!"

When Blithe dumped him, he felt as though a support was being wrenched away and he had sought to pull it back with desperate words he would never normally have spoken.

After lunch, he had English with Blithe, an hour concrete in time. The looming horror of this made the morning seem almost bearable.

Thankfully, he did not expect a group activity or discussion; he expected a practice exam but, as little revision was required, he hadn't made a mental note and now could not be sure.

The teacher, Mr Farrell, knew what had happened. When informed of the existence of the clip, he'd appeared to take it seriously but didn't see it as his role to interfere in the private lives of his pupils.

Robbie hoped that the classroom door would be open and a teacher present, those were the only things he prayed the teacher would deliver.

Mr Farrell would have been on time if the photocopier hadn't jammed but it did, and so Robbie found a locked door. Behind him, the class quickly queued up; Blithe appeared last, like a rat creeping around the periphery, avoiding wide open spaces. She stood some yards from the queue. Her classmates noticed but no one needed to draw attention to her.

Robbie stared into the brick wall with his hands firmly in his pockets – he looked as sad as he usually did but, expecting to find misery, the students found it in his resting face. Robbie was quiet and usually ignored, but today they observed him and diagnosed depression, brought on by the girl lurking down the corridor. Blithe saw Mr Farrell approach first and rose up from leaning, waited, and then walked slowly alongside him. She stopped suddenly, ensuring she remained behind her classmates as her teacher unlocked the door. Noting her presence behind him, a boy threw his words to Robbie at the head of the queue.

"Seriously, you could do so much better!"

There was a pause. Robbie and a few others walked in, but four moved aside for Blithe.

"After you."

She turned. They remained in a line against the wall, boys and girls with sneering faces led by Madeline's friend Josie.

"Fuck'n come on!" Josie spat, "because I'm no turning my back on you."

Blithe knew immediately that was just an excuse to say something. Josie always had to say something. It was Blithe's turn to sneer as she went in ahead of them.

She wasn't shoved, she wasn't jostled. If she was spat at, she didn't feel it, but she waited for it, as she had been waiting all day.

Earlier attempts to trip her had only made her stumble, as she made sure to take steady steps. As she made her way through the crowded corridor to her final class of the day, she moved too fast. She didn't know whose foot succeeded, but her hands hit the floor and her body skidded after. Halfway to picking herself up she froze and heard a girl's voice.

"Watch yer step now!"

She didn't look up to see who was gloating. With her hands on the ground, she drew her legs together and slowly sat back, pausing before rising, using her position to check that her bag was properly closed. As she began to stand, she looked down the corridor to see Robbie looking back at her. He had seen her fall and had been waiting for her to get up. When he saw her looking, he hurried on.

It was sheer relief that urged Robbie down the swelling corridors at the end of the day.

Even though he was keen to slip away, he moved to the side, away from the stream and cast his eyes around between the three emptying bottlenecks of the school.

He saw Jamie first, coming out of the doors on the other side of the courtyard. He was easily identifiable for two reasons: he was tall, and he moved slower than everyone else. Robbie waved him over before casting his eyes further afield. Blithe approached the gates. The crowd separated them, and he kept losing sight of her. She'd been running, or almost running, until a group stopped her in her tracks. She was too far away to hear, too far away to read facial expressions but a split second of body language made the situation clear.

Then Jamie was at his side, saying something about someone putting porn on one of the computers, but Robbie didn't follow because he could tell that Blithe was shouting back. A girl, Codey Gallagher, moved forward, thrusting her face into Blithe's then, forcing her further back by the volume of her shouts.

"Look!" Robbie pointed, "Do you see that?"

Jamie followed where Robbie indicated as once again, Codey rammed her face forward, as though to head-butt. She thrust her clawing hand at Blithe's face, Blithe slapped it away. Codey grabbed at her collar, shouting words they couldn't hear. Blithe shrugged free.

"Walk with her. Walk with her Jamie."

He'd been clear before but now, he spoke quickly with a tremor in his voice.

"What! Why?"

"Well – look! As soon as she's out of the gates, she's fucked."

Jamie craned to a clearer view of the scene, grimaced and looked away.

"Aye but... Whose fault's that?"

"Walk with her."

They looked at one another, waiting to see the resolve of the other.

"Why me?"

"Shall I just pick someone at random? Who else am I going to ask?"

Jamie wouldn't have minded being charmed just a bit, he wasn't so full of self-confidence that he could easily resist it. He was disappointed when Robbie's persuasion took a turn the other way.

"They don't go for you. They never go for you, you just get words, put some fucking headphones on you've got nothing to worry about. They're feart of putting you in hospital again, it's just too much hassle. They don't go for you, even the girls don't go for you."

Wishing to appear unmoved, Jamie looked at what was happening to Blithe with a steady and, he hoped, impassive expression.

He lost sight of Blithe, now Codey was directing her shouts

downwards.

"Look, will you just see her on her way?"

Jamie hesitated. Blithe got to her feet.

"Go on, she's getting up. Go!"

Jamie scowled and walked towards Blithe. Robbie let him walk ahead before following. He moved so slowly Robbie thought he might miss her.

As Jamie walked, the grounds emptied and he could see Blithe very clearly as she tried to walk away, but Codey grabbed the strap on her bag. Blithe yanked and raised her fist.

Jamie was angry at the implication he was incapable of defending her, and that it was his disability that made him the best person to walk with her. He saw her disappear around the corner and decided that if he couldn't see her when he rounded the corner, he would give up and go straight home.

However, when he turned the corner, he saw Blithe trying to get past Codey and her friend, Aleesha. They had an audience, clearly entertained as Connor, Codey's boyfriend and Kaiden, Aleesha's younger brother, perched on a wall nearby. Jamie looked over his shoulder, planning to gesture at Robbie as much to say, *'what am I supposed to do now?'* Robbie was just visible, walking in the opposite direction with his head down.

"You fuck'n look at me!" Codey screeched. "You don't fucking go around blaming ma pal. You don't blame anyone fur your own shit, own it! It's yours, if you try to put on it anyone else, I will fucking smash yer face in!"

Jamie continued towards them.

Blithe shouted back, "Ye just want to squirm yer way up her arse!"

'Blithe shut up, fucking shut up', thought Jamie. He'd have preferred it if she'd tried to ignore them until they became bored.

There was enough space for Jamie to pass on the pavement but as he drew level, he subtly gestured to Blithe to walk in front of him. Blithe was not expecting this and so Jamie repeated the gesture. Instead of walking where he indicated, Blithe made to push her way past Aleesha. As she did, Aleesha's broad shoulders slammed against her, and she stumbled into the road.

"Fuck's sake..." Jamie muttered.

As Blithe stepped back onto the pavement, Jamie walked alongside her. The boys didn't get off the wall and so the group stayed put but Connor shouted down the road after them.

"She's on the market again! Go for it! No spoilers but, I'll download it later!"

Jamie blushed; he didn't know how much as he hobbled to keep up with her. She glanced at him angrily, but he continued after her, humiliating enough as it was. He didn't look over his shoulder, much as he wanted to know if they were being followed.

"Are ye following me?" she demanded.

"It's not my idea... Robbie wanted me to walk ye home because ye were about to get yer arse kicked."

"You don't live near me - do you?"

"No."

"So what are ye doing?"

Jamie glanced over his shoulder and was relieved to see Codey and her friends crossing the road away from them.

"Look, either I stop ye getting yer arse kicked or, I watch ye get yer arse kicked. I've not decided yet."

Blithe had a determined frown on her face.

"To be honest," she said, "I don't like him doing me favours."

"We didn't plan it. We just saw you on the way out and it just seemed like the decent thing to do."

Unlike Blithe, Jamie kept looking over his shoulder. The group's abrupt absence made him uncomfortable.

"I can't see anyone behind us." He said.

"Well, you can fuck off anytime you want to. Who am I going to complain to?"

"That's true."

He wasn't going to spare her feelings but at that moment Connor reappeared, jumping out from a shop doorway. He seemed to grab Blithe but just as quickly, ran away. Jamie watched him rush off and when he looked back, he understood, he'd wiped something brown and sticky down Blithe's cardigan.

"Oh fuck."

Blithe speared him with a glance, a direct instruction to say nothing. She tore off her black cardigan. There was a bin nearby, she only had to carry it a few yards, but she threw it in like it was on fire.

"Lucky it wasnae your face…"

Blithe wasn't comforted. She glared at him, she didn't think he understood, nor would he ever understand, so why was he there? That was the only black cardigan she had, and they'd know if she washed it and wore it again.

For the next twenty minutes, they walked in silence. Jamie, hobbling a few paces behind, sensed that Blithe was tearful and saw no point in forcing conversation and anyway, he had nothing reassuring to say. They reached a steep flight of dingy concrete steps that led up to the car park at the foot of the tower block.

There, Blithe left Jamie with a quick mutter of, "This is me".

Jamie watched her run away up the steps and made his way home.

Blithe ran inside and into the lift, closed her eyes in time with the doors and breathed slowly, as she was carried up to her empty flat on the ninth floor. When the doors opened, her frenzy began again as she dashed to her front door. She fought with her keys, rushed inside, and bolted straight down the corridor to the bathroom, her bag still on her back. She kicked her bag into a corner, blasted on the bath taps, hastily undressed, and climbed into the tub as it filled. She lay in the bath with her ears under the water, listening first to the tumbling water and then, the calming echo of her breathing.

She wasn't sure that she could stand another day like the one she'd just had.

* * *

Half an hour later, Jamie arrived home to his narrow mid terrace. A rectangle of overgrown shrubs encased in railings, separated the front of the house from the pavement. On setting foot inside the house, there were always shoes, bags and umbrellas to trip over.

Immediately to the right on entering the house, there was a small living room cluttered with DVDs, books, and magazines. The family were often on the move, and so their time together was generally spent at the kitchen table, the family room forgotten in favour of the airier room at the back of the house. From there they could view their overgrown garden, decaying toys not quite hidden among the flowers.

Jamie normally found his dad, Stephen Gilchrist, sitting at the dining table, fiddling on his laptop instead of working in the windowless office. Today he stood behind the table, dithering. He didn't acknowledge his son when he walked into the room and unusually there was no dinner cooking. Jamie went straight to the fridge and, after pouring himself a drink, said hello, loud enough to shake his dad from his reverie.

Stephen looked up dazed and muttered, "Nightmare, fucking nightmare..."

Jamie sat down. "What have I done?"

"What have you done?"

"Nothing,' Jamie grinned.

"Then don't grin at me like that, you'll have me wondering what yev been up to. No, your Gran wants to go into a home."

Jamie nodded vacantly, not immediately seeing the problem.

"See, normally it's the children who put their parents in a home. See, one day you might be like, 'Sorry dad, I can't look after you and you can't look after yourself. I've got my own shit to deal with.'"

Jamie didn't know what to say. He was slightly flattered that his dad should confide in him.

"Well, if she wants to go into a home... isn't that up to her?"

Stephen gave his son a withering look.

"No. Her pal Janice has gone into a home, but that's fair enough. Your Gran visits her regularly, thinks 'this is nice and clean, I get meals brought to me, nice garden, bingo and the crossword. Where do I sign up?'"

"Oh well, she probably just wants to be with her pal."

Stephen frowned. "Aye but it's so expensive. She understands, she's not stupid, but she puts on these blinkers. The thing is, she doesnae need care. She should be grateful fur her independence but no, she's wanting care. Care that other folk need, that they're crying out for, believe me. I ask you, who wants to be put in a home?"

Jamie paused for a moment. "Someone who's lonely. Maybe you should visit her."

Stephen sat further back in his chair and tapped a pen against the table. Jamie began digging around in his school bag for his phone.

"How expensive is it?" Jamie asked, from the depths of his bag.

"If I paid it to you, you'd live like a King."

Jamie placed his phone on the table and zipped up his bag,

"Money you've not got. If you've not got it, you've not got it."

Stephen nodded and left it at that, wishing that it could be so simple. He stared at his son, who was too absorbed in scrolling through his phone to notice. Stephen thought that Jamie's hair might have been acceptable in the 70s or early 90s. Wasn't he meant to be fashion conscious at his age?

When Stephen was Jamie's age, he had tried to blend in, keeping his hair short and spiky. Strands flicked up around Jamie's ears, which he smoothed whenever he noticed them. His overgrown fringe swept over his eyes, and if the back were straightened out, it would extend beyond his neck. Not quite a pudding basin, but enough of one to irritate his father. Now as Jamie stared down at his phone, his face was almost entirely obscured by hair, so perfectly that Stephen wondered if that was the intention.

At Jamie's age, Stephen hadn't stayed out of trouble, but he'd avoided getting caught. He was glad that Jamie didn't seem to take the same risks but, it irked him to see his son looking so feminine, at an age when he should be doing everything in his power not to look pretty.

Stephen counselled himself not to mention his hair. Jamie's mum had no problem with his hair but if she did, she'd probably tell him he looked young or cute. At that age, Stephen would sooner have been a skinhead than been called sweet, and his internal teenage self was screaming, 'Look at the state of his fucking heid!' He leant forward reasonably.

"Are you still growing your hair?"

"No. It grows on its own."

"Let me know if you need money for a cut, if that's all that's putting you off."

Jamie murmured, not really listening. He was messaging Robbie at that moment.

Robbie didn't know how to feel when he received a message from Jamie.

Jamie: Didn't get her arse kicked but got smeared in shit.

Robbie: But they left you alone?

Jamie: Aye.

Robbie: Will you do it again?

Sitting in his kitchen at home, Jamie considered.

Jamie: Probably.

He thought it sounded vague, but Robbie knew it meant yes.

Robbie: I knew they wouldn't go for you.

* * *

A year ago, Robbie, Jamie and Jamie's girlfriend, Molly, were on their way to a youth orchestra event in Edinburgh. As instructed, they'd been ready and waiting outside the school at 8 am and spent fifteen minutes waiting for the coach and champing in the icy morning mist. When the coach, at last, turned into the street, it was too much for Molly. Perhaps it was a rush of love or just the prospect of escaping the cold, but Molly ran towards Jamie and jumped on his back.

Robbie joked afterwards that as she jumped, he gave a warning shout that he genuinely recalled in a theatrical, slow motion, "Nooooooo...' Jamie recalled that Robbie simply froze.

When Molly landed on Jamie's back, all three heard his knee crack. Jamie's wasn't braced for it, his bad leg was not straight, and so one weakened socket that had undergone several operations, suddenly took her full weight and a little more. The injury just below the kneecap re-opened and like a rock on the surface of a frozen lake, the fracture spread down. Molly knew it was delicate but, as Jamie's recovery had been going very well for quite some time and he was moving normally, it was easy to forget.

Robbie froze, waiting for the scream, the fall, whatever it was going to be. He saw nothing, blood drained from Jamie's face and then seemed to rush back and his eyes bulged. Molly landed on the ground, cupping her face as the enormity of her mistake dawned on her. The doors of the bus opened, and Jamie astounded them both by dragging himself up into the coach, relying on the rail and dragging the leg like a dead weight.

Robbie wished later that he had prevented him from struggling his way on.

Jamie threw himself down into a seat in the second row. Robbie moved in front where he made his appeal over the back of his seat. Jamie didn't say a word. His bulging eyes didn't blink, and his skin faded from red to drowned cabbage. The bus moved off. Their teacher, meanwhile, made her address standing in the centre of the isle. Robbie watched as Jamie began to perspire, his breathing became shallow and, though his face didn't crumple, his eyes watered, Robbie's cue to shout.

"Miss!"

Jamie tried to argue but the pain had knocked him rigid. The teacher came, and Robbie swapped places with her. As he made his way to another seat, he, and everyone else on the bus heard Jamie cry out.

"Don't touch it! Don't touch it!"

The teacher called an ambulance. The bus driver cursed and swore as he pulled over. Ten minutes later paramedics boarded and had to manoeuvre the tiny gangway. They carried Jamie off in an absurd sideways shuffle. Molly's jump resulted in a fracture and a broken knee-cap.

Jamie had sustained the same injuries in the past and coped very well. Robbie had expected that he would cope once again but, this was not quite the case. Having been there before, Jamie detached himself from the process, waiting to get better without participation. Robbie recalled the inertia of the unfocused glazed eyes, staring into space. A slightly protruding lower lip was the only indication of the feelings that lay behind it; intense frustration mounting to the most self-destructive anger. He would not ask for assistance; he would not do his exercises and he would not tell the story of how it had happened. Just as well then, that Robbie was a witness. He was not the only one.

It was not forgotten. Jamie was called the brittle boned-bawbag or Poundland man as he seemed to possess the durability of the worst products from Poundland. Jamie and Molly preferred to forget that they'd ever been together. Jamie knew that he was treated with kid gloves. Who wants to be delicate, Jamie wondered? Even women can't be arsed with it.

* * *

Blithe's mum, Lynne, sat on the sofa with her feet up on a battered pouffe. In the space between her leggings and her thick woollen socks, two inches of mottled skin bulged. The blinds had not been drawn during the day, and the unnatural light was harsh over piles of paperwork and dried and drying clothes that needed to be sorted. The peach walls had become chipped and marked after a decade of wear and tear, a grey wallpaper border was very slowly peeling and had become dog-eared in places. The kitchen was accessible through the living room, and Lynne could clearly see her daughter serving up dinner through the doorway.

She turned her attention back to the television, wider than the TV cabinet on which it was balanced. The cabinet had been made when TVs were boxy, which her second-hand TV was not. She raised her voice to Blithe in the kitchen.

"D'ye want a hand in there, hen?"

"No."

Blithe came through with a tray of steak pie, chips, and peas. It was not suitable for someone with type 2 diabetes but her mum rarely planned meals that were and accepted it gladly. Blithe returned to the kitchen for her own meal.

"D'ye see yer brother the day?"

Blithe shook her head as she came back in.

Lynne gestured to her plate. "This is good hen."

Blithe watched her mum shovel food into her face. Her mum very slowly continued to gain weight. Her blouse used to hang but had become very tight across her breasts.

Lynne used to joke that Blithe should take some of her weight, but eventually she could not ignore that Blithe never smiled when she said this.

"Are you watching this?" Blithe asked.

Lynne was half-watching a soap opera.

"No, turn it over if ye want."

Blithe turned off the television and started to eat her dinner. Lynne watched the little figure hunched over her plate, eating so fast she thought she'd choke, desperate to scuttle back to her room.

"Ye alright hen?"

"Aye."

Lynne stopped eating and observed the scowl on her daughter's face.

"How's school?"

"Same."

Lynne nodded. "Yer brother used to say that. Something's no right. Is it school?"

"School's shite."

"Ahh. Don't let them get ye down."

Blithe laid down her cutlery. "I've no pals. I hate it there."

"How can ye have no pals? Don't you let them win."

Blithe nodded, openly humouring her mum.

Lynne sighed. "I had this with yer brother…"

"So don't say the exact same things to me!"

Blithe, who hadn't intended to raise her voice, went back to eating her dinner.

"Don't you talk to me like that, ye hear me?"

Blithe didn't even look at her. She faced her tray and droned, "Aye maw."

"Yev no been out this week. Ye had a falling out?"

Blithe ignored her.

"That's it, isn't it? Would be easier if ye just telt me."

Again, Blithe cast down her cutlery and gritted her teeth.

"I broke up with Robbie, now everyone hates me!"

Relieved by her answer, Lynne smiled.

"He'll get over you and then they'll forget. Least ye didnae keep stringing him along eh?"

"Definitely didn't do that…"

The blank screen created an uncomfortable atmosphere for Lynne, who felt better with background noise to coax her thoughts along.

"See, if yer brother had said, I could have done something."

But Blithe could equally have said something, she'd been in on the conspiracy from the beginning. When Donnie skived, it never occurred to her to report him. They communicated these deceptions like spies; it took less than a finger to the lips, barely even a look, almost an instinct that he could trust her to cover for him. She assumed that one day he would return the favour. Blithe supported the lies he used when he came home without his coat, or with scorch marks on his arm. She understood enough, though he did not confide in her, all the more reason then, that when he did need her to conspire, she did.

"Aye well, same shit school, different kids, different problems." Blithe muttered. "I'm not putting myself through it fur nothing. Don's got practically nothing to show for it, but I will. Head down, get on with it and get out."

Lynne nodded. "I'd fight for you if I could."

This was true, Lynne would have done anything for her if only she had the information to act on, but that wasn't what Blithe heard. She heard her mum essentially say, that she was incapable of fighting for her.

Later, Blithe sat cross legged on her bed, her laptop balanced across her knees. In the bottom left of the screen a message popped up that she'd been tagged in a photo. She hadn't started her revision yet, so she opened the image. It was a picture taken years ago, when she was at primary school. A glorious sunny day under the trees. A shallow burn trickled down in the middle of the picnic area at New Lanark, the 18th century mill village where she had been taken on a school trip. She picked herself out quickly, one of the few children aware of the photographer, lunchbox protectively in her lap, head down, peeping up towards the camera under a straight black fringe, an expression that suggested someone had been unkind, but that wasn't necessarily the case. Blithe was a child who was rarely sure of anyone. A boy nearby responds to the camera with a look-at-me grin. The parent helpers take centre stage. Blithe noticed Codey Gallagher with her gran. Everyone knew Codey's gran because she was one of those adults who was always around to help with school trips or to offer assistance in the classroom. She was a big cheerful woman with closely cropped grey hair and a snub nose. Codey leans heavily against her gran, her face against a fleshy shoulder, sulking or shy, it was hard to tell.

Blithe recalled an even earlier school trip when she had lost her lunch box. She went to Codey's gran, who had led her by the hand, soothed her with her singsong smoker's voice and solved the problem. Blithe now stared at her face and smiled; *Now your granddaughter wants to smash my face in, what do ye have to say to that?*

Blithe didn't know that Codey had lost her gran to breast cancer two years ago. Why would she know? Who would have told her? If Codey had lost a parent everyone would have known. But family attachments are not always linked in the sequencing of generations, one welded to the next. The links that were prized from Codey were as solid and sustaining as those of a parent. Now with childhood vanishing, no one could replace them.

* * *

Donnie did not come home that night, but neither Blithe nor Lynne noticed as he was expected back so late. Even he did not really know what happened that night.

Donnie worked in a pub in the city centre, three or four nights a week. When a shift ended, he found himself, more often than not, in a deserted city centre where revellers could be heard but not seen. Disjointed voices, like beacons, demonstrated the opportunities of the hour for those with friends, money and stamina.

Going home after a shift meant staying awake, playing video games until the sun rose and beamed into his head. Morning was sobriety, a swaying pile of all the things he had to do to reverse the slide. He was like his mother, caught in an accelerating descent, that moved too fast to be halted just like that.

Donnie had no close friends. On leaving school, he'd severed all ties and, in the four years since, had not really succeeded in forging new ones. He quietly tagged along after Aldo and Jack, colleagues and friends who could be found on either side of the bar and were always in the pub long after kicking out time. Donnie followed them, laughed at their jokes and when he wasn't smoking, he was rolling up; he had to do something with his hands.

He often fell asleep at Aldo's after work and would be woken by voices demanding that he leave.

"Kicking out time! Mon. Fuck aff."

Aldo would cease to operate as a friend. Invariably Donnie was too tired to argue, too heavy to move anywhere other than the direction in which he was pointed. This time he had not gotten far. At 5am, he lay on a park bench on the southside of the Clyde, halfway to being home.

Donnie couldn't remember anything more of the previous night. He still had his phone, bank card and wallet but no cash. He didn't think he'd been robbed but he couldn't be sure whether he'd spent his money, or if he'd had any notes to begin with. He could vaguely remember taking half a dozen blues early on, maybe more. Blues were a cheap form of Valium but the chemical compound varied. Some came via fraudulent prescription, others were pressed locally; generally blue but sometimes white. Some lasted the night, sometimes the effects wore off within two hours. Donnie sought to banish aches, anxiety, and intrusive thoughts. That was all.

He staggered home, past the factory workers waiting for their minibus. He noticed nothing. Not the bats, not the fox that he'd have seen very clearly, if he'd looked up for long enough. He always noted the factory workers waiting for their minibus. They waited like ghosts, in the dark, in silence, too tired to talk or move their faces. Donnie was no better than they were. He thought his own situation was partly due to a lack of intelligence and doubted the same could be said of them. These people had only to break a language barrier. It wouldn't have surprised him if they already had better qualifications. He belonged with them as much as he belonged anywhere.

* * *

BLITHE SHITS HERSELF UP THE FRONT.

Jamie was impressed that the words were so clear and consistent. The message had been sprayed on a wall facing the sports field and each letter was twelve inches high.

Up the front of what?

After some thought, Jamie was sure they'd said exactly what they'd intended to say. He had to walk past the message several times that day. It drew the eye.

He heard that Blithe had been hiding in the school office, otherwise he would have assumed she'd skived. He decided that he didn't want to go through the gates with her and so, at the end of the day he went out the back, across the playing fields, through the hole in the fence and along an alley. He had to walk fast but he did so almost without limping. The alley opened into a small housing estate linking directly to the main road.

He did not need to hurry. Blithe had ducked into the same estate. Staring into her phone, she was late in noticing him. She'd reached the end of the cul-de-sac and planned to follow it round, hoping that no one would notice she'd taken such a pointless walk.

She looked up from her phone when Jamie was close enough to cast a shadow. Childishly, she screwed up her face.

"Is Robbie paying you to stalk me?"

"Aye, he's pimping me out."

Blithe rolled her eyes. "So what are you going to do if I get my head smashed in?"

"Call an ambulance."

Blithe raised her simple phone and waved it slowly in front of Jamie's face.

"Ah," he countered. "But can you make calls?"

"All phones call 999."

Jamie lazily let his hand loll round from his wrist as he thought of another reason.

"No, but you need to be conscious."

"Well if yev got nothing better to do..."

They emerged out of the estate back onto the main road. Up ahead they saw the crowd from the day before, but they were far beyond earshot and walking fast. The crowd did not look behind them but Jamie and Blithe ground to a halt, waiting until they vanished from sight. The boys walked as though they had something rammed up their arse, and the girls tripped forward on flat feet, as though flat shoes were unnatural.

Blithe and Jamie continued towards an old parade of shops, more than half of which had been shuttered up for as long as they could remember.

Jamie sighed and glanced at Blithe.

"You been hiding?"

Blithe didn't answer. She wouldn't call it hiding.

"Did you see the wall?" Jamie asked.

"Of course I saw the fucking wall! The teachers saw the fucking wall! Why else did they let me eat my lunch in an office?"

"Did ye tell them who ye thought it might be?"

Blithe smiled to herself. "No."

Jamie wouldn't have told either. He knew that what Blithe was suffering was a hounding that would last. It would get worse before it got better, and that's if it ever got better. If it had happened to him, he would have demanded that his dad homeschool him. They'd fall out within a week, the teaching would be judged harshly by his mum, creating a tension capable of destroying their marriage and even then, it would still be worth it.

So far, he'd tended not to look at Blithe. Walking alongside her, he easily avoided her face but, with regular glances, kept a careful eye on her profile. Her eyes were half closed; she breathed heavily and steadily, her small nostrils flaring just slightly.

He looked down before she might notice him staring. Jamie was starting to think it was all a bit pointless when he was reminded of why he was there. As they came to the end of the parade of shops, something flew through the air. It flew between them, landed with a crash, and splintered into pieces. It was a rotten bit of wood, pulled from an old window or door frame, possibly from one of the abandoned shops.

Jamie turned around; the figure's hoods were up as they fled through the car park. He would not follow. He turned his attention to Blithe, standing by the splinters, very still and swearing under her breath.

Jamie was for walking quickly on, but Blithe didn't move.

"Come on, keep going."

He walked on but she had not moved, her hand raised to her eye as she swore under her breath. She began to pull at her eyelid for the foreign object that was causing her so much pain. Through her gritted teeth, she muttered.

"Ah that kills."

"Shit. Did that get you?"

Jamie looked back and saw Connor returning with his brother, an older, uglier version of himself. Codey and Aleesha walked behind them. The boys were grinning, Aleesha screeched out a staged laugh. It was hard to tell if she was amused or if she just wanted to announce her presence.

Jamie stepped behind Blithe and pushed her into the

newsagents. This irritated Blithe and, she tutted. Her vision blurred and she stumbled on the steps as Jamie shoved her.

Jamie pushed her from the shoulders and steered her mechanically to the very back of the shop, where there was no natural light and shelves were either empty or half full of cleaning products and the odd sheet of wrapping paper. Blithe kept her hand clamped against her eye.

"Do you want me to have a go at getting it out?"

"Just have a look, see if you can see it."

Blithe revealed a very bloodshot eye. Jamie held her eye open and craned round, trying to see the offending object without blocking the faint light.

"Look up. Look right. Look down. I can't see anything."

He pulled her under the light and then exclaimed.

"Wait now! I see it. Do you want me to try and get it?"

A splinter of dried white paint nestled in the crease of her lower lid.

Jamie took Blithe's silence as a yes, put his index finger in his mouth and gave it a quick suck.

"What are ye doing?" she demanded.

"Look, do you want it out or don't you?"

Blithe leant her head back in the light, and after a few rapid blinks she held still as Jamie stuck his finger in her eye and dabbed gently. He was as gentle as possible as he searched it out. His moment came with the object appearing as she blinked again. Slowly but surely, he removed the offending chip of paint and displayed it triumphantly on the tip of his finger. Blithe let her focus sharpen on his twinkling green eyes.

The shop keeper had been watching her on the surveillance. He called out to her as she marched past the counter.

"You alright there, hen?"

Blithe smiled and nodded as she passed the counter, Jamie followed behind and did likewise.

Blithe quickly checked left and right before stepping back out onto the pavement.

"They'll be waiting in the car park down the road, probably..." said Blithe. "But if they think they've put my eye out that might be enough for one day."

They continued down the road, past the shops where there was nowhere to quickly duck into. Now, Jamie was very nervous; they were coming up to the car park on the corner of a busy crossroads, where semi circles of steel, indicating each bay, made an acceptable place to sit and wait. From there, the concrete steps leading up to Blithe's tower block could be seen almost directly across the road. In order to avoid walking past, they would have to go the long way round the crossroads. Such an obvious avoidance technique would make matters worse.

Jamie became aware of an older boy with dark hair jogging towards them. His heart sank. The boy slowed to a walk as he came alongside them.

"Ye aff home?"

Spots and acne marks stood out on his pale, pinched skin, and his Adam's apple looked more like a misplaced bolt in his neck. His short black hair was greasy and his tracksuit bottoms and hoodie hung off him.

"Where are yis both aff to?" he asked casually.

"Home!" Blithe exclaimed with unnecessary frustration. "Schools finished for the day."

"See, I don't even ken what day of the week it is man."

He grinned at Jamie, who couldn't help but smile back. He should have recognised Donnie; he'd been vaguely aware of him years before, but did not remember him looking so gaunt and lantern-jawed. Donnie faintly recognised Jamie.

"Do I know you?"

Jamie shook his head, not sure what he was after, not sure whether he'd assumed they were a couple.

Donnie's nose wrinkled as he considered his sister. "You okay? Yer eye's a wee bit sore?"

Blithe nodded, too fed up to even complain.

"Got followed. They flung something at us, got something in my eye. Never mind, it's out."

"Who did that?"

"Cuntrags in my year Donnie, who d'ye think?"

Donnie turned to Jamie. "Is that right?"

Jamie grinned. "Aye, I had to be eye doctor."

Donnie nodded, a little crestfallen, and shoved a fag packet in Jamie's face. The packet contained roll-ups that Donnie had spent hours rolling while waiting in the bus station. Not wanting to offend, Jamie took one and stood waiting for the offer of a light. It didn't come.

"Cheers for that." Donnie called. "See ye."

Blithe and Donnie crossed the road and headed up to the flat. Jamie looked at the roll-up in his hand, gave it a quick sniff, and pocketed it.

* * *

Robbie sat alone in his living room with the curtains closed and the lights off. His school bag lay undisturbed at his feet, exactly where he'd dumped it when he came home. As he pulled a remote from between the sofa cushions, his phone buzzed.

Professor Baw-Bag: Have you seen this?

Robbie did not know Professor Bawbag. He watched with a grim fascination as a video slowly buffered. His finger moved a fraction and hovered over the back button. With it all at his fingertips, Robbie was tempted to watch his humiliation. Every day the memory twisted into something a little worse.

This wasn't the first time he had received the video, but it was first time he had dared to watch it. The screen froze on his own face, his flattened nose, his small chin and dimples. He clicked 'back' with repulsion – if he couldn't stand to look at his own face, he shouldn't taunt himself with the horror in action.

His phone rang. It was his mum calling from the supermarket, wondering if there was anything he wanted her to pick up. She didn't normally do this, but he knew she wanted somehow to make it all better.

He tried to reel off a list, but his imagination disappointed him.

"Could you pick up a machete? And you'd better get some more paracetamol."

She chose to ignore his childishness, which irritated him, though he knew it was reasonable.

"Okay. You don't have anything dangerous nearby do you?"

"No."

"Right. See you soon. Don't go anywhere."

A message came through from Jamie as he hung up.

Jamie: Walked B. Bit fucked up. Stick thrown, no blood. I'm ok.

Robbie: Stick?

Jamie: You're not coming up on Snapchat.

Robbie uninstalled several apps to cut down on the channels of communication, but he felt no safer. If anything, it left him feeling worse.

He wanted to ask how she was, but that would lead to other questions and, although he trusted Jamie, he didn't want him to even suspect genuine concern. He wouldn't ask any more questions. In this way, his feelings would stay safely within.

Jamie recalled how he had managed to extricate the object from Blithe's eye. He was proud of the care he had taken in the poor light, as though he were a doctor working on the battlefield.

The following day at school he looked out for her, wanting to see whether her eye was still bloodshot, but they weren't in any of the same classes.

It had been overcast and wet, gusts whipping across the many puddles. Nothing had a chance to dry out and the damp permeated the sterile rooms, carried on feet and jackets. By the end of the school day, the rain shrunk to dew in the air. Blithe made her way out of the main gates, seizing her opportunity while the coast was clear.

Jamie walked after her. He didn't need to catch her up immediately, as long as he remained just behind her. He watched her rapid little steps, her head raised high and vigilant as he struggled to keep up with her. Eventually, several minutes later, Blithe turned and gave him a curt nod.

"How's your eye?" he asked.

"I can see your smug face perfectly."

Jamie was relieved that trouble seemed so be elsewhere, but Blithe felt all the more anxious for it.

"Ye don't have to do anything," she said. "See if I was a guy, you'd let me get ma head kicked in. You would enjoy it as well."

Jamie doubted that this was true but tried to consider it seriously.

"I could watch revenge but not physical pain, I don't like seeing people in pain."

Blithe observed his limp and nodded. She didn't flinch at the mention of Robbie, and so Jamie decided to go further.

"Why did you do that to him?"

"Don't know."

"Well, see, if I was a girl, I'd probably go for Robbie..."

"Ye could be a girl," quipped Blithe. "Shove another "A' or "I' in yer name, maybe a hyphen, take some pills and boom! Pair of tits bigger than mine."

Jamie glanced towards her chest. She was a small skinny girl and Jamie thought that pills wouldn't be necessary, a month of big portions and no exercise would probably do it.

"He's a good guy."

Blithe nodded. "He is. He's so nice, I'm so lucky but, fuck what I actually think."

Jamie replied coldly. "When you bag yer raging hard man, I hope you'll be really happy, I hope you cream yourself every time he puts yer windaes through!"

Blithe stopped to stare at him, wondering what other gems would slip from his mouth. He had expected her to get angry, but instead, she seemed faintly amused. The anger and defiance he'd prepared for deflated out of him like a slow fart and, he stood speechless and embarrassed.

"I don't want out with every single nice guy, being decent does not get you whatever girlfriend you want. There's loads of nice girls and maybe you'd be happy with any of them like some, fucking, nature documentary. Man enters the arena, there is a girl, she will do, and they will fuck. Fuck's sake Jamie."

Jamie smiled and Blithe tried not to.

"Okay," he said, "I ken what yer saying and if yer not feeling it, fine... But why film him? That's what nobody gets."

This was the first time anyone asked her directly. She sighed as her heart sank. It was a reasonable question and, after a time, she said.

"I don't know, I've already said I don't know. I didnae think he'd ever know or ever see it. Honestly, I ken yer not going to believe me."

Jamie didn't say anything. He didn't want to accept this explanation, but he did.

Codey and Connor waited with their friends on the corner where their paths would cross. As far as they were concerned, an injured eye did not constitute a job done. Rather than follow Blithe as before, they decided to surprise her. They had taken a different route, with Connor cycling at the front, his older brother Jason and Codey, jogging alongside. Aleesha and her little brother, Kaiden, lagged at the back with Leanne Kelly jogging along somewhere in the middle.

As planned, by the time Blithe became aware of the group,

they were already waiting.

As they passed the carpark on the corner, the only indicator Blithe gave that she had seen them was a quick little bat at Jamie's hip. It was a warning to be on his guard, not to say anything or come out with some stupid exclamation. This, he managed. They walked past the car pack without increasing their speed, aware of all eyes on them.

Connor sat upright on his bike with his feet planted squarely on the ground and his hands in his pockets.

He watched Jamie and Blithe very closely. There was a symmetry in where they faced and where they looked. Though Jamie's walk was asymmetrical, Blithe managed to keep to the same rhythm. Connor glanced over at Codey; she had been talking to his brother Jason and now watched her enemy passing with arms folded.

Connor watched the figures striding past and smiled. He wanted to bring their nerves to the surface. Generally, all he had to do was stand on the street corner, stare and sure enough, he'd note shoulders arching, footsteps quickening, heads dropping down or eyes unmoving or moving too much.

The group used their stares to intimidate, until Leanne burst out laughing as Blithe began to cross the road.

Jamie looked over his shoulder and momentarily made eye contact. As soon as he did this, Leanne stood up and walked towards them.

"Hey!" she shouted. "Bitch face!"

She'd been waiting for him to turn around. Her hair was piled messily on her head and her nose scrunched up when she shouted, pulling at the greasy fleshiness of her face.

Jamie muttered to Blithe, "Is that you or me?"

"It's me."

Then they heard another angry shout, this time from Codey.

"You feart of a girl!?"

Blithe was quick.

"Don't reply."

"Should I see you to yer door?"

Blithe shrugged.

"I'll see ye to your door, then she can kick my head in so that I can prove that I'm not scared of her."

"Ye are though, aren't ye?"

"Of course I am. I'm still doing this stupid walk with a miserable bitch. And by the way, I don't always do what Robbie tells me. I wouldnae need to be so fucking nice to him, if you hadnae been such a massive fanny."

Blithe had been waiting for him to say something like this. In the silence, they glanced at each other simultaneously, Blithe because she regretted sneering and Jamie because, having been so honest, he now felt guilty.

"Ye know, ye could just bolt... hobble away home." Blithe suggested. "Robbie would never ken, who would tell him? Me? Fat fucking chance of that."

Jamie sighed. "I'm not all that comfortable lying to ma friend, and if you show up at school tomorrow with yer face kicked in... I'm not sure I'm comfortable with that either."

'Me getting ma head kicked in?"

"It's not for them to do it. They're... shit!"

A small stone struck Jamie on the back of the head. He knew not to look back and heard laughter and hooting.

"Ye alright?" Blithe asked. Before waiting for a reply, she turned to face the group.

"See if ye were trying to hit me, yer aim is shite!"

Another missile was hurled. Blithe ducked it and shouted, "Still shite!"

Jamie looked at her in horror.

"Look, they've started," she explained, "so that's it. No point keeping quiet now!"

The group moved closer towards them.

Codey took a run to the front and shouted out, "What are you saying? What's that yer saying?"

At that moment, Blithe noticed that the lights had just changed further down the road. A stream of traffic was about to pass, but she had just enough time to cross before it did. She began to run, and Jamie ran after her.

Jamie could run but not as gracefully as Blithe. Once they had crossed the road, the way to the tower block was uphill. A steep alley of concrete steps cut up from the road to the tower. When they reached the alley, Blithe pounded up the steps. If it weren't for her hefty, ink-stained rucksack, her sprint would have looked sleek. Jamie couldn't follow so easily; his eyes took in the looming steps above him. They were small, awkward steps, like a leaning stack of concrete shoeboxes. Still, he climbed, the aches increasing with every step. One leg had to take all the weight of his body; his legs did not share the task of climbing. Blithe stopped and looked back. Everyone knew Jamie was slow on stairs. He waved her on, already out of breath, shaking his head.

"I'll wait at the door," she called.

Jamie watched her bound up the last steps with easy strides. At the top she turned back to see how he was doing, her face remaining expressionless as she turned away, hurrying on without him.

He was almost at the top when the group reached the bottom. Jamie heard familiar calls behind him, but he did not turn, he wanted to get to the top of the steps before he was trapped there. The focus of this little ambition took the edge from his fear.

The group enjoyed watching him climb as much as they had enjoyed the sight of him tearing across the road.

"Hey!" Aleesha shouted. "Could you run any less like an uptight fucking giraffe?"

"Don't ignore her ye brittle boned bawbag!" Connor spat.

Jamie reached the top of the steps. He faced the levelled carpark surrounding the tower, and fifty yards away, saw Blithe under the awning as she vanished inside. He walked as fast as he could over the cratered, crumbling asphalt. He could not run anymore.

Aleesha, a short chunky girl with a black greasy bob, jogged alongside him.

"Are you going in there to fuck her? Can ye even fuck standing up?"

Connor joined her and added, "Na, his knees'd drop aff, he'd end up as fuckn, Dopey the dwarf."

Jamie tried to look straight ahead, but pulling a disinterested face was beyond him.

Jason, Connor's older brother, moved in front of Jamie, shouldering him as he walked alongside.

"Sorry about the rock, ye ken, but that happens when ye move around with a target, ye ken, like, fuckn... dressing up like Isis in some fuckinanistan or wherever."

Compared to his big brother, Connor was an Adonis. Jamie glanced at a nose that had been broken and piggy, eyes in a pinched and knobbly face that he should have been able to keep at bay until at least twenty-five. Repeated pummelling of the face can do that.

Jamie could still feel roughly where the rock had hit.

"It's fine," he muttered.

The main door was not far away, just a few yards.

"Oh that's great. Can ye fuck standing up? Just honest curiosity, I swear to God."

Jason watched Jamie turn bright red and grinned.

"Have ye tried? Aye probably not, just watching ye there I was thinking that it's probably no for you. Tell her to go on top. I've heard she'll dae anything, not very well but, hey, a hole's a goal."

Jamie had to walk round him, and he was now very afraid that when he reached the door, Blithe would not be behind it. If he reached the door and it didn't give, he would have to turn around and face them. He couldn't buzz, he didn't know the flat number. It wouldn't be easy to look through them then. They followed him to the door and watched as Jamie gave it a push.

Sure enough, the door didn't give. Jamie was so crushed that, for a second, he looked back at Jason despairingly. Laughter burst around him. He had tried to be expressionless, but his lips parted in a silent groan.

At that moment, the door was pushed ajar as Jamie was suddenly pulled inside, so quickly that he fell on his side. The door slammed, the laughter continued even after the door slammed.

"Ye alright?"

The sound of his fall and the slam of the door echoed around the bare lobby. Jamie rose shakily from the old orange tiles and nodded. His knee hurt, and he didn't want to go out again. The words cut so close to the bone, they were impossible to ignore. He didn't know that he was still very flushed. He'd walked her home expecting exactly the kind of thing that had just happened; he could hardly be outraged.

"Don't listen,' Blithe said. "That guy boasts, he's like, 'Rarr! Make way bitches and put out! But he does think a hole's a goal, which is just as well by the way, because I don't think his Tinder profile could say much more than, 'Hole wanted, preferably small and warm.'"

"You'd know eh?"

"No!" Blithe slapped his arm. "But he will fuck anything, and he can say what he likes about me. Yev got to leave those bastards to think what they like. I ken how stupid they are and if ye heard the kind of stupid shit they come out with, you'd find it easy too."

"What kind of shit?"

"Like, 'I'm never buying that minging mango chutney – it funds jihad."

Jamie's frown was sceptical.

"Honest, I did," Blithe continued. "Trust me, if you're looking to buy guns and ammo, making chutney is no good."

Jamie covered his mouth; he didn't want to laugh. Blithe noticed that he tended to cover his mouth when he grinned.

"Are they going to wait outside for long d'ye think?" he asked.

Blithe shook her head.

"Wait five minutes. They've no business being up here, none of them live this way. They just want to wind you up. You'll be fine going back the way ye came."

"Well, you don't have to hang about here waiting," Jamie muttered, feeling cowardly at having to sneak out.

"I'm up on the ninth floor. I'll be able to see them from my bedroom window. Wait on the stairs, and I'll call down when they've gone. Alright?"

Jamie followed her through to the staircase. He watched her mounting the stairs and hesitated before taking a seat on the step. As Jamie waited, a numbing anxiety set in as he thought about getting home. There was no easy way out, he could be jumped whichever direction he took.

The main doors of the flat opened. Jamie held his breath while the footsteps approached. A boy a couple of years below him entered the stairwell and looked at Jamie suspiciously.

"Awright?" Jamie smiled.

The boy only nodded slightly and glanced over his shoulder as he walked past, as though he expected Jamie to spring something on him. Just then Blithe, at the top of her lungs, shouted down the stairs.

'They've gone! I've just seen them leave. Yer fine!"

Then the boy paused, suddenly understanding,

"I passed Connor and that on the way here. You'll be fine if yer heading back Shawlands way."

Jamie smiled.

"...But no one here's afraid of that cunt."

CHAPTER 5

Robbie's textbooks covered his pillows. He lay on his front, pen in mouth but he wasn't doing anything. Studying had become more difficult. Long passages of text seemed foggy, hard to follow and hard to care about. His dormant brain just wasn't sparking to receive anything, only what had happened, what he should have done and failed to do. He went over what people had said and therefore, must be continuing to say. His brain connectivity re-wired and hardwired to a mess of paranoia, shame, and embarrassment.

He had a notebook out; in the margins he had drawn an owl and a laughing face. His phone sat propped up between the open pages of his textbook. A message appeared.

Jamie: We should bulk.

Robbie sneered; there was something distinctly stupid and patronising about Jamie's efforts to cheer him up.

Robbie: Eat some fatty shit.

Jamie: Predictive fuckity fingers.

Through half closed eyes, Jamie's message became clear.

Jamie: Busk.

Robbie moved the phone further up his bed by the headboard. He started to read his textbook but the little light coming on in his peripheral vision demanded attention.

Jamie: My sister could film it. If it's good we could post it up but if you want we could delete it.

Robbie groaned aloud, momentarily moved the phone away

from him, and pulled it back to type.

Robbie: What are you wanting to busk?

Jamie: The usual.

Jamie sat at his desk, also under the pretence of revising. He too was finding it hard to concentrate, and though his messages were light-hearted, that was not how he felt. He slumped in his chair, hand supporting his head as his fingers typed swiftly. He was unperturbed by Robbie's responses, reading them eagerly and moving on before an expression could pass his face.

Jamie: No surprises, maybe some Marley. If my sister comes she'll want to sing an Amy McDonald, but if we can't think of anything else, I'll no be able to stop her.

Robbie: You just want to prove that you can sing.

A frown creased Jamie's forehead. Robbie was not a trained singer whereas Jamie was, but Robbie had a love and instinct for it. His voice a little raw, perhaps, deeper than you would think from looking at him but he had a spirit that Jamie lacked.

Around the age of fourteen, Jamie became embarrassed in his own skin, viewing himself critically from the outside. When he had sung as a child, he enjoyed being good at something, he'd relished the attention. Attention was something he increasingly shrank away from. He didn't feed off the audience, he ignored them.

Robbie could be withdrawn, but he was not self-conscious. With the right conditions he could be the entertainer. He could, Jamie reasoned, bask in the centre of attention. Though he'd not tried it before, Jamie was convinced that an hour of busking would have restorative powers.

Now, reading the texts, he wondered if it were naïve of him to suppose it could be so easy to repair Robbie – they disagreed about music. Robbie liked music that he said you could dance to; he didn't seem to especially hate anything, not even boy bands. Jamie couldn't dance, he couldn't leap about, couldn't really mosh and his ears were easily offended – as he was the choosier, he chose. This time he would be more self-sacrificing, he wouldn't baulk at whatever Robbie chose.

Robbie stared at his phone without replying. He wasn't going to say no, but he should have felt nervous to agree. He felt nothing.

Robbie: Where?

Jamie: Below Princess Street, on the platform.

Robbie: They'll not be able to hear us.

Jamie: There's fewer trains at the minute. Bigger crowds. It's the most miserable place in the world.

Robbie: You singing Radiohead will cheer them up?

Robbie: What about a Samaritans gallows building and knot tying team day.

Robbie: Or splatter the hamster holiday club for traumatised children?

Jamie was tempted to throw his phone.

Jamie: What do you want to do?

Robbie: You never do anything crowd pleasing.

Jamie: I hate crowd pleasing.

Robbie: So don't busk you moron!

Robbie laid his phone face down and managed to get on with some work.

His mum arrived home from work a little later than usual, due to transport upgrades in the city centre. She asked him if he had eaten, he said he had, but he had eaten nothing since lunch.

In the bathroom he stared at his face, barely moving a muscle. Facially he was still a child, his lips were too prominent, his chin too weak. If he allowed some weight to fall from him perhaps, he thought, it would take his dimples with it.

* * *

When the bell rang at the end of the day, Blithe had waited behind. While Jamie waited at the gates, Blithe was in the head teacher's office.

She sat on a cushioned chair that felt a little like luxury. The office was spacious, the desk larger than the rest but, strangely empty of paperwork. Perhaps the head had hidden it, you've got to be careful with what you leave lying around when you invite a pupil like Blithe into the office. Blithe noticed that the rain had started to come down and she smiled. No one would hang around waiting for her today.

Mrs Smith, the head teacher, was a large woman with red hair in a neat bob. She'd never really spoken to Blithe before, as there had never been a reason. Now she hurried in, slightly breathless.

"How are we today Blithe?"

She smiled. Blithe simply nodded.

"I've spoken to a few members of staff about what's happened. I think I get the picture; I appreciate you coming forward and I appreciate your honestly. It's meant that we don't have to sieve the fact from the fiction – it all seems fairly clear to me."

Blithe nodded again, her stomach in knots.

"Now, I am horrified that you could circulate something like this. I realise that this is something you have done in your own time, but your parents should be informed. Now, what's circulating around the school is another matter and there is a feeling, unanimous among the staff I've spoken to, that you are sorry, it hasn't made your life easy has it? No. I bet not. I've considered the matter long and hard. You've chosen to give yourself isolation detention in effect. For another couple of weeks, I am happy for that to continue. This is a punishment – you must continue to stay in the study room at break time, you may eat your lunch there. It won't help your learning to have you burn out this close to exams. You need a break but all the same, I suggest you use the time well. After two weeks I would hope the matter will start to die down. If it doesn't, my door is open to you. The teachers are there to support you, we're still behind you."

Blithe almost looked over her shoulder and nodded again.

"You've said nothing since I called you in here, Blithe."

Blithe nodded again and croaked, "Thank you."

Mrs Smith leaned across her desk.

"Are you alright?"

Blithe nodded and chewed her lip. Mrs Smith didn't look convinced.

"Sure?" She searched Blithe's face. "Okay then. I won't keep you. Goodbye, Blithe."

"Yes," thought Blithe, "You know my name, well done."

It was heartening to walk out on the mouldy concrete and hear only her own footsteps. The sky was heavy with muted white clouds, seeming to push down from above like a headache. Walking through an aftermath of chaos in perfect safety, flicking rainwater with many light steps. She was almost happy and then, as she rounded the corner, she saw the familiar figure at the bus stop. He turned to look at her and even from the distance of fifty yards, he saw her relief before she had time to wipe it from her face.

She called out, "What are you doing?"

She drew closer and saw how wet and bedraggled he was. When the rain was at its heaviest, he'd been tempted to give up waiting and jump on the bus. He'd given her five minutes, then another five minutes. He was relieved when at last she appeared, but he was the bearer of bad news.

"I know you look after yerself…and there's fuck all point in me being here…"

Jamie rubbed his arms. As his blazer was wet, it made hardly any difference.

"There's a 'but' coming," he added.

Blithe smiled. "Yours or someone else's?"

Jamie shook his head. "You're weird today, did they drug you or something?"

He paused for a second, not used to her playfulness.

"But there's things I overheard; Codey Gallagher has been bragging about what she's going to do to you. I heard it a couple of times, I thought ye might have been held back because she'd already hurt you. Don't walk on your own."

Blithe didn't react but she wasn't surprised. Codey couldn't let conflicts fizzle out, she had to demonstrate some kind of win.

"Well, I've no change for the bus, I'm gonnae have to walk. Ye don't have to come with me."

Blithe began the walk home. Footsteps followed behind as Jamie struggled to catch up.

"You're not going the usual way?" he asked.

"It was raining, she'll no have waited. She doesnae live at my bit."

"Do you want to know what I heard?"

"Yer gonnae tell me. On ye go."

"She said she's going to smash yer face in on the way home."

Blithe shrugged. It was as she expected. She didn't know what Jamie wanted her to do with the information.

"She had an audience," Jamie continued. "She's bragged to too many people. She said she'll break your nose and yer jaw. She said she doesnae care if she gets into trouble, it'll be worth it to rearrange yer face."

"You overheard her?"

"Aye, in snatches. I went up to Daisy, who was there, and I asked her."

Blithe didn't look convinced.

"Mon now," Jamie coaxed, "Daisy's a nice girl."

"Bet she didn't give two fucks."

"She didnae think it was funny and I tell you, loads did. Why don't you go somewhere else? Walk through Pollok Park or something, where she'll not be waiting."

"That's in the other direction."

"It's not. Gives you a wee bit more time. Fuck sake, if I can walk it, then you can."

* * *

The clouds were beginning to break in places. As the wind blew, sunshine cracked through here and there, a warm stroke on the back to counter the breeze. Blithe was tired, but not so tired that the walk in the park was a complete drag. The wet grass and sodden ground permeated her shoes and walking aggravated her blisters, which made her and Jamie equal in their ability to cover the distance.

"Why doesn't Codey like you?" Jamie asked.

"I don't think she's that bothered about me."

Jamie grinned. "Oh, you didn't hear her."

Blithe smiled and focused on Jamie.

"Oh right, she's going to stamp my face unrecognisable? Where does she think she is? I'm just convenient. Because I've no friends, she'll use me as an example, like, look what I can do, I could also do this to the people who fuck you off. I'm a fucking advertising sample. She wants folk to see her standing up for her pals, she wants to be seen as a tough hard-ass bitch."

Jamie nodded. "We're too old for this shit."

They emerged through the trees and walked by the lawn, on towards the museum. The glass panels on the east side of the museum ran parallel to a grassy slope which rose up to the building like a hem. Jamie left the path, took a couple of steps up the slope and sat down. Blithe followed slowly, wet grass seeping into the sections of her shoes that were not already waterlogged.

They sat in silence, staring into the wide-open green that was, for now, all their own. Birds called clearly from the woodland yet the trees entirely drowned out the traffic beyond.

Blithe kicked off her shoes and examined the soles, sodden at the base and fraying at the toe. She wiggled her toes, sat back and diverted her attention to the sky.

She glanced at Jamie, whose hair was only just beginning to dry off.

"D'ye not have a home to go to?" she asked.

"I'm a fucking gentleman," he replied.

Blithe kept her twinkling eyes on him, a smile teetering on her lips.

"If I get home and my mum sends me out to get the messages, there's nothing you can do then."

"And I'll no feel bad if something does happen. It's not like I can help you at school is it?"

Blithe had nothing to say. Her expression turned cold as she looked away into the distance. Jamie took his phone from his pocket; he thought he'd heard a buzz but there was nothing.

"I think I could use a bit of abuse," he said. "I need to toughen up. I dinnae want to be scared all the time."

Blithe scoffed. "Seriously?"

Jamie continued to stare ahead with neither denial nor embarrassment.

"Well you should be careful what you wish for," Blithe muttered.

"I know but... I've got to stand up for myself. There's a lot of cunts about these days."

Blithe considered this carefully.

"If yer constantly getting grief, you have to be an arsehole. If ye live a nice life where people aren't constantly trying to smash yer face in, then ye don't need to learn to defend yerself. There's nothing wrong with that."

Jamie nodded, pulling at strands of grass absentmindedly.

"It's not an ideal world though,' he said. "What about something in between? I shouldn't be sheltered, I should be punched around a bit. Not too much, just a wee bit."

Blithe pursed her lips. "Ye don't get to specify."

Jamie started to scroll through his phone. He became aware that Blithe was sitting silently by, without a phone to distract her. He tried to find a clip that he could share to guarantee a laugh, but eventually, he sighed, pocketed his phone and rose to his feet, with his knees still stiffy bent. Blithe watched with a raised eyebrow as he took a deep breath and tumbled head over heels down the slope. It was an ungainly tumble as knobbly ankles were for a second revealed before he crashed to the earth at the bottom of the slope. Jamie lay on his back for a while, listening for comment and, when none came, he sat up and rubbed his knee.

"That's more uncomfortable than it used to be."

Blithe grinned at the grass that stuck to his hair and plastered, yellow and slimy, against his blazer.

He turned, noticed she was amused, and made his way back up to her, ruffling his hair.

"Do you want to go inside?"

Blithe had not been in the Gallery since she was small. She was unaware that she did not need to pay. Back when her mum had energy, she had been taken along with her brother to various things in the park but, her recollections of the art collection were vague.

Once inside, she said nothing to Jamie, who either seemed to be just ahead of her or just behind her, staring at the exhibits with an unreadable face. Obeying his sense of reverence, pretending to be cultured or bored, it was impossible to tell. Jamie wasn't sure, it might have been the first time he had ever walked into a museum by choice. He felt just as much of an imposter as she did.

Jamie and Blithe emerged from the woods into avenues sheltered by vast oaks. They left the green behind as they passed under the long, low railway bridge, emerging from the tunnel to be once again assailed by both noise and smell. The bridge locked the city away but now they faced a long walk home on concrete beneath grey skies.

As they walked towards the crossing, Blithe dived across the main road. On his own, Jamie would have waited, but he tore after her, across several lanes of traffic. A taxi hooted at him, but he didn't care and didn't see the driver jab at his temple in fury.

They walked alongside a fenced-in wasteland, where once a petrol station or tyre yard had been. Now there were weeds, gravel, and a rusty supermarket trolley. They should have been careful walking there but were too tired to be vigilant. The driveway remained but now it went to nowhere and was only good for a getaway. Jamie was relieved that their pace slowed before they made their way uphill.

Jamie felt safe because Blithe seemed relaxed. He caught her smiling to herself slightly, even though her aching heels had started to affect her gait. Trudging uphill, she seemed to weigh so much more than before.

Across the street, a girl walked towards them. Jamie didn't register her at first, still looking out for uniforms like his own. He took a long drink of water; the girl drew closer and just as he replaced the lid of the bottle, he saw her poisonous glance before she had time to avert it.

Her name was Leanne Kelly. She'd changed out of her uniform into tracksuit bottoms and a lime green hoodie.

Her shark eyes swivelled in Blithe's direction, and she did a complete about turn. It wasn't the turn that was alarming, it was the marching of a girl with important business.

"Shit." Blithe exclaimed. "Move!"

They hurried on uphill, finding a shot of energy from somewhere. The final section was not so steep. As it levelled out, Leanne ran around a corner ahead of them and shouted.

"They're here!"

Jamie had not approached the building from this side before, but knew his bearings from the red awning over the main doorway, battered and loose. As they mounted the slope turning into the carpark, they heard the sound of running trainers hitting concrete. Aside from Kaiden, the boys had left the group. The girls did not have the audience they had hoped for.

Codey, Leanne and Aleesha rounded the corner and made a dash. Codey caught Blithe just as she reached the main door, grabbing at her sleeve and scrunching it in her fist, as Blithe pulled back towards the door. Blithe reclaimed her sleeve with a sudden yank, Codey staggered back and threw herself towards Blithe with her arm raised. Blithe deflected the punch and stumbled backwards to the main door.

Leanne gave Blithe a shove and placed herself in front of the door. She craned past Blithe and Jamie, hoping to see an audience gathering behind Codey. Only wee Kaiden emerged from around the corner, with a carrier bag bulging with cans.

Codey shouted over her shoulder, 'Get yer fat arse down here!"

She turned back to Blithe but kept glancing over her shoulder. She was just a little nervous, just a little hesitant. She wanted her friends to see what she was about to do far more than she wanted to do it.

At this point Blithe became aware of Jamie's head moving up and down in the throes of nausea, his hand to his mouth and then his throat. As she looked away, she heard the splatter as copious amounts of liquid spirted out of his mouth – voluminous and heavy as it landed.

Leanne jumped back from the door in revulsion. "Fuck sake!"

Blithe slammed her key in the lock and pulled open the door. Jamie managed to squeeze inside first but as Blithe followed, he pulled the door closed a little too early and her leg became stuck. As he widened the gap, Leanne had a chance to stamp on Blithe's ankle but, whether it was Leanne's kick or Jamie closing the narrow opening, Blithe grazed her leg against the door as she slipped through. She also lost a shoe, but all that mattered was the heavy battered door between them, now slamming shut.

A barrage followed against the door, like hail in a hurricane. Blithe moved down the corridor but Jamie stayed, his hands against the door, convinced they were about to ram their way inside. They could be heard taking run-ups and the sounds of their bodies hitting the door were as painful as they were pointless.

Anger was not a feeling to be wasted. Anger garnered respect, anger got things done and punctuated life for worse but sometimes better. It therefore made sense to throw yourself repeatedly against metal and wood, if just for the chance to display it.

Jamie stayed by the door. "They've probably worked out that I spat water at them."

Blithe heaved a great sigh and turned her attention to her foot. She wouldn't get that shoe back, and the scratch on her ankle was beginning to bleed. She watched the blood through the hole now gaping in her black tights. She felt at the graze and was almost weepy that this had been done to her. She was getting so tired of it, but either she got used to it or it would wear her down.

"Shit!"

Jamie had heard a key in the door and bolted around the corner to the lifts.

The door creaked open a fraction as a hoarse voice called, "Get tae fuck!"

It was the voice of Donnie. Blithe didn't want to see her brother. She dashed round the corner after Jamie as Donnie made his weary way inside. Blithe shoved Jamie past the lifts and ran round another corner. Jamie followed her down a short flight of steps to the door of the cleaner's cupboard.

They listened as Donnie approached the first lift, pressed the call button, walked towards the second lift, and came into view. They waited. If he turned, he would see them. The doors opened and he stepped inside, keeping his back to them while the doors firmly closed.

In wonder at his own power of evasion, Jamie cooed with a

childish, 'Ooohhh...' Blithe nearly did the same thing. The lift rattled loudly as it carried Donnie up.

"I'm not going to go up yet," Blithe said. "Mum'll rip into him."

This wasn't exactly true. Blithe could discern a lot from his tone of voice and Donnie was returning home angry and exhausted. Now was not the time for questions but Lynne would demand answers, nonetheless. Blithe did not want to be there when she did. He would not talk, he would not confide, and you couldn't make him.

Something heavy was thrown at the main doors.

"What's the deal if they get in?" Jamie whispered.

Blithe was uncertain. "They'll think that we'll have gone on up to my flat. Why wouldn't we?"

Blithe moved further up and sat on the step.

"Doesn't that smell of piss?" Jamie asked.

"Piss and disinfectant," Blithe corrected.

Jamie moved up to sit with her. He assumed that basement steps in a tower block would invite piss, but the only smell he could pick up on, was industrial disinfectant.

They heard another bang as something heavier still was hurled at the doors. Jamie checked the time on his phone and messaged his dad to say he would be late. He didn't want to go out alone. The rage at the door had left him with a clear image of bricks or bottles flying towards his face.

"What about you?" he whispered, "Are you just going to sit here?"

Blithe sighed. "In ten minutes I'll head up. Have a look out the window, see if they're still about outside."

Nothing was said for a while. It had gone quiet outside, there was no need to wait ten minutes. They were aware of their elbows just touching.

"What about your mum though? Yer brother's a big guy."

"Is he fuck! He's tall but there's nothing of him!"

"Still," he continued, "Yer mum's not well. Do you think she'll be okay?"

"She's a big fat tank, ye cannae get past her. What happens, what always fucking happens, is shouting and slamming doors. It disnae get better, disnae get worse, it just goes on and on."

"Are you going to be alright though?"

At first, Blithe frowned.

"What? From them upstairs?" she laughed. "I'm not going to get battered or anything."

Jamie turned to face her, tilting his head. "That's still shit though. I'm not saying my home life is perfect, but I've never not gone home because of a fight. Not one that someone else is having, anyway."

Blithe sighed, 'They're not that bad but... ye can hear everything and Donnie wants me to back him up, mum wants me to back her up."

Blithe didn't confide much. She struggled to believe that someone outside her family could understand. It was hard to talk about their situation without seeming to list a catalogue of failure. Further explanation never helped, it offered only poor excuses. Still, she tried.

"I ken that I slag my brother off and he deserves it but he's still a poor fucker. He's got nothing. I feel sorry for the pair of them. It's like Donnie was just dropped. I never had my dad at home, he moved out before I was born so it's fuck all to me. With Donnie though it's not like that, he's been dropped by dad, by school, by pals. He's just abandoned, d'ye understand?"

Jamie nodded, a little worried that his earlier assumption was offensive. He'd pictured a physical fight: thrown crockery, soap opera screaming, and she probably knew that. He wished he'd kept his mouth shut.

Blithe knowingly cast her eyes above. "Soon something's going to happen. He'll do something stupid or something stupid will happen to him."

Jamie struggled for a while to think of anything reassuring to say. "Aye well, he's a big boy."

Blithe faced Jamie critically. He stared back with wide innocent eyes, afraid once again, to have said the wrong thing.

Blithe wiggled a finger at him.

"See, I knew you were going to say something like that. That's what everyone says; 'he's a big boy', that's part of the problem. You think you're going to go from being Poundland man."

Jamie looked at her reproachfully. "Don't call me that."

"Okay...to fucking Mad Max. I'm asking you?"

Amused, Jamie considered.

"I probably won't feel that different. I hope I won't make so many stupid mistakes."

Blithe seemed to be getting worked up. "But if you do, they'll be serious mistakes, no job, no money mistakes."

"Is that the kind of stuff you think about?" Jamie exclaimed.

"I think about other stuff. I think about Codey drenched in pigeon shit, I think about her desperately trying to be a boxer, only she's shit at it, and gets all her teeth get knocked out."

At first Blithe thought Jamie was suppressing a yawn as he draped his hand to cover his mouth. Green eyes squeezed to black crescents, and he giggled.

Blithe smiled to herself. She didn't really care what was going on upstairs. She would care a lot when she knew, but for now, it didn't matter.

Jamie listened out but now all he heard were seagulls screeching and heavy drizzle tossing against the windows. A tranquillity settled into the silence. Amid the sterile tiles and the bare cream coloured walls, they'd huddled themselves warm. He turned towards her, this time he had nothing to say. Moving like a reflection she turned at the same time.

They froze for a moment, breathed a little deeper. Neither inclining away, close enough to feel the breath of the other. Like reflections joining, they moved together. It came so naturally, without pressure, only the urge to feel the lips of the other and with a gentle flicker, tongue found tongue. Like sinking into sleep, sinking peacefully together, until they came apart.

Jamie couldn't resist tucking her hair behind her ear and stared at her intently.

Blithe restrained her smile for as long as she could, making it all the more wonderful when she gave way and let it light up her face. Then he had to kiss her again, a little clumsier this time because now she wanted to laugh.

Then he noticed her bleeding leg and had no qualms about examining it, but she pulled away. She didn't want him feeling at her horrible old tights.

"I'll go on up now."

Blithe stood up and climbed the steps, keeping her injured leg tucked away behind the other.

"It's fine," she assured him. "Just needs a clean."

"You're not going to get that shoe back, are you?"

"I'll no want it back. Those were my only pair of school shoes."

"What shoe size are you? Maybe I can give you an old pair of my sisters?"

"A five but don't you worry."

"But they'll send you home, you'll not be able to get other ones today. Could your mum maybe write a note?"

This was the least of her worries. Jamie remained on the step, reaching out for her ankle and looking up at her with a half-smile. Blithe pressed for the lift. It seemed to respond instantly, landing on the ground floor. Donnie stepped out. The sight of him drew a sharp, audible intake of breath from Jamie and he withdrew his hand. Donnie raised his eyebrows and made a suggestive clicking noise. He wasn't stupid.

"Ye alright?" Donnie addressed him.

"Why are you back down already?" Blithe demanded, before Jamie could reply.

Donnie shook his head, as though it was down to some madness that couldn't be helped and marched outside without another word. Blithe shrugged at Jamie and stepped into the lift. Jamie licked his lips and slowly made his way outside, hoping to follow on the heels of Donnie.

* * *

"Ye'd better be hungry."

Blithe found her mum in the kitchen, resting her hands on the kitchen surface to steady herself. A warm cottage pie sat on the top of the oven.

"I thought I was doing tea fur three. He's fucked off again."

"He was quick about it."

Lynne sighed. "He was, aye. He's been let go."

"Why?"

"Oh, fur sleeping in."

Blithe screwed up her face as the news sank in.

"He disnae start till like, one!"

"Aye, earliest is twelve. He says he's no sleeping, but I says to him, why d'ye not get yerself to the doctors. If yer sleeping through that alarm something's no right. Get it sorted. I cannae be giving him pocket money. I cannae help him!"

"What did he have to say to that?"

"He was aff. That's it, he knew tea was in the oven but off he slipped, like a fart out a wetsuit."

"Was he...okay though?"

Lynne turned to face her with wet eyes. In answer, she dashed down the dishcloth, and threw up her hands, defying concern.

Blithe left her alone and made her way to the bathroom. At that moment she didn't give two fucks what had happened at school, and she wasn't especially concerned about Donnie. She'd even forgotten about the hole in her tights. Now reminded, she sat down on the toilet and calmly pulled her ankle across her lap to properly inspect the graze. It didn't really hurt anymore.

Lynne set Blithe's dinner down on the old glass coffee table. She moved towards the window and stared out across the parkland and the white council houses beyond, her pinkie in the corner of her mouth. She had to sit down as, all of a sudden, she felt very lightheaded.

Blithe came in and smiled, a cheeky little smile.

"Ye alright ma?"

Lynne nodded and, with a wheeze in her throat, went back through to the kitchen for her own dinner. Whatever he was doing, he was doing it for pennies.

Her boy had no money.

* * *

Jamie and his younger sister, Krissie, walked through the city centre. Krissie carried a guitar case but still managed to march with a giddy energy while Jamie walked with purpose.

Krissie glanced up at her brother, but Jamie looked straight down. She'd made him late.

Robbie was waiting by the entrance to Buchanan Street underground station. He was surprised to see Krissie, suddenly looking so much older than thirteen. Her black hair was coiled in ringlets around her face, falling down to her shoulders. Her age was apparent if you looked very closely, her rosy lips and full cheeks were doll-like and somehow gave it away.

Robbie had few tools for looking older. A moustache would work but come at the price of looking like Super Mario. He secretly persevered with the diet, hoping that his body would use, as an energy reserve, the puppy fat around his face. So far, it hadn't worked. He thought his wrists might have narrowed but nothing else.

"Ye ready?" Jamie asked.

Robbie should at the very least have been nervous, but he felt nothing, he didn't feel a part of the plan. He was aware of his apathy but put it down to Jamie taking control. In reality, that was not the cause; he felt very little about anything.

Jamie and Krissie had already walked past many buskers; the best pitches were taken but, Jamie had not planned on performing in any of the usual places. He did not want the crowds to walk past him, he wanted to be where they were waiting.

"Shall we head down then?" Jamie spoke with a nervous speed.

"Are you sure? On the platform they'll not be able to hear us." Robbie said.

"That's what I said!" Krissie exclaimed.

They could both see that doubt was starting to cloud Jamie's thinking, but the idea that played in his mind remained too perfect. He'd seen clips of people singing on the London Underground, the singers received gratitude and applause, so thrilled were the commuters to be momentarily released from drudgery. Jamie hadn't doubted that he too had that power, until the escalator down was in sight.

"The trains are fucked at the moment," he explained. "They'll be waiting in the cavern of despair and we'll do our thing."

Robbie turned his attention to Krissie for the first time,

"What are you playing?"

"I'm not. I've been asked to film yis."

Robbie looked back at Jamie and frowned.

"What?"

"If it's shit, we'll just delete it."

Krissie was the better guitar player; she'd been playing since she was nine and could sing well enough. It seemed very odd that she be there only to film. Robbie should have filmed them. Musically, the siblings ought to complement one another, but he knew this was an exercise aimed at improving his self-esteem. Never mind that it rested on skills that only the Gilchrists possessed.

"Are you wanting to do something Krissie?" he asked. "We

need all the help we can get."

"Don't encourage her!" Jamie exclaimed. "She'll sing in that stupid Irish accent, sound like a hiccupping Irish nun."

"Amy McDonald isn't Irish...'

"She is the way you impersonate her."

Robbie didn't find their squabbles amusing and was tempted to walk home.

"Fuck off Jamie! You sing like a whale!"

"You sound like Gran on fucking helium."

"Well, you sound like Gran on fucking Viagra."

Repulsed, Jamie had no reply, he only sneered. Krissie's triumph plummeted.

"Probably."

Robbie massaged his temples. "Sorry, what are we doing? Are you seriously going to sing Radiohead in the cavern of despair?"

"What's wrong with that?" Jamie spat. "You can play that, you could play that a few weeks ago. Have you not been practicing?"

Robbie narrowed his eyes. "I've exams."

"So what are you saying? That you can't play it, you've forgotten?"

Robbie shook his head. "No I can do that just about. Are you sure that folk in the cavern of despair are going to thank us when they're made to listen to Radiohead?"

Krissie laughed but Jamie refused to see the funny side and said, stony faced. "I would."

"Aye but that's you. You listen to your dad's music."

Jamie was on the verge of storming off.

"Look..." Robbie soothed, "If that's what you want, okay, but then what?"

Krissie piped up. "I can do the song from Juno!"

Jamie dismissed her. "No!"

Robbie rolled his eyes. "But she's been playing longer than me, unless you want to sing 'A Horse with no Name' – badly, because

I can't do the complicated bit in the middle or Mull of Kintyre then maybe she'd be better."

"You can play Mull of Kintyre?"

"It was the first song I learned to play; it came with the book...'

"Look!" Jamie interrupted, "Don't bullshit, you can play more than that. Let's do one song and see what happens. Can you sing the horse song? Because I don't know how it goes."

"I do."

"Krissie shut yer face! No, we're not doing it because if you know it, it's almost certainly shit."

Robbie made to turn but instead twisted back reluctantly.

They made their way down through Buchanan Street Subway. Jamie had always thought of it as the most miserable place in the world, the vastness of an aircraft hangar coupled with the pressure and darkness you might feel in the belly of a whale. Here, everybody was simply waiting and here, he was sure, his intervention would be welcomed.

However, the commuters Jamie had had in mind were not to be found late on a Saturday morning. A few solitary people were milling around but there were also clusters of young people on their way to somewhere worthwhile, already loud, and cheerful.

Krissie and Robbie were not so sure, exchanging glances when they thought he wasn't looking. Robbie felt quite cheerful. He wasn't singing, he wouldn't look nearly so stupid, no one would notice his mistakes – if they could even hear him.

They moved far down the platform where they wouldn't be collared by staff. Robbie took his guitar out and practiced the opening cords. He could not really hear himself. When the announcements came it was harder still.

'THE NEXT TRAIN TO ARRIVE ON PLATFORM 8 IS THE 12.13 TO MILNGAVIE."

When the Milngavie train arrived, Robbie couldn't hear the cords he was playing, but he kept trying. Jamie was showing Krissie how the camera on his phone worked. From the expression on her face, it was clear that she thought the tutorial unnecessary.

Jamie's ambitions had sunk, but while an opportunity to salvage them remained in view, he wouldn't give up.

As the train pulled out, Jamie gave Robbie a nod. Robbie, without knowing why exactly, nodded back. Krissie stared into the phone, Robbie could tell she was grinning behind it.

Jamie straightened up, tilted his head back and began to sing.

"A heart tha-at's full up like a la-andfill...'

Standing beside him, Robbie could hear him quite well. He'd heard him do the song many times, but he was still far from being sick of it. Strumming what he hoped were the right cords, he could see the measured breathing, the chest rising and falling and hear the very sweet voice that emanated from it. He wished he could use another word to describe it, but sweet it was. Robbie marvelled that someone so shy could sing in public so effortlessly.

"A job that slowly k-iills yo-u"

- "The 12.20 to Helensburgh will arrive on platform 3..."

Robbie stopped playing at this interruption. Jamie looked at him out of the corner of his eye, a quick glance, a cutting condemnation for being so unprofessional. Robbie laughed; he couldn't really hear that either.

"You look so tired unhappy

Bring down the government..."

"WE REGRET TO INFORM PASSAGERS THAT THE 12.25 TO SPRINGBURN IS CURRENTLY DELAYED BY TEN MINUTES."

"They don't,

They don't speak for us..."

The travellers were taking some interest. One man was laughing openly, otherwise, they were bemused. Krissie was holding the camera but her hand was shaking.

"I'll take the quiet life...

A handshake of carbon..."'

"PLEASE REMEMBER THAT SMOKING IS NOT PERMITTED ANYWHERE ON THE STATION PLATFORM"

"With no alarms

And no surp...'

"IF YOU SEE ANY SUSPICIOUS PACKAGES...'

"And no surprises!" Jamie raised his voice, making himself heard in the war of sound.

"No alarms and no surprises

No alarms and no..."

"PLEASE DO NOT LEAVE LUGGAGE UNATTENDED ANYWHERE AROUND THE STATION PLATFORM."

"Silent...silent."

"ANY SUSPICIOUS PACKAGES WILL BE REMOVED."

At this point Robbie decided to call a halt, mainly because, in the effort to hear and not laugh, he couldn't recall the next part. He bowed his head and lowered his guitar to his side, motioning to Krissie with a swipe to his throat to stop filming.

"Hey you!"

Robbie looked over his shoulder. A large man in his forties, clearly on his way to an old firm game, had been paying attention behind him. His Rangers strip was tight around his belly, his neck and bald head were swollen red.

"Why are you playing that wrist cutting music ye fanny! Like the worlds no fucked up enough!"

Robbie looked back to see how Jamie would respond, but he noticed he had turned sullen and red in the face.

"See. I'm fucking late today, I cannae be late the day, ye ken what I'm saying? Play something else – right and I'll sing, really loud because I couldnae hear ye well."

Jamie remained sullen.

"Oh, I'm sorry wee man, I'm sorry, but I'm just trying to help you out, right. Can youse play anything I'd ken?" He pointed to the guitar case at Krissie's feet.

"Can you play that sweetheart?"

He rubbed his hand over his bald head, glanced at the board and grimaced. Krissie knelt down to open her guitar case. Much as she didn't like being sweethearted, she was keen to show off.

"See, she's fucking gorgeous. You two don't know anything about marketing yerselves."

Jamie glowered as Robbie leaned forward and tried to project his voice conspiratorially.

"That's his wee sister!"

"Oh shit man, no offence like, no offence."

Jamie shrugged again. Krissie returned her brother's phone, picked up her guitar and began to strum a tune from a well-known film. After some listening, the man began to nod along and once, he had fully recognised it he began to clap his hands. Others along the platform watched in amusement as something closer to the original vision came to pass, and this time, Jamie recorded it. The stranger clapped his arm over Robbie's shoulder and sang into his face, seeming to roar with the gases of lager. Jamie could see Robbie momentarily grimace as flecks of spit came his way.

The bald man was clearly competitive, determined to drown Robbie out, his volume extending at the expense of its limited ability. Robbie found it hard not to dance with him, the beefy arm stiff over Robbie's shoulder, meant that he was dragged around, forced to copy the shuffle, if only to save his feet. Krissie could have stopped it; her guitar had the power of The Red Shoes, but she was enjoying herself too much. As Robbie sang with him, he even became quite theatrical, extending his free arm comically and raising his voice as they brought the song to a close. As if that weren't enough, when he freed himself from the man's grip with a little spin, ending in a bow, relieved to be free.

It was strangely uplifting to dance and sing with a menacing guy who stank of booze and fags. Such people approach strangers all the time and this was, without a doubt, one of the best possible outcomes. He'd come with a grievance and been charmed. The whole exchange had left a sour expression on Jamie's face, who felt they were all united in taking the piss out of him.

Jamie deleted the first video, he didn't doubt that he couldn't be heard and in fact, he couldn't bear to watch it.

When Jamie returned home, he watched the clip of Robbie on his laptop, from where he could view it critically on the larger screen. He watched his friend, at last, being funny and playful. The footage could warm a memory, even if the experience had been underwhelming, what he'd taken from it showed a side of his friend that he wanted to see more often. He had no qualms about sending it on.

Robbie turned the video off before it was even halfway. He saw himself, a small precocious boy with a chubby face, not a serious human being. At the time, he felt that the humour was directed at the ridiculous man, but he then saw with jaded eyes, that he was the one being laughed at and belittled. The boy he saw was not the young man he wanted to be. This was not how he imagined himself. It cut him to be so ridiculous and, it twisted the knife that this stupid footage could sting his eyes. He blinked away the frustration and embarrassment and messaged Jamie.

Robbie: Delete it. Now.

He then lay back on his bed and waited. Jamie read the message almost instantly but did not reply. He was now irritated by his friend's ability to sap all the joy from everything they did. Meanwhile Robbie lay on his bed, waiting for the confirmation. After ten minutes he messaged again.

Robbie: Have U?

Robbie waited for two torturous hours before Jamie confirmed that it had indeed been wiped from the face of the earth. Jamie reluctantly deleted the footage that showed his clever friend, relaxing again, taking on an arrogant fucker and laughing at him.

* * *

"Krissie. What shoe size are you?"

Krissie was eating her breakfast over the kitchen sink. She'd spent a lot of time getting ready and had left little time to eat. Milk dribbled down her chin; she traced it back to her mouth with her finger.

"Something you're not telling me?" she asked.

Jamie sat at the kitchen table, unashamed and, he hoped, mysterious.

"Four," she answered.

Disappointed, Jamie's face puckered.

"Why? What size you after? Mum's a five."

"I don't think mum has school shoes."

"Go up and look."

Jamie was reminded of a store of old shoes in his parent's wardrobe. His dad had gone out early to attend a job interview and, with less than ten minutes before he had to leave, Jamie was able to find three black pairs of shoes, all of them dusty. He asked Krissie which of the three would be best for school. Krissie was, by this time, rushing around and at first said that none of them would do. Jamie managed to collar her coming out of the bathroom and she eventually selected a pair of scuffed lace-ups.

Jamie concurred, wrapped the shoes tightly in a plastic bag and tucked them inside his blazer.

He left the house first, refusing to wait for his wee sister but, as ever, she caught him up further down the road.

"Does that girl need shoes then?" she demanded.

Jamie would have denied it had there been any point. He nodded.

"She might start to really like you if you keep helping her."

Jamie tried to look as though he was concerned by this possibility until Krissie added.

"But yer fuck ugly and you smell, and no-one can stand you."

Blithe arrived at school in plimsolls that had once been white but were now a dingy grey. She had better trainers, but she thought she'd be less likely to be sent home for wearing something that was plainly not a fashion statement.

Already on walking to school her footwear had been noted. Connor cycled past her several times, sometimes with a menacing silence, but more often calling out and speeding away before she could reply.

"What happened? Did ye forget to staple yer shoes together?"

"Could ye no find the end of the roll of tape?"

She managed to walk into her first class without attracting any more attention. Her shoes would be noticed eventually, and she'd have to offer some explanation. She would not tell the whole truth and was working out her excuses as she made her way to her second class.

She stared straight down at her shoes and her weighted steps as she mounted the stairs from the first floor.

She was pinched gently on the arm and something was shoved at her side. At first, she thought this was a little dig for the sake of giving a little dig, only it was too little to be that. She glanced up for a second. Jamie stared at the crowds coming down, going to great lengths to avoid eye contact. His eyes were wide open as he concentrated on not looking, with a slight curl at the side of his small mouth. She took the package and felt the unmistakable feel of rubber soles. Without examining them, she put them in her bag.

In History, sitting at the back of the classroom, she changed her footwear. The shoes would do well, they were more comfortable than the ones she had lost and would not be pulled off so easily.

* * *

The day passed without violence. Comments were thrown at her, but she managed to ignore them, no matter how loud, no matter how threatening. As she stared down at her feet, it surprised her how easy it was to get through the day.

On the way home, Blithe was well aware of Connor on his bike, silently circling her like a vulture. He cycled past her, turned and rode in the direction of oncoming traffic, bouncing up onto the kerb and cycling back towards her once again.

He cycled close, hoping she might flinch. Without looking up she elbowed him, sending him into a swerve. He recovered and pretended it hadn't happened.

Jamie saw all this from a distance. Having spat on the cyclist's girlfriend, he knew that his presence would likely make it worse. He couldn't bear to be a coward and sped up. Connor made his way back. He looked Jamie in the eye, jerked his head towards Blithe and shouted.

"Ye getting that fanny fur free like?"

Jamie ignored him and became aware that Codey was now behind him. As Codey overtook, she elbowed him in the side, slapping his arm as she passed.

"Oot ma way!"

She glanced over her shoulder at the useless obstacle, quickly catching up with Blithe, who hadn't looked back once. With her boyfriend now cycling at her side, Codey marched towards Blithe. Her hand shot out, and she grabbed the black ponytail in a tight fist, planting herself secure and immovable as Blithe's neck and back arched backwards. Blithe kicked behind her with her heel. Blithe scurried ahead once Codey let go, but felt the edge of a slap against the back of her head. Connor cycled after her for a bit before twisting the front wheel to a sudden stop; he looked back patiently but Codey no longer wanted to follow.

Instead, she turned to Jamie and sneered. Without Blithe, he had no reason to take that route, which would be more obvious if he suddenly turned around. He walked on slowly and Codey waited for him.

"Is she sorting ye out?" Codey demanded.

Jamie didn't reply. He scowled, transmitting the genuine feelings of disgust he felt towards her; she was just a maddening, lesser form of life. Blithe wouldn't have made that mistake. If she had something to say she would say it, but she wouldn't look at people like that. She knew how it felt.

"What ye fucking looking at?"

"I don't fucking know." Jamie muttered.

Codey blocked his path.

"We know yer going in there to fuck her, ye dirty cunt."

Codey took a sharp intake of breath and spat. She'd aimed for Jamie's face but that was, fortunately, too high and so flecks of saliva sprayed over his shirt. He felt a sudden horrible anger rising in him. He glanced at Connor and tried to swallow the urge to shove her and walk on.

"Ye wanting to slap my girlfriend? Try any of that and I'll break yer fucking neck."

As Jamie walked on, seething, he didn't hear the bike coming behind him, but he heard the unmistakable shot of saliva and felt the impact on his blazer. He could no longer see Blithe, he walked simply to get away.

He decided that he would walk round the long way, if he came out onto the main road and still couldn't see Blithe, he would go home. If she were there, he would see her to her door but of course, it looked bad if he went into her flat. As he neared the main road he slowed and looked around for Blithe. He gave himself time to be sure that she hadn't waited.

A kiss can be nothing. A kiss, he thought, if that's how you're going to cheat, is barely cheating. It can be an experiment, with no conditions. It means nothing. Both Jamie and Blithe knew this; they didn't have to think far back to recall when kisses were for experience first and pleasure second, if pleasure was anticipated at all.

And then he saw her sitting on a wall. Although she was almost obscured by the hedge, he recognised the slender pair of legs stuck out from the bush, toes pointed to better display his mum's old shoes.

She leaned forward and smiled sympathetically; he was flushed and felt infected by the spit on his clothes.

She lifted her legs daintily to indicate the shoes.

"Cheers for these."

Her grin glowed with gratitude. Jamie hadn't seen her smile like that before. It was lovely to see but he was not ready to smile back, not whole-heartedly.

"Are you here to see me home?" she asked, aware that she'd pretty much made it home on her own.

"If you'd not waited for me, you'd probably be home by now."

Blithe conceded with a shrug. She had no objection to him walking her the remaining distance.

"They gobbed down yer back?'"

Jamie nodded miserably and felt the anger rising again.

"Just a wee bit of gob, it'll come out in the wash. Ye got another blazer?"

Jamie nodded.

"Ah, come up and get a flannel on it. No bother. My mum's working in the charity shop till gone five, not that it would matter if she were in but...since you think she's rough as fuck, I thought I'd mention it."

Blithe's flat was cleaner than Jamie expected. Days before, Blithe would have been less inclined to invite him up, when the flat had the power to shock. The smells from the bins had been sour and sweet like bile, the living room was dingy with dust and detritus. Lynne had been busy the day before. It wasn't easy for her to take the bins down to the ground floor and lob them up and over into the massive stinking stack of rubbish. The rubbish chute hadn't worked for some time, and they had been advised not to use it. She'd often have to leave her rubbish on the ground where the bag would inevitably be torn open. Blithe argued that it was Donnie's turn to sort the bins and finally, Lynne had had enough and ploughed through the much-needed housework until she sat panting in her chair, fearing her irregular heartbeat.

So, to Jamie's eyes it was surprising, the decor seemed a bit dated, the smell he detected was the odour of a dusty hoover and the residue of the previous mess.

Blithe indicated the bathroom. Lynne hadn't cleaned it but, Jamie found it just as untidy as his own.

He caught sight of his red face in the mirror and gazed intently back, as though telling himself off for caring, and perhaps, for being embarrassed at being there. He didn't know which of the flannels were clean and wasn't sure about rummaging around in the cupboard. He was still angry and roughly pulled off his blazer, turned on the hot tap full blast and stuck the soiled parts of the blazer under the jet. When he could see more closely that the mucus had stuck, he took some toilet roll and tried to prise it up to prevent it simply being smeared across the fabric by the force of the water. The wet toilet roll peppered the blazer.

To be forced to make contact with their bodily fluids felt like a defeat. He saw his grimacing reflection and gave up on the job, hanging the soaking blazer over the bath. His shirt would be harder, but he took a damp bar of soap and simply drew over the spit, thinking that at least it was something sweeter smelling. The soap tracks looked worse and so Jamie splashed the still hot water over his shirt, until it was so wet in places that his bare skin shone through.

He untucked the shirt to stop it sticking to him and made his way through to the kitchen, where Blithe was getting a drink. She turned from the sink, glanced at his wet shirt, and let out a single laugh.

"If that's how ye felt ye should have said. D'ye want a shirt?"

"No, it'll dry."

"Sure? I've a big girl's blouse."

"No ta."

"Suit yerself."

They walked through to her bedroom. It surprised him, not because it was untidy, but because it was as much a child's bedroom as a teenager's. Her single bedspread was faded purple with butterfly prints, knickknacks of childhood adorned her mantelpiece including a picture of a baby, one of her many half-siblings, in a tacky frame. The picture was a relic from the days when she regularly saw her father and his family. A round purple-grey rug, curling up at the edges, lay beside her bed. This was more of a child's room than his wee sisters. He wanted to examine the items on her desk, the strange toys that must mean something, not part of a collection, not part of a decoration but there for some other reason. At least he understood; he had a few of these things, ugly objects that kept a memory clear; a rusty badge, rock and tacky souvenirs that a well-meaning loved one had thought about. These days, he kept them in a drawer.

Blithe knelt on her bed, opening the window the few inches it would allow.

She looked over her shoulder and saw Jamie casting his eyes around her bedroom. At that moment, his eyes fell on her jewellery box, clearly cardboard under the pink and her pink CD player, covered with stickers. Unplugged, it hadn't worked in months, maybe years, but Blithe played her music through an old and temperamental iPod.

Blithe thought about reassuring him that it was all junk, junk was all she had, but instead she indicated the window with a jerk of her head.

"Look."

Jamie followed, and they knelt on her bed, staring out of her window at the pupils far below. Codey hurried past the flats,

Conor slowly cycling along beside her. Blithe turned to Jamie, but he had cast his eyes further afield and turned his head to the east where he could see, bright in the distance, parks, and freshly growing woods.

"It's a handy view, eh?"

"You're the king of the castle,' he said, pressing his nose against the glass.

Blithe sat back on her pillow and reached by the side of her bed, where she kept a small biscuit barrel. Hearing it open, Jamie turned from the window.

"I keep these for breakfast in bed; a cup of tea and a couple of biscuits."

"Don't you get crumbs in your bed?"

Blithe grinned and nodded. "By the way, whose shoes are these?"

"My mum's."

This was the reply Blithe had predicted and she nodded,

"She's got comfy shoes. Does she mind me having them?"

"She doesn't know."

"I'll get new shoes at the weekend...hopefully."

"Dinnae worry about it, she'll no notice."

She offered him the biscuit barrel. As he leant forward to take one, he stroked her cheek with his index finger, gentle and deliberate.

"What was that for?"

For a moment, he looked confused and hesitated.

"Sorry. I was just being nice."

He bit into the biscuit, staring at her with uncertainty. Sitting on her bed, he felt for the first time that he was in his friend's old territory. As time went on, Robbie would have less and less of a right to feel upset. He felt guilt, but the urge to kiss her was stronger.

Blithe leant forward and drew herself up on her knees. She

placed her hands very firmly on his shoulders, but rather than reaching in for a kiss she seemed to stare him out. He ceased to feel bashful and stared back, placing his hands on her hips, and letting his thumbs roll where her waist narrowed.

He craned towards her and she joined her lips to his. His fingers left the warm soft skin as his hands went to her face, smooth and cold.

They fell side by side and his hand settled on her waist. He still had nothing to say, but he stared at her until his eyes closed peacefully. He'd go no further, with his eyes closed and his hand on her skin he simply basked. Blithe understood the silence.

"Would Robbie mind d'ye think?" Blithe whispered.

He kept his eyes closed. "Probably wouldn't be happy about it."

Blithe rolled onto her back and stared at her butterfly lampshade, filled with cobwebs.

"I sent it to one person. I sent it to one person, and that's it! One fucking person."

"He's still not right."

"You should hate me." Blithe muttered.

"Oh, I did."

Blithe sat up and looked at Jamie lying still on his side. He stared back at her with a steady gaze, a little like anger. She recognised the look for what it was, too calm to be bitter. He could not undo what had been done, saw no point in talking about it, but he wouldn't lie to her.

"I sent it to one...' She repeated.

"The wrong person," Jamie said flatly. "I wish ye hadnae as well but... there we are."

He rose up on his elbow and kissed her arm, hoping to soothe her frustration. Sitting up, he stroked the silky black hair, mesmerised as it slipped so easily through his fingers. She lay back again and his arms slipped easily beneath her. He held her tightly against him. She could feel where his shirt was still wet but even then, she found her eyes closing, the need to worry ebbing. In symmetry, they held each other so protectively. It was hard to see how anyone from the dingy world below could possibly hurt them.

* * *

Jamie made his way home through light drizzle. He concentrated hard on his leg, trying to gently increase the pressure on the delicate joint, then transferring his weight to his stronger side as he straightened the weaker. To passers-by, the boy was dealing with a stiff leg. He was not aware that Conor was following him. The bike was elsewhere, and Conor appeared to be alone.

"How was it?" Conor called out.

Jamie turned around as Conor hurled a small stone at him. It flew over his shoulder.

"Don't look round man!"

Conor shouted without threat, as though Jamie was reckless for having looked round in the first place.

"I'll have yer fucking eye out. Don't be stupid now! Keep yer head still man and walk straight, fur fucks sake!"

He continued flicking stones until, bored, he enquired.

"Did ye get yer end stuck in there?"

Conor could see, even from behind, just how Jamie bristled.

"No? Fuck man, I didnae think she was bothered. She's screwed fat Boaby and he cannae tie shoelaces, he's got fat strips of Velcro. Ye ken who I'm talking about?"

Jamie didn't reply. Conor hurled another small stone and it hit the back of Jamie's head.

"I thought everyone kenned fat Boaby. Got turned away from the trampoline park fur being a fucking trampoline, the wains ricochet aff him." A stone clipped Jamie's ear. "When he gets turned away, he goes tae Greggs, sits at the wanker's bar along the window, asks for a tablecloth and sticks a fag in a pie, fur his birthday tea. Ye must ken fat Boaby." Another stone found its target. "He lives in the old park in Newlands under the climbing frame, every morning he takes a piss down the slide, stops him getting stuck on the way down, works like grease. Ye should ken him, he's been where you've been. He's been wi' her mum as well, met her on the beach during walrus mating season."

There'd been a few fat Boabys over the years. Any unfortunate, overweight gormless guy that Conor happened to encounter would be assigned the name.

Conor walked a few paces behind, his palm now empty of stones, though Jamie could feel where many had landed, even if they hadn't broken the skin.

After a prolonged silence Jamie dared to turn around; he only allowed himself a glance and saw Conor waving from across the road. He'd been waiting for Jamie to check his whereabouts; he enjoyed the power and relished rubbing it in, even when there was no one to see it.

Jamie walked on and found a lump growing in his throat. It stayed even as he tried to swallow it away. He sat down at the next bus shelter he passed, leaning on the thin plastic bench that substituted seating. He pulled his bag onto his lap and after a little rummaging, found the roll up in foil that Donnie had offered him days before. It was largely flattened and as he straightened out the foil, some tobacco blew away. The roach was almost entirely out and Jamie pushed it in with his finger, and, unflattening it with a few squeezes at the creases.

After further rummaging, Jamie found a lighter and lit the pathetic thing, hoping for a distracting or calming effect. He sat up straight in the shelter, looking around him. Fag in mouth, he put the lighter back in his bag and decided to make his way home.

As he took deeper breaths, he seemed to detect a fishy aftertaste, specifically sardines, something tinny to it. He took a deeper puff but, the aftertaste of the cheap tobacco tasted stronger. He flicked what remained of the roll-up into the road and continued on his way home.

When Jamie entered the house, he noted his father's coat hung over the bannister, where it had recently been chucked. His dad didn't call out to him, but Jamie heard him open the fridge and mutter and so decided to leave him alone. He headed upstairs to his room and threw his bag on the bed, fingers trying and failing to find any lumps on the back of his head. While his laptop loaded, he went downstairs for a drink.

His dad leaned against the kitchen side. There were no preparations for cooking, no work in progress, he simply stood with his arms folded. He glared at his son, who, under the threat of interrogation said nothing, only ran his fingers through his hair, brushing it temporarily out of his face.

"You stink."

Jamie frowned; if anything, he smelled like cheap soap. He took a glass from the cupboard and made his way to the sink.

"I drove down Pollokshaws Road, just now."

Jamie realised what had happened and clenched his eyes shut in frustration.

"You stupid wee... just round the corner. Where's your brain?"

"Go on up, search my bag."

He spoke quickly, before his anger grew. He would not tolerate this on top of everything else, and he would not apologise or back down. He'd felt vulnerable enough, he'd been proven to be weak, and it was not a role he would resume at home.

"Are you denying it then? What was in it?'"

"Smoked fucking sardines." Jamie snarled.

"Answer the question!"

"I don't fucking know what it was! I didn't roll the fucker, if I had it would probably have tasted better!"

Stephen took a step back and tried to laugh but, there was an angry tremor in his chuckle.

"Then you are even more of an idiot. If you're going to be that stupid at least know what you're taking."

"Cheap tobacco, dad. Cheap tobacco. Good luck getting that tested, I didn't want to take it down to the station because I didn't want to look like a fucking idiot. Next time I'll hand it on to you."

"If I catch the smell of that on you again… If I catch you, I'll take your phone for a week, a month maybe. Do you understand? I don't know why I don't take it now."

Jamie took his phone from his pocket and skimmed it across the table. He would miss it as soon as he was upstairs, but he wanted to get away.

"And since it's my money that you're spending I'll stop that an a'."

It was an odd thing to say and if Jamie hadn't been so desperate to get away, he would have taken more notice of it. Instead, he replied bitterly.

"Well, that won't be hard."

That was meant to be it, but as Jamie turned to go, he received a slap across the cheek. He froze, and his father's eyes widened at what he had just done.

Jamie moved quickly out of the kitchen, down the passage, and, thundered up the stairs to his room.

He bit his lip and clambered over his bed to where his laptop was ready. He plugged in his speaker, selected an album, and followed the routine he had planned. But a number of things had changed. Now he wanted his door locked and bolted. All he could do was place a chair on its back, perfectly filling the space between the door and the bed.

Then he began to curse to himself, muttering like his father, lamenting the odds of being seen at that moment. He looked in the mirror above the fireplace and was not sure whether the redness of his face had anything to do with the slap. He felt a sudden urge to smash his face against the mirror and bowed his head, almost to counteract it.

He covered his face with his hands. His instinct was to run back to the flats, back up to Blithe's. He imagined holding her until he fell asleep and waking up next to her in the dark. He checked that fantasy; he didn't want to want her.

Then, there was a knock at the door. Jamie knew this was an apology. He didn't want that either, he wasn't sure he deserved it, but he certainly didn't deserve the embarrassment that would come with it. He waited, hoping he would just go away, but the knock came again and then his father's calmer voice.

"Can I come in?"

Jamie gently picked up the chair from where it was blocking the door. He opened up and took a step back. Stephen stepped inside, waxy faced and unbearably tense.

"I'm sorry."

Jamie remained standing, staring down and nodding numbly. His father cupped Jamie's cheek, and he looked up into a face so anxious and shattered. He did not want to be touched.

"I'm sorry," Stephen repeated.

"It's okay. I didn't mean...I didn't mean to..."

While Jamie rambled, Stephen put his hand in his pocket and brought out Jamie's phone.

"Are you okay?"

Jamie took his phone and looked his dad in the eye.

"Aye. Are you?"

Stephen shook his head. "It's not been an easy couple of weeks."

"I know. Earlier, I had stones chucked at me, I got spat at and... look, I was just trying to calm down."

"Why did you not think to tell me? Where I was living, when I was your age, you'd get glassed for next to nothing..."

In their own way, both pleaded, Stephen to forgive and Jamie to forget and return to a time, not so long ago, when he hadn't goaded his cash strapped dad until he struck him.

The front door downstairs banged open as Krissie fell inside. Stephen ignored her.

"There's things I understand, ye should know that."

"Aye but, when you were my age, what did you tell your parents?"

"But that's different."

Jamie began to struggle. It seemed his dad was waiting for another outburst, but he wouldn't provide it, though he was desperate to move beyond this suspended state. Stephen shook his head and walked away, slowly thumping down the stairs. He recalled Jamie's furtive little glances. Those glances told Stephen that he had failed to be the parent he'd vowed he would be, no better than his own father who had belted him.

* * *

His forehead pressed against the slanting glass; Jamie pushed his arms through the slight opening in Blithe's bedroom window. He could not get his arms out beyond his elbows but felt the cold breeze on his hands and wrists and noticed how much stronger the wind became higher up. The howl beyond the glass had beckoned him to reach out. Low cloud bled into drizzle; he was positioned at that melting point, obscured to the people on the ground, half swallowed in sky. He felt the increasing droplets of rain, his bare chest curved away from the glass and the sludgy condensation.

His school trousers stayed on, as did his socks. White shirts lay in a heap on the purple rug, they'd pulled them over their heads and let them drop, never minding that her floor was peppered with fluff and papery debris. Her skirt lay crumpled at the pillow.

When Blithe returned, she was charmed to see him against the window as she recalled doing the same thing a long time ago. Jamie, as though suddenly aware of the cold he'd let in, dived beneath the covers.

A mop of hair emerged from the sheets and then most of his

face until, like an animal smelling something out, he stopped moving when his nose emerged. He watched her.

She wore an oversized cardigan belonging to her mum, her bare legs were smooth and elfin. Her ankles were so delicate, he could link his fingers around them. A cold breeze reached around her legs and she hunched her shoulders and leapt onto the mass of sheets. The limbs underneath rose up against her pressing knees and worked quickly to find a way to let her into the warmth once again. Her cold feet found his ankles, where his trousers had rolled up. He cried out at her freezing feet and kicked them from the cuffs of his trousers. Then, he held her very tightly, uncomfortably so. His grip pinned her arms against her sides and it was an effort to free them, his legs too clamped against her thighs.

She freed herself to breathe, to pull back and focus on the face above her.

"Are ye alright?"

A sneer was all she saw in response. She moved up towards the headboard, so they could lie face to face.

"What?" she demanded.

"Promise you won't laugh."

Blithe pondered for a second. "Fucking idiot. I'm going to laugh now!"

Jamie grinned. "Remember yer brother gave me a fag? Well I smoked it yesterday but, at the exact moment my dad drove past."

Blithe laughed, a little too much.

"Fuck! So Daddy burst yer balls for that? Bet it was a shit fag." Jamie nodded.

"You shouldnae have taken it. He wanted to be yer pal, but all he could do was offer a pre-rolled fag. Once some wee boys, I swear they were about twelve, were waiting outside the shop and asking everyone that came out for a fag. I swear when he gave those boys a fag, it made his day. Didnae make theirs mind you."

"Not if it tasted like the one he gave me. A lot of it blew away, and it still tasted like shit so I chucked it into the road. I don't think ma dad saw that. He didnae bust ma balls, just ma face."

Blithe pulled away a little further to look at his face.

"Does he do that loads like?"

"No, he's not done that since…a long time. Years."

"Did ye greet?"

Jamie frowned. "No. Why did ye ask me that?"

Blithe shrugged.

"So," she said, "You came in the door, he turned around and was like 'Bam! Smoking's bad fur ye, ye wee bastard, take that!"

"No," Jamie grinned but only briefly. "I was so fucked off, I mean, what are the chances?"

"Where were you?"

"Round the corner from my house."

Blithe brought her face closer to his on the pillow,

"Then the chances were high."

Jamie pushed his face closer still so their noses were touching,

"Ok-ay. That's true."

He kissed her quickly on the lips and adjusted his head on the pillow to see her properly.

"Here's the thing; he's a freelance writer, also used to do a bit of web design but, he admits, pretty basic stuff. Over the last year there's not been a lot going on for him, he's not bringing a lot in. Or he has to do it for free, people expect his work for free. I can mind him saying, years ago, he shouldn't ever work for free but then, he went back on that because he had to get out there. I don't know if it made any difference. No, he's not sitting on his arse doing fuck all but, he's not getting paid – I know that. My mum's got a proper job that just about pays the bills."

"Ah right, so he sees you wasting money and goes batshit."

"Well, I smoked it because I didn't want to waste it, the opposite of wasteful. He threatened to not give me money and

I said like it wouldn't be hard to cope without his money, and it wouldn't be hard, because it's not his money, it's my mum's."

"And then he hit you?"

"Aye."

"Not fucking surprised! You arsehole!"

Jamie leaned over her. "Are you joking?"

Blithe pushed him off her. "No!"

She sat up and turned to look at Jamie, lying with his head on her pillow, staring back at her with a frown.

"Don't tell me you're an angel," he said.

"No! But I don't hit my mum right where it hurts."

"Ye said your mum was a big fat tank."

"Aye but she wouldnae hear me say that! That's the stuff I widnae say to her face."

Jamie sensed he would lose this argument.

"It's not that bad. My family aren't loaded but we're not fucked. If we were going to lose the house, then I'd be hitting him where it hurts. It's no excuse, he shouldn't do stuff like that."

Blithe lay back again and closed her eyes.

"Yer dads not Jesus, ye can only piss him off so much. Maybe he can't take any more shit. I can understand that, that's how ma mum feels, that's how I feel."

"What's up with yer mum?"

"Arthritis, type 2 diabetes, ME... depression too probably. She wouldnae lash out though, she'd just fret and get sick. Yer alright though, aren't ye? He didnae hurt you?"

"No. He shocked me though."

Blithe decided to forgive and turned to trace a line down the side of his face.

Jamie liked this but wasn't ready to resume.

"Why did you ask if I was crying?"

Blithe didn't know, perhaps because there was something delicate about him. Jamie rolled on his side and propped himself up so he could stare down at her face.

"You think I'm pathetic, don't you?"

Blithe stared up at him, with a pout which Jamie took to be assent.

"You do! You so fucking do! You've me down as a pure whinging snot face."

"No! You're just different. What have I said like?"

"Nothing but you make faces. You smirk and that. You baulk."

"Boke?" Blithe laughed.

"Baulk. You pull a massively fucked off and disgusted face."

Blithe sighed and tried to remember. She raised her hands, gently cupping his face as it leaned over hers, sliding her fingers slowly up through his hair and then pulling his face down closer to hers.

"I wasnae sure about you before," she said "You weren't sure about me. You hated me. You don't hate me now."

"I don't hate you much."

He grinned. He'd been zoning in on her mouth and kissed her. They lay caressing underneath a duvet that was older than them both, possibly put together.

There was a chill against their bare shoulders and a stuffiness where clothes clung against them under the winter duvet. Blithe loved this, she thought she could sleep for days with her head resting in the crook of his arm, she liked to hold his head against her chest and feel his arms at her sides. He appeared to fall to dreaming but, he wasn't asleep. He liked feeling her fingers running through his hair and sensed she would be less likely to do if she thought he was awake. Instinct recognised instinct as perfectly as bare skin sealed against bare skin.

Suddenly they heard the front door open. Blithe knew at once that it was Donnie, the speed of his footsteps made it clear.

Jamie's face shot up.

"Hiya!" Blithe shouted out.

She grinned at the alarm on Jamie's face. She put her finger to her lips as they listened to the sound of cupboards banging within the kitchen.

"Should I go?" Jamie whispered.

"Not cause of him."

"But what if he knocks on your door?"

"He won't."

Jamie pulled her against him and inhaled the sweet fruity smell of her hair.

"You're not like your brother, are you?"

"You're not like your sister."

Jamie looked at her critically.

"I don't look like her but we're plausibly from the same family. He's alien."

"Not to me he's not."

Jamie jerked his head, letting the duvet fall back from his shoulders.

"He's nothing like you. Nothing like."

He brought his head down, resting his chin against her breastbone until she squirmed, and he lay his head to one side.

"He's been rejected," she whispered. "A lot."

"He's hardly the only one whose dad left."

Blithe narrowed her eyes.

"When my mum was pregnant with me, dad ran back to his first wife. How many people do you know who've had that happen to them?"

"Were you like a secret family or something?"

"When my mum met my dad, he was married with kids. I ken what yer thinking though, stupid cow to break up a family."

"I wasnae thinking that."

"Well I do. The way she tells it though, he was like a victim of domestic abuse from the whole family he married into. It's a family that sticks together no matter what, they'd support each other through murder. Half the time they hate each other but they'd absolutely, 100%, go to war for each other. My dad struggled with that, understandably there's like 99 cousins, aunts, uncles. That's a lot of people to hate you if you step outside it. He still lives in it, the human tribe. If you're born into it, it's probably okay, but if you're not used to it... That's not a family, it's more like a gang. At the head of that family is my dad's mum-in-law, Granny Boyle, she's an old witch and she hates me. She's got thirteen kids, over forty grandkids and I think thirty odd great-grandkids and counting. Christmas is something..."

"That's insane!"

Blithe enjoyed the shock on Jamie's innocent face.

"So you don't like that side of your family?" Jamie asked.

"I just don't belong in it. When my dad met my mum, he tells her that Jimmy, his brother-in-law, was threatening him. Mum was getting over someone else, someone much better. Rebound."

There was a momentary silence at the word 'rebound' and then they heard Donnie coming through from the kitchen, his bedroom door slamming and the TV coming on. Blithe lowered her voice.

"Anyway, Jimmy was threatening to do something, chib him or something."

"Was that true?"

"Oh probably, Jimmy's an arsehole. Anyway, they get together, within the year, Donnie is on the way. Dad's gone from this massive mad family, to just him and mum. He still needs to see his other three kids, my mum agrees on that, obviously. Anyway, he needs to see them, and he always takes Donnie with him, sometimes leaving him with Michelle, the wife he married twice. Life's not so easy, big family is tough but, yev got all the hand-me-downs, all the help. Life with mum was hard, no money, no help because his family were pissed off that he'd left his first wife. My mum doesnae have a big family. He couldnae hack it and back he goes, soon as he hears I'm on the way, he packs his bags and off he goes. He needs to have a pack leader telling him what to do, that's what I think."

Jamie's fingers gently swept across her brow.

"Do you see him?"

Suddenly, the sound of gunfire erupted from the next room. Donnie had turned on his console.

"Now and again, on my birthday and stuff like that. Dad used to make more of an effort with Donnie, he'd take him out with his other three kids. He did that a lot when mum needed a rest and that. Donnie didn't belong. He wasn't happy. I mean, we're all bastards but he really felt like one. Donnie was too young to be able to explain it, so he acted up. That's fair enough, he acted like a real wee shite, visits with dad happened less and mum struggled. Well, that's what I've been told. I don't remember, I was in my cot, dreaming of *Teletubbies*."

"No wonder he's fucked up."

Blithe shoved Jamie away.

"You don't get to say stuff like that. I'll say if he's fucked up or not."

"Sorry, I was just saying that that's bound to mess you up."

Blithe nodded. "My dad's not a bad man, just a weak man."

"So yer mum raised you by herself?"

Blithe nodded. "I don't think I'd have minded having a stepdad, but she never brought one home for me to try out. If it made her happy, I'd have been okay with it, *we'd* have been okay with it I mean."

Jamie kissed her again. "While he's machine gunning, I'll get out."

"I'm allowed to have you round, it's my room..."

"I know but still...what would I say if he walked in?"

Blithe grinned. "I'd tell him to get out. Maybe ye are a bit pathetic...'

"Don't say that."

Jamie got out of bed, picked up his shirt and gave it a shake before putting it on. As he buttoned it up, he watched her, the top of her head peeping out from beneath the sheets. They both wanted to laugh, neither knew why.

CHAPTER 6

Stephen and Jamie waited in the car outside Robbie's house.

"Just go on, chap the door." Stephen urged, "Get out and walk a few feet."

Jamie was determined to organise using his phone. This was how he normally did things, and he wouldn't leave the car if he didn't need to. Robbie knew that they were waiting, but if he could have gotten away with it, he would have made them miss the entire party. He also didn't like having to travel to the other side of the city, as it prevented him from leaving on his own terms. For Jamie, the party in Milngavie seemed to be a perfect opportunity. There would be some familiar faces who wouldn't be hung up on what had happened with Blithe, but the majority would be friends Ross had made since moving to the west. Robbie could talk to them as though nothing had happened and enjoy the balance of the old and the new.

This was not the way Robbie saw it. When, days ago, the first message came through inviting him to Ross's, he sensed pressure and ignored it. Jamie messaged him again. Only on receiving the third message, when Robbie thought that Jamie was becoming angry, did he reply,

Robbie: Okay.

He'd sleepwalked to agreement.

Finally, Robbie shuffled down his driveway. Stephen watched him climb into the back seat and noticed that he did not apologise for keeping them waiting, something he would have expected this unfailingly polite boy to do after five minutes, let alone fifteen. Waiting at traffic lights a little later, he glanced in his rear-view mirror and observed a disgruntled look on Robbie's face. Stephen thought he needed to be shaken out of a sad daydream and projected his voice to the back seat.

"Must have been fun for your dad when Nigel Farage turned up at the University."

"He doesn't work in that building," Robbie replied vacantly.

"He wasnae tempted to get involved in the protest no?"

"No. Hardly anyone turned up."

"Well, Farage disnae really sell well in Glasgow. Still, I'd have been tempted, if I was yer dad.'

"It wouldn't have been appropriate."

"Sure...sure. I understand but *I'd* have been tempted to chuck an egg at that racist cu...creep."

As he listened, Jamie smiled to himself and decided to interject.

"Oh, I can see you in your baseball cap, with your carton of free range eggs. Bounding in like, 'How do you do fellow kids?'"

"Aye well," Stephen laughed, "you're not going to kill anyone with an egg."

The monotone voice from the backseat finally had something to say. "Someone still has to clean it up."

Neither Jamie, nor his dad, knew what to say to that. The injured voice had attempted dignity and failed. Two awkward seconds passed; Jamie felt a smile forming. He glanced at his dad, who was also fighting a grin. Jamie covered his mouth and looked out of the window, but Stephen could not, and Robbie knew they were silently laughing at him. Stephen cleared his throat and tried again.

"You sure you're up for this Robbie?"

He barely heard the reply.

"Sorry, Robbie, I'm just saying I can turn around."

Jamie turned around from the front seat, and there was

communication of some sort. Stephen couldn't quite make out the distracting mutterings.

"What's going on boys?"

"He's fine!" Jamie replied.

'Just shout Robbie, if ye decide to head back. It'll be no bother."

Robbie remained silent in the back. Stephen was happy to, once again, be useful to his son. He asked if Ross's parents were aware of the party, Jamie admitted that he didn't know, but honestly doubted it.

"Oh well, I cannae warn them eh? Be respectful though, dinnae do anything stupid."

Hours after Stephen dropped them off, Jamie and Robbie sat in Ross's bedroom, huddled round Robbie's phone watching clips on YouTube.

The crowds had gathered downstairs. The house itself might have been no bigger than the old place in the south side but the garden was bigger, and the kitchen opened out into a large dining room and conservatory. People huddled all over the place, and music overlapped with different songs playing in different areas.

The party did not extend to Ross's bedroom. Whenever they thought someone was coming to join them, the door was slammed shut no sooner than it had been opened, as though they were making out.

Jamie drank a beer. He'd put the rest of his stash in the fridge and was concerned that it would be gone before he had a chance to drink any more of it. Robbie had a quarter bottle of rum in his jacket pocket.

Jamie contemplated dragging Robbie downstairs, or simply leaving the miserable bastard to his clips.

Robbie scrolled. "Oh, have you seen this?"

Jamie gave a "Humph."

"No?"

'Probably, Robbie – to be honest I've not been paying attention.

Come on, let's head down."

Robbie sighed and sat up straight, to better judge the noises rising from below.

"Listen to it,' he muttered.

Jamie listened to sounds that were exactly what he would expect of a party; regular laughter, a bit of screaming and the sounds of several girls singing along to Adele. It was a horrible noise but not out of the ordinary.

"Aye so? Let's go down and find some people we know."

Robbie bristled. "Who else did Ross invite?"

"I don't fucking know. I don't stalk him online. Does it matter?"

"Aye, of course it matters. You go, and I'll stay up here for a bit."

"No. Come on. Don't be a fanny."

"Don't bother – leave me to finish my drink."

"No, take it with you like a normal person. I ken what you'll do if I go...I don't want people to slag you off for being the sad bastard that sat watching clips of seals."

Robbie slammed his drink down on the side.

"You don't need to look after me."

"If you wanted to spend the night on yer phone, you shouldnae have come to a party."

"I didn't want to. You forced me."

"No, I didn't. If you'd said no, I would have left you alone."

'Like fuck you would."

"You'll never know, because you didnae say no."

Jamie hadn't needed to persuade him, but he would have if necessary. He paused and said calmly.

"Don't be a dick, just come downstairs."

"Wait a second, I'll neck this back."

"Why? Bring it with you, walk and drink."

Robbie didn't want to know these people; he knew enough from hearing them screech. They were far more likely to bind him in his anxieties than encourage him to relax.

Many were deep in conversation as they made their way downstairs, Jamie made an effort to smile as he passed a small crowd of girls. He was sure that Robbie belonged in the kitchen with the talk. At the foot of the stairs they saw Ross, their host, lean from the living room doorway. He gave them both a wave and Jamie could tell from his gait that he was already a little drunk.

"What were you doing in there all that time?" He called.

Jamie looked over his shoulder at Robbie, who shrugged.

"Watching stuff."

A girl from the living room called out, "Looking at porn! They were looking at massive cocks!"

Robbie thundered past Ross, down the corridor to the kitchen. Jamie followed, making a face at Ross to show that he at least, could deal with a few jibes.

Harry and Lisa stood talking in the kitchen. They had been a couple for over a year and throughout that time had been engrossed in each other, at the exclusion of anyone else, inspiring both envy and irritation. Robbie crossed the kitchen and wedged himself in a corner behind the breakfast bar. For once, talking was all Harry and Lisa were doing, so Jamie went to them rather than Robbie. He'd known Lisa since primary school and he and Harry had taken violin lessons together for years. Lisa gestured towards Robbie.

"What's up with him? Has a seagull shat on his cake?"

Jamie looked over at Robbie, still staring into space.

"Oh, he's the same... I don't think he's trying, to be honest."

Lisa considered Robbie, whose gaze evaded eye contact.

"Is he trying to score tonight? Is that why he's here?"

"No. It's an experiment that's clearly not worked. Why? Is there someone interested?"

Lisa seemed surprised.

"I thought you were. Yer a cute couple..."

Harry nudged her; she stopped and gave a guilty smile.

"Well, he's no being sick and he disnae smell so he's in with a shot. Ye ken those lassies? They were destroying Adele, one of them might be up fur it – the wee ones anyway. If he's not pissed up, I can see if Carmen is..."

Her eyes rolled as an idea formed.

"I'll get Carmen! Oh, she's a miserable bitch as well. Honest! They'll spend an hour taking about death in the garden. Then they'll get fucked up and hug. I should so get her!"

Jamie smiled and shook his head.

"Just leave him."

Harry put a protective arm around Lisa.

"Did you run a brothel in a past life?"

Lisa laughed.

"I'm just trying to help."

Harry considered Robbie.

"No. Dinnae throw Carmen at him. Together they'd open a black hole into a world of...poetry."

Lisa shook her head dismissively, made her way over to Robbie and gestured to Harry and Jamie to follow but she was shoved back by a girl who urgently needed the sink. The girl wretched a little; a prelude to the real thing.

Harry muttered. "That's not on, gonnae no chunder over the dishes. There's two toilets."

"Not everyone wants to stick their head in a toilet,' Lisa pointed out.

"I wouldnae have to pick bits out of a toilet!"

Robbie turned to the breakfast bar, filled with various litre bottles and cans, and poured himself a drink with his rum and someone else's lemonade. The sick girl slowly straightened her neck and looked over her shoulder. Her eyes narrowed, focusing first on the lemonade, and then the boy who held it.

"Fuck aff!"

As first, Robbie was not sure who was being spoken to and turned around by degrees. The girl was still gripping the sink, but she faced him squarely now. Robbie turned back and screwed the lid back on the lemonade.

"Cheap bastard!" she cried. "Buy yer own!"

Robbie left his drink on the bar and walked out into the back garden, leaving the patio doors open. The girl picked up the glass and poured the contents into the soiled basin.

By this time, the garden was in shadow, fenced in by thick bushes. Light from the house cast onto the decking, but Robbie deliberately stepped just beyond the periphery of the light.

The wind was getting up. Two girls had been chatting on the decking but skipped inside when Robbie came out to pace the lawn. Robbie wasn't sure what his plan had been; he normally had one, he was methodical; even when sulking he had some notion of the purpose of the next half hour. He stood alone in the garden, with as much purpose as a grazing cow.

"You coming in?"

Jamie leaned out of the patio doors. There was a note of impatience in his voice, small but still incendiary.

"I'll wait," Robbie replied.

"You cannae stay in the garden all night. Come on!"

"Out here, I can be avoided."

Robbie turned and tried to focus on the bushes in the gloom. He tried to see something in the bigger picture of the bushes against the night sky. Jamie slipped into the garden and slid the doors closed carefully behind him. Now outside, he heard giggling and mutters from the driveway around the corner.

"Why won't you talk to Harry or Lisa, or Ross who invited you?"

"Because this party is full of pissed up fucks, who don't care what they do."

"Keep your fucking voice down!" Jamie dashed towards him in a moment of rage that passed when they stood face to face.

"You're talking like you're better than everyone else. You're just fucking miserable!"

Jamie faced the wind. The late spring still threw an icy drizzle, which danced in the night air. Jamie rubbed his arms and glanced back at Robbie with impatience.

"Do you want me to bring you out a beer?"

Robbie stared off into the bushes like a reprimanded child.

"Have a drink and come inside."

Robbie said nothing but sat down on the wet grass. Without a word, Jamie returned to the kitchen.

Robbie huddled up and looked at the house and the goings-on inside – illuminated from his view in the shadows. It had been relatable once, but now it was another planet; he could hardly breathe the same air. He couldn't talk to them, he could only interrupt. He could either be ignored or break their conversation and weigh it down to where he waited, a tethered lump.

Jamie returned wearing his coat and made his way across the grass. The bottle necks grasped between his long fingers, swung slowly at his side like the tools of an unpleasant job.

"Maybe it's not too late to get the train. I'll see." Robbie unlocked his phone.

"No." Jamie muttered. "Not on your own. Not when you're like this."

Robbie smiled. "What do you think I'm going to do?"

Jamie shrugged and began to open the beers with his keyring.

"Sorry for ruining it," Robbie muttered.

Jamie shook his head and passed over a bottle, froth running down the sides. "It could definitely be a lot better, but you've not ruined it."

Robbie took a swig, despite not really liking the taste of beer.

"Imagine if it had happened to me," Jamie said. "If it was me that..."

He smiled, hesitating, mentally rephrasing, not wanting to say her name.

"If all that shite had happened to me, what would I be like?"

"Unbearable," Robbie replied flatly.

Jamie frowned down at the bottle grasped in his hands.

"When my leg was fucked, you didnae say I was unbearable. Well, I'm trying to return the favour, ye know what I mean? Because shit happens."

Robbie narrowed his eyes. "What are you going to do? Are you going to sleep on the floor here?"

Jamie shrugged. "Maybe stay awake all night, you up for that?"

Robbie shook his head.

"Well look, just come inside. Find the adult. D'ye know that Ross' boyfriend is twenty-one?"

"No! Is that legal?"

Jamie laughed. "There you fucking go, there's a responsible adult, sort of. He disnae look twenty-one though, but he'll put up with you. He's got nothing better to do. I don't think he's enjoying himself either, disnae like being stuck with the kiddies."

Robbie moved towards the kitchen door and glanced at Jamie uneasily.

"Don't leave me alone with these fucking people."

Jamie sighed.

"At some point the locals will want their beds. Just wait it out. You'll feel better when there's less people."

Inside, the mix had changed and the kitchen was now full of strangers. The sink, despite the earlier accident, was now full of cans and bottles. A smell of caramel wafted through the kitchen, blown in by a girl vaping at the door. Jamie looked down the corridor, hoping to see a familiar face and caught sight of Harry, still animated and energetic. Jamie hurried through the kitchen with Robbie trailing after him. By the time he saw who Harry was talking to, it was too late.

Lewis Moir turned around and gave Jamie a wave.

"You talked Robbie af the ledge?" Lewis enquired with a smirk.

Jamie could only mouth, "don't start".

Jamie was not afraid of Lewis; he was just an arsehole. He glared at Harry, who remembered with electrifying urgency, the special care that needed to be taken and clapped Lewis on the back.

"Don't. Come on."

Lewis didn't budge; the glances, the panic, and the pressure to tread around Robbie as though on eggshells, amused him. He nodded, a grin slowly spreading across his face.

"Ahh bless, the wee soul!" He raised his voice; he was positioned by the doorway into the living room and below the staircase, where a group of girls had congregated.

"Hey, Hey! Everyone, can we get a big aww for the wee man! One, Two, Three, Awwwww!"

With a drone, the call was copied from the living room, as though at a pantomime. Robbie closed his eyes. Lewis enjoyed the response and called for his audience to try harder.

"Awwww. A huge fucking awww!"

Jamie hung his head; he heard the sound of Lewis's body crashing against the wall as Robbie shoved him. He glanced up and saw his grinning face, still enjoying the agony.

"Shut the fuck up!" Robbie roared.

Lewis stumbled again but the grin remained.

"Yer an angry wee lion."

"Shut your fucking mouth!" Robbie cried again.

Lewis seemed to straighten up calmly but then, with a speed, punched Robbie on the cheek.

"What ye fucking daen?"

Jamie ran in between them, Harry grabbed Lewis's shoulder. The intervention was not welcome; it put them both in the wrong. Lewis shook free of Harry and Robbie slapped Jamie away, before making for the front door. The door slammed, and Jamie glared at Lewis.

"Don't shit stir. It's not fucking funny."

Lewis simply grinned, his lantern jaw inviting a smack. Jamie gave a quick shake of his head and ran for the door just as Ross clumped downstairs to see what was going on. Throwing open the door, Jamie directed his anger up at Ross, now hesitating on the stairs.

"Why's he even fucking here!" he gestured angrily to Lewis, 'Fuck sake Ross, ye ken what he's like."

Before Ross could reply, Jamie slammed the door behind him.

Robbie recognised the thud of trainers, the flagging breaths of irregular hurrying and didn't need to look back. He'd predicted it, just he'd predicted that the party would be full of pissed up cunts.

'Where are you going?" Jamie called. "You've left your bag."

Robbie glanced over his shoulder as he marched on.

"I'm not going back in there Jamie. I'll walk back if there's no trains."

With some effort, Jamie jogged past Robbie and faced him square on. Robbie stopped and exclaimed.

"I don't want my bag. I've got my wallet and phone here."

Robbie side-stepped Jamie and turned right into an alley, without knowing where it would lead.

Jamie followed and called after him.

"You didn't need to shove him!"

Robbie stopped for emphasis. "Oh yes I fucking did."

"Well, it disnae matter." Jamie called after the retreating figure, 'Only because ye shoved the right man. Could have been worse."

"I knew who I was shoving." Robbie shouted over his shoulder. "I won't be humiliated by that cunt!"

The alley opened on to yet another quiet residential street. Robbie would have continued down a deserted country road, so strong was his impulse to get far away from where he had started. One side of the road gave way to a wooded area where light flickered through the trees, not urban lights, but starlight reflected in a pool deep in the woods. Robbie crossed over towards the woods, in the dark it was hard to see whether it extended beyond the pool. The sky over Glasgow glowed red in the east, providing a little orientation.

Jamie didn't often see the night sky quite like this; travelling just that wee bit further out of the city had unveiled the universe. Jamie paused and stared, making out what he supposed were constellations. He assumed Robbie wanted to be ignored and was surprised to hear him say.

"Why are you being like this?"

Shaken from his star-gazing, Jamie turned back.

"What?"

"Are you wanting me to canonise you?"

Jamie didn't know what that meant but even if he did, he would let it go.

Robbie sat down on an old wooden bench that backed onto the woodland.

"I've heard you're walking the bitch to her door."

Sober, this might have made Jamie nervous but he was feeling a little sleepy. His leg ached and he wanted to join Robbie on the bench. He made no effort to protest, found no impetus to care.

Robbie continued, "You've been in the flat..."

"We were being chased. I hung out in a pissy lobby for ten minutes, then I went home."

"When I asked you to do her a favour, I didn't mean that."

"I know, but they jumped us, more than once."

Robbie took a quarter bottle from his coat and took a swig.

Jamie barely raised an eyebrow at the solitary selfish drinking and murmured.

"She's a nice girl."

He waited for the attack.

"Well she's gonnae be *nice* to you. No one else'll go near her, but don't think no one sees you walking her, you ignore her at school and as soon as you're out of the gates you think, what? That nobody can see you?"

Jamie nodded vacantly but couldn't leave it at that.

"I don't think she did it to piss you off," he said quietly. "I don't think she did it to... up herself."

"Just a whoops?"

Jamie nodded. "Aye, that's what I'm saying. I think."

"You're an idiot."

"No! You were saying the same thing! You were saying that you thought she came clean to the school about it. Who was it then if it wasn't her?"

"Aye she did that but not to help me. She did it because she didn't want to get into trouble."

"Robbie, don't bullshit, you felt sorry for her. That's why I started walking her."

Robbie took another swig and grimaced. He had nothing more to say.

"Look, if you don't like the taste of that stuff, don't drink it," Jamie said softly.

"I'm cold. It gives me a warm feeling; it burns my throat in a good way. You're not going to start going out with her, are you?"

Jamie made a noise, a grunt that was intended to sound baffled and amused. He was no good at pretending.

"Because I couldn't hang out with you if you did. I couldnae hear about her. I couldn't."

"You've got nothing to worry about."

Jamie's instinct told him to flee from the tension and surface into breathable air.

"Ye cold?" he said. "I'll run back and grab the bags. Don't move."

He didn't wait for a reply, turning and walking as fast as he could. Every so often, he sighed in relief, eyes still rolling up to the stars. The walk allowed him to vent before he stepped back into the dregs of an unsuccessful party.

He had to knock on the door several times before it was answered by Lewis. As Jamie stepped inside, Lewis gave a quick glance left and right.

"Where's yer mad dog?"

Jamie ignored him and staggered up to Ross's room where, it quickly became apparent, Ross and his boyfriend were having an argument. Again, Jamie knocked several times before loudly announcing he was coming in. He swiped the bag as though fearing gunfire. Ross sat on his bed looking contrite, still with the expression of lost little boy while Ross's boyfriend, angry at the intrusion, paced.

Lewis had heard Jamie thundering down the stairs and waited blearily by the front door, eyeing Jamie with puffy eyes.

"Is that you off now? Off to tuck him in? Give him some milk?"

The tired expression on Jamie's face angered Lewis.

"No?" he continued, "Just a quick hand-job before you turn out the light, send him off to dreamland."

But Jamie wasn't riled and reached around Lewis to open the front door.

"Lewis, if that picture does it for you when you're alone in bed, on ye go and dream it...."

As he slammed the door, he heard Lewis shout back,

"Well, I ken what you'll be daen the night!"

He tried to jog back to the woods. With a few drinks inside him and no one to watch, he was no longer self-conscious about the strange loping he resorted to.

His eyes were still adjusting as he stared at the outline of trees in the distance, though he knew exactly where the bench was, it was so dark that it took him a while to see it. It was empty. He called Robbie's phone, but it was either switched off or drained. He stood and listened, calling for Robbie, trying not to throw his voice too far.

He walked to the end of the road and there was nothing but empty windows and his echoing footsteps. The more the night wore on, the less Jamie cared about waking the locals. Twice he walked to the end of the road and then back again. He considered making his way to the train station.

Doubting that Robbie would go off and leave him, he walked back to the bench and shouted at the top of his voice.

"I'll get louder. Where are you, ya bastard?"

He listened again but all he heard were cars in the distance. He then noticed the patch of trampled ground by the bench, leading to a path where the woods began.

He sighed, groaned and then marched in; hands raised against the branches. His eyes adjusted a little but the ground at his feet remained a great black hole. He could make out where the trees thinned and started to make his way more clearly, using his phone as a torch. He heard rustling and called Robbie's name, but his voice was not as loud as it had been. Still blind to what was underfoot, he assumed the worst; the soil threatened to burst with fungal spores, slime or faecal remains.

A bat swooped, then another, and with that Jamie found his voice.

"Robbie!"

He waited, fighting the urge to run from the woods. He heard something and called again. He made out a muffled sound and ran blindly towards it through the trees or bushes – he was in no position to distinguish which.

"Hey!"

Closer now, he heard the swish of foliage as a body rose through branches. Robbie stood to make his presence known and slumped back down into the ferns at the foot of a plane tree. Jamie moved towards him and lit up Robbie's squinting face, pale and waxy in the dark. Robbie waved his hands in front of his face in protest at the light and Jamie caught sight of a graze on his forehead.

"What happened?" Jamie demanded.

"Nothing."

"You're bleeding!"

Robbie put his hand slowly to his face.

"It's a scratch, from a tree, I made contact with a tree."

"Get up!"

Robbie curled up and closed his eyes, pressing himself into the tree trunk behind him.

"Get up! Fucks sake man look what yer lying in!"

Robbie didn't move, and so Jamie exclaimed,

"Dog shit!"

Robbie glanced down and sniffed at the air,

"No I'm no!"

"You could be. Mon, get up. Come on, you cannae sleep in the woods."

Jamie crouched down and grabbed at Robbie's collar.

"Did you drink the rest of that bottle?"

"No."

Robbie took the bottle from inside his coat and swirled it, so Jamie could hear the unmistakable swish.

"How come yer fucked?"

The black shape shrugged. "I've not eaten since lunch."

Jamie pulled him to his feet.

"How not?"

"I telt my mum I was eating here, that we'd order a pizza."

Jamie slung his arm over Robbie's shoulder and manoeuvred with care.

Robbie speech was a little slurred, but his thoughts were coherent enough when he managed to focus them steady.

"You are so lucky I found you."

Jamie gritted his teeth and raised his only free arm to shield them both from brambles.

"Sorry." Robbie mumbled. "I want to not exist... for a while."

They emerged from the woods. Robbie sat back down on the bench, took back his bag and hugged it against his chest.

"Yer not still thinking like that are you?" Jamie asked.

"Don't know... Aye. Everyone does though. My Dad said there were three questions you can ask to reveal a liar. The first one is something like, have you ever, like, worried that you're shit in bed?

Jamie grinned. "I've never wondered that... give it time."

Robbie nodded. "I've wondered if I'm a good kisser, same thing. The next question is, have you ever enjoyed taking a dump and thirdly, have you even thought about killing yourself to get back at someone. Everyone has! If you don't answer yes to all three, you're a liar."

Jamie kicked at the dried earth around his feet. He considered the three questions and said eventually,

"When I was wee, I'd get angry and I'd think to myself; I'll make you sorry, I'll throw myself into the road and then you'll be sorry, then you'll wish you'd been nicer to me. That's not the same thing. I thought that because I wanted to imagine my family sad. To picture them sad, would remind me that they loved me."

"It's perverse." Robbie whispered.

"That's not the same as being suicidal. You wouldn't seriously though?"

Robbie had been calm, his face very still, but for a second it seemed ready to cave in from the effort.

"You're right. I imagine them devastated. You too, actually." Robbie cleared his throat. "But it still makes me want to. That's awful isn't it?"

Unable to respond, Jamie stood in shocked silence.

"There's not that many of you to miss me. I don't know, I have lots of thoughts, it's like a labyrinth but the brick wall of every turn tells me that it would be so simple to just stop existing."

"But you wouldn't go back to that party and let off an

explosion, would you?"

Robbie smiled drunkenly to himself. "Maybe."

"For you, it's very fucking final, but it wouldn't be for your parents or for me. A parallel world where you don't exist doesn't just suddenly stitch itself up. You'd leave devastation, you may as well let off a bomb, you know that, you're just too self-absorbed to waste time imagining it. Think about what you'd do."

"I do."

"What am I supposed to do when you tell me this stuff? Do I tell your parents and freak them out and fuck things up for you? Or do I do fuck all?"

"Ye could just listen. I don't expect much."

"But if you did something I'd be the mess because I could have done something and didn't?"

"Don't tell them!"

Jamie froze and then reanimated with a groan.

"Are you not listening?"

Robbie nodded. "Shut up now."

Jamie knew that he was getting to him and continued.

"You don't fancy Blithe. You're not jealous. Are you?"

When Robbie spoke again his voice was thick, not just with booze.

"No. Pretending was good."

"Pretending what?"

"I wasn't in love. I pretended. Reality is so shit, man it's grim... Love's a nice idea. I'm so fucking stupid though, I don't know why I wanted to pretend, with her of all people. She's so..., hostile."

"She needs to be. That's just how it is,' Jamie said to himself. "You okay?"

Robbie might have nodded a little.

"Are we sleeping on Ross's floor?" Jamie asked.

"No!"

"Taxi?"

There was no reaction to this, and Jamie began to walk.

"Get up," he called over his shoulder. "We'll head to a main road, flag down a taxi and get as close as we can with fifteen quid. If you can greet, that'd be good, we might get taken straight home."

The temperature had now dropped. The roads were largely empty, and vehicles took advantage of this by zipping past beyond the speed limit. The houses were unlit and the streets unfamiliar.

Taxis sped by, dashing their hopes as quickly as they raised them. Jamie made a phone call but hadn't considered that he would need his bearings and frustrated many taxi drivers.

"Where do you want picking up fae?"

"Uhhhhh..."

Jamie struggled to access the internet on his phone. He was running out of data, and maps loaded intermittently in little glimmers of hope that ultimately cut out. After using his phone as a torch, it had dropped down to 5% battery. He had one conversation with a taxi driver, who seemed patient until he realised that Jamie only had fifteen pounds. He gave up asking Jamie to describe his surroundings and told him to call back with a clearer location. When Jamie called back, the phone rang out.

Over the course of an hour Jamie's limp morphed into a drunken stagger. Finally, a taxi pulled over across the road.

"Where yis heading?" the driver demanded.

"Southside but we've got..., we've got £16.25. Will that get us to Pollokshaws or Shawlands?"

"Disnae matter. Both are completely out of my way." He squinted at Jamie, his bulldog jaw like a punchable extension.

"Can you take us some of the way? Please."

Jamie was interrupted by loud clicks as Robbie tried the back door desperately.

"What ye fucking daen?!" The driver erupted.

Robbie jumped away from the vehicle and crumpled to his knees. Jamie couldn't blame him, he felt ready to do the same.

The driver was enraged.

"See if he's sick... I'll no have another wain being sick in my car! What are you daen with him anyway, he's a fucking state."

He gestured to Robbie kneeling on the pavement.

Jamie was about to protest that they were the same age but said instead.

"I've plied him with vodka and I'm going to rape him. What do you think?"

"I think yer af yer fucking heid!"

With that the driver drove away. If he'd looked in his rear-view mirror, he would have seen Jamie gesture furiously with his hands. Robbie stood up but his straight back soon curved again and in the loudest moan he'd managed all night he wailed.

"Rape isn't funny!"

Jamie glanced at Robbie and noticed the empty bottle in his hand, a bottle that had been a quarter full when they started out.

"Yer already fucked! Why?"

"Tickles ma throat and... that," Robbie explained.

"Ye never offered me any!"

Robbie held the bottle at arm's length and judged it critically.

"Sorry, sorry" he said. "You never... you never drink spirits. You should have left me in the woods... where it's warm, with all the trees..."

A battered red car past slowly alongside them and took a while to draw to a stop by the kerb. Jamie limped alongside, as lame as it was possible to be while remaining upright. The passenger window wound down.

"Have you been walking all this time?"

Jamie peered into the car. It took him a while to recognise Ross's boyfriend. He'd avoided looking at him when he swiped his bag. He didn't even know his name and wondered whether it was too late to ask.

He nodded and Ross's boyfriend grabbed his phone from the passenger seat, waiting while it rang, staring ahead.

"Ross? I've found yer friends. Aye, the one with the leg and the other one...' He looked over his shoulder at Robbie, stumbling along the pavement towards them. "Aye, I'll sort them out a lift but after that I'm going home. Look, kick them out, not your problem... Ross! Shut it a minute... Yer gonnae have tae tell the bams to leave. Aye, kick them out. You'll be fine. I'm hanging up now but I'll call you tomorrow... Byyye."

He grinned, firmly pressing the button to hang up. "Fuck sake."

He glanced up at Jamie. "You getting in?"

Robbie had stopped several feet from the car and looked doubtfully at it. Jamie hesitated, then decided to text Ross with the last of his battery to ensure that, even if they were chopped into pieces and dissolved in acid, Ross's boyfriend would be caught.

Jamie opened the passenger door and slid inside, eyeing the driver carefully. He had a small, neat frame, thick dark stubble and undercut hair, carefully sculpted at the top. From the short sleeves of his black shirt a Celtic Knot tattoo was just visible.

Robbie pulled open the door, fell across the back seat and lay still. On hearing the driver cough, he sat up and angrily slammed the door.

"You're the guy that started on that... is his name Lewis?"

Jamie nodded guiltily as the car pulled onto the main road.

"Did you just nod? I'm watching the road."

"Aye, that was me."

"That guy's the devil. After you left, neighbours called the police, they arrive, then one of the girls is accusing Lewis of groping her. He says he grabbed her breast accidentally when he fell off the sofa."

Jamie tried not to laugh, but sniggered.

"It's not funny."

Robbie leaned forward between the front seats and said conspiratorially.

"Jamie thinks rape is funny."

"I do not!"

Robbie shook his head blearily and then tapped at the driver's shoulder.

"Where are we going now?"

"My name is Callum, we're leaving a shit party and I'm taking ye home. Okay?"

"No. I think I'm gonnae be sick."

Callum roared in frustration.

"Fucking kids! Fucking wee bams! Listen, I cannae pull over the now. Don't you be sick!"

Jamie turned round in the passenger seat and instructed Robbie to sit back and take slow, deep breaths. All the way home, Robbie groaned, belched and tossed his head but he wasn't sick. Jamie imagined knocking on his door, pictured his mum's face when his knocking dragged her out of bed. He glanced at Callum, who'd been driving with gritted teeth, and instructed him to drop them both at his.

* * *

Jamie was sober enough to open his front door with care. They tipped into the dark, unwelcoming house, over the clutter in the hallway. Jamie groped his way to the kitchen; it did not occur to Robbie that he could follow without invitation, and he slowly fell to sitting on the staircase.

Quickly, Jamie returned, holding a tumbler in each hand. Robbie felt a foot prod him in the elbow and he knew to stand and follow him upstairs. He stumbled into Jamie's room and sat on the bed with his back against the wall, head tilted back, mouth hung open. His last spark of energy ebbed away. Jamie moved quickly around him, turned on a sidelight and threw him a t-shirt. Robbie's head lolled but he showed no sign of moving, slowly kneading the t-shirt in his hands without caring to look at it.

Jamie went to the bathroom, very hastily brushed his teeth to remove the bitter, acidic taste that water wouldn't wash away. He then stuck his head around his parents' bedroom door and whispered. He was not sure from the murmurs he heard whether they were awake or not.

He was surprised when he returned from the bathroom to find Robbie still sat on the edge of his bed, silent and sorrowful.

"Ye alright?" he whispered.

Robbie continued to stare down through space. Jamie cleared his throat, but Robbie wasn't registering hints, so Jamie started to undress. It took a few seconds for Robbie to realise what he was doing, and at last he lurched from the room. Jamie pulled out a vest from his bottom drawer, just about managed to put it on properly, and fell into bed.

Bed swallowed him, like the embrace of a great cuddly god. He was falling asleep when he became aware of his door opening and Robbie droning.

"Uhhhh."

Jamie ignored it, but Robbie made the noise again.

"What?"

"Where do I sleep?"

Jamie was not going to get the camp bed out. He was not going to creep around finding bedding.

"Get in or on. Don't care."

A pause and then, the mindless noise.

"Uhhhh... Uhhh... Could I sleep on the floor?"

"Aye. Go on."

Robbie lay on the floor parallel to Jamie, who lay completely buried beneath his sheets, nonetheless, he kept hearing the shuffling by his bed and so poked his head some of the way over the edge of his mattress.

Robbie lay positioned as though in a coffin, his eyes flicked in Jamie's direction and returned to the ceiling immediately above him, martyrdom complete. He'd changed into Jamie's t-shirt, but his jeans were still on.

"I'm not really going to rape you. You can get in."

"Uhhh."

"Have you not slept with yer dad before? When there's no room?"

Robbie stared up at him blankly.

"Robbie. Get in for fucks sake."

Robbie rose uneasily. He sat on the edge of the bed but didn't get in.

"You know what everyone's saying?" he said.

Jamie rolled over to face the wall.

"If anyone knows...about us...sharing a bed, you know."

"Sleep on the floor then, wake up feeling like shite. No one will know you're repulsed by me physically."

Robbie lay down on the bed. As soon as his head was cupped in the pillow, he wanted to stay there. His brain throbbed, his stomach rolled, and he could only ease his suffering by closing his eyes.

He wanted to kick off his trousers and slipped beneath the sheets, but did not want to seem eager. The result was that he moved around, irritating Jamie who was on the cusp of sleep when the sheets tugged, or Robbie elbowed him as he tried drunkenly to slip between the sheets by stealth. Robbie pressed down on the duvet between them, creating a barrier over which he hoped their bodies wouldn't touch. Jamie rolled over, taking the barrier with him; Robbie slammed his arm down as though to imbed a boundary line on the bed.

Jamie snapped into a spasm of rage.

"Fucks sake! Get in or get out! Fucks sake man!"

Robbie quietly obeyed, shifting over to the very edge of the bed, as far over as he could get without falling out and in a sad voice he whispered.

"Sorry. I'm really sorry."

"Shut it!"

"You don't have to hang around with me…"

"Shut it Robbie! I'm no talking the now."

"I ruined it. I ruined it. I ruined it…"

Jamie rolled over towards him.

"No, you didnae ruin it man. Go to sleep."

"You wanted to make it better. I made it worse."

He was working himself to tears. Jamie had no sympathy, only a desire to sleep.

"Look, you should see a doctor. I'll always, you know, help but I'm no a doctor, it's too much…" He yawned. "Too much, for me. You should see someone."

"No. I'm not worth helping. I'm not worth putting back together. I'm not. I'm a fucking idiot…"

Jamie reached out to place his hand on Robbie's chest.

"Please. Stop talking."

Robbie reached for the hand on his chest and held it still while he thought about flinging it away, ashamed that he could not relinquish it. Soothed, he squeezed the hand gently and within minutes heard soft snoring at his side. He stared at the face, mostly in shadow, slightly minty breath whistling out. He wondered what it would be like to kiss him but then reminded himself that he was drunk. Still holding Jamie's hand tight against his chest, he stared up to the ceiling until he too fell asleep.

* * *

The curtains had only partially been closed and, the morning rays fizzed into the back of Robbie's head as though concentrated under a giant magnifying glass. He moved his mouth, ungumming the stale flavours of the night before, then he realised that the warm body lying alongside him, nose pressed against his shoulder, was Jamie.

Instantly, he feared that Krissie could have crept into the room and taken a picture. Robbie wanted to feel disgusted, it was his method of making the potential rumour untrue, to strengthen his denial.

Downstairs the washing machine whirred and the radio played.

When Jamie opened his eyes, Robbie was perched on the edge of his bed, fully dressed.

"Can you let your family know I'm here? I really need a piss."

Jamie gave a bleary grin and croaked, "Go back to sleep, honey."

"Shut it! Can you let your family know I'm here?"

Jamie rolled over, pulling his sheets tight against him until Robbie snatched them away. He gave up and followed Robbie out of his bedroom, stopped in his doorway and called down the staircase.

"Robbie needs a shit! Is that alright?"

Robbie clenched his jaw and raised his fist, as though to strike Jamie with all the force of a marshmallow.

"There you go!" Jamie exclaimed brightly, gesturing to the bathroom before returning to his bed.

Conversations would soon be interrupted by the bell. The glow from the clouds cast silver on the windows on the east side of the school, where the wind was kept at bay. Blithe stood, looking longingly at the houses beyond the school wall. Five minutes ago, she'd considered making a run for it. Not now. Her elbow ached, and her forehead was grazed from where it had been pressed up against the wall and she'd tried to break away, only to be forced back into position.

Jamie and Robbie were making their way down the corridor on the second floor when Jamie saw her through the window. As the light bounced off the glass, she could not have seen him.

Robbie stared out. "Look at the state of it."

Jamie stayed silent but kept his eyes on her.

"So fucking stupid what she's done to herself. Has she got any friends left, do you know?"

Jamie shrugged; he genuinely didn't know. The bell sounded,

and the friends moved in opposite directions.

Blithe stayed still. She waited till she could escape the crowds in the corridors, till she would almost be late. Just as she was starting to make her way inside, Jamie met her. His eyes widened at the new graze on her face.

He glanced down at her arm as she attempted to cover it with her sleeve.

"You okay?"

She sighed and raised her arm to save further questions. '*Fannybaws*' was written on her forearm in thick marker pen.

She made to push past but Jamie blocked her way.

"If it won't come off, you could change it."

"To what?"

"... Banny Balls...?"

Blithe managed a completely straight face.

"It's Baws, with a 'w', no with two 'll's."

Jamie looked confused but then smiled slightly, before restoring his genuine look of concern. He touched the graze lightly with his forefinger, sighed, and let her go on her way.

* * *

Hours later, they sat side by side on the edge of the bath in Blithe's flat. Blithe failed to get the marker pen off and Jamie was having a go, not because he'd do a better job, but he didn't like to see Blithe scrubbing so harshly at her pale skin.

"You got any dry skin cream?" he asked. Her skin was scarlet from rubbing and '*Fannybaws*' was still clear. Blithe reclaimed her arm and examined it.

"No. Maybe I'll have a bath and see if I can soak it off. Unless you can think of something to change it to, something better than fucking Banny Baws."

"It's hidden if you wear long sleeves." Jamie pointed out.

"Aye, and what's the betting tomorrow's hot."

"Mind you, now it looks more like Funnybaws – that's a wee bit better."

Blithe scoffed. "Aye, cause nothing's betters than an infected scrotum. No trouble going about with that on my arm."

She stood up, leaned over the sink and made the water as hot as she could before she plunged her arm in.

Jamie smiled to himself until he saw that Blithe had taken a nail brush to her arm, he rose and took the brush out of her hand.

"Don't."

Blithe wondered who he was to be giving orders, and once again plunged her arm into the soapy basin, before drying it on a towel. By now, her sleeve was soaking and she removed her shirt.

The band of her tights appeared over her skirt, just above her bellybutton. Her white bra had been washed too many times to still be white, the cups were a little tight and the underwire rubbed at her sides. Jamie tried to look her in the eye, rather than the chest. He'd held her before but had not seen her body as clearly as he saw it now. He looked at the line down her back and her breasts moving within the bra as she dried her arms. He wanted to pull her towards him from the small of her back, and had to look away.

"So what happened?" he asked.

"They found me."

"They just came up to you and did that?"

Blithe frowned and kicked the toe of her shoe against the pedestal.

"I'm just asking!" Jamie exclaimed. "Don't be like that."

Blithe groaned, walked through to her bedroom and unhooked her bobbly red dressing gown from the back of her door. Jamie followed.

"I was waiting, out of the way, you know, near where you saw me. They walked past and had a go."

She pulled on her dressing gown and plonked herself down on her bed. Jamie sat down opposite her on a little white stool. Blithe's bedroom was tidier than normal. A few of the tacky nick-knacks had gone.

"But what happened to make them do that to you?" Jamie asked.

"They were like, 'Hey you! Fannybaws!' I was like, 'Get tae fuck!' Then it was all this."

"Fuck sake, Blithe. I'd have just ignored them."

Blithe's eyes glowered with a mischievous glint.

"Oh aye, does that work? Where's yer self-respect? Look, ignoring works with the verbal but they are not verbal. You're lucky, cripple. You get verbal."

Jamie raised his eyebrows and leaned in towards her.

"How am I lucky? I was pretty much fully recovered when Molly jumped on me. Years later, I still haven't got my leg back to where it was when she jumped on me. You heard about that right?"

"I heard that yer knee snapped like a twig."

Jamie narrowed his eyes. "It fractured, it didn't snap."

"And that you were greet'n."

A look of uncertainty passed Jamie's face.

"A pain like that knocks the wind out of you. I don't remember shedding tears but, it's possible. I was in shock. If you're in pain for ages, it wears you down and, you just can't take it anymore but, shock's not like that. Maybe when your kneecap pops out of place and your bone cracks, you'll be fine. Well, when it happens to you, maybe you can tell me not to cry."

Cornered by reason, Blithe had to lash out.

"Fuck!" She marvelled. "Do you think it's taken years off your life?"

Jamie had been leaning forward conspiratorially but sat back suddenly and gave a shape intake of breath.

"Why d'ye ask that?"

"Sorry. I don't know, can you forget that I asked that?"

"No."

"I didn't mean it like that... I meant it's a good war wound. Ken what I mean?"

"No it's not. It's really not. I was on holiday, decided to go off on my own, didnae tell anyone where I was going. You couldnae write a better cautionary tale. Do you mind that time, when you were just getting used to going out on yer own?"

Blithe frowned. "No. Going to the shops probably."

This response disappointed him. He'd craved his independence, but his parents had been slow to give it, the lead they kept him on was let out very cautiously. His had been a calculated, controlled growing up, whereas Lynne had not had that luxury when it came to raising Blithe. Self-sufficiency wasn't an earned privilege; it was something she required her children to have.

For Jamie, his first taste of freedom felt like a spiritual awakening; he could understand the appeal of religion, if it felt like that. Aged thirteen, he had been on holiday with his family in the Highlands. After dinner, he had gone out on his bike. He wanted to climb and so abandoned his bike and continued on foot. He could still recall walking away through the dying sunlight, on a path that elevated him steadily over vast rolling tracts of bronze. At the foot of the mountains, the sky was so clear that looking up gave him a falling sensation, as though he could feel the earth turning.

The darkness surprised him; one minute the landscape was clear at an almost microscopic level, and then the shadows had eaten into the very brightness that had drawn his eye.

"When you're wee, walking is about getting from one place to another," Jamie explained. "You don't appreciate what's around you unless there's a swing park. I wanted to see what was round the corner and see how far I could get but it got dark fast," he explained. "When I was walking there was generally a barrier to the slope at my feet, a wall of untrodden turf – it varied from a foot high in places to just a ridge. I was plotting my way down and I just fell, I couldnae tell you how far. It happened so quickly, I don't know how I managed it, but I must have thought the bank was there and it wasn't. I'd expected to roll, but instead I was in the air and the first bit of me to hit something solid was my knee and the solid thing was a big rock. It was a while before I was found by a walker, who carried me. Fortunately, she was built like a brick shit house, but she would have been better off getting help. I'd be better off now, if she'd not done that, just left the leg alone until I was winched to safety. I used to be really into sport, I was a great wee runner, probably because I was one of the tall ones, I had these really long legs."

"You still do. Bet yer parents were..." Blithe struggled to complete her sentence.

Jamie grinned. "Were what? A mess? I don't know, I passed out. I should think so."

"Did ye hit yer head?"

He placed his hand on one side of his face. "This is the part of my face that hit the ground, I willnae forget."

"Did it hurt?"

He paused and stared at her with world-weary eyes.

"I screamed for a while and passed out. The hospital was up in Fort William, it specialised in mountain injuries. I'm told they made a fuss of me because I was so young, though that's not how I remember it. My memory isn't reliable, but the first thing I remember is that my eyes were closed, and my hands were up under my chin. I think I must have been being put to bed after an operation, I was being shunted really slowly and carefully, or maybe something was being laid underneath me – that's more likely. I don't remember voices – I try but it's a tangle of sound and I don't remember having control, my brain had stepped out on its own, floating in black soup. Have you ever come round from an anaesthetic? Well trust me, I didn't have awareness in any normal sense, but I knew the smell of my dad, he was holding me, keeping my arms tight across my chest and my head rolled against his jumper. I didn't know anything but, I knew his smell. I keep that jumper now. I wear it when I need a comfort blanket – it's bobbly and grey."

"Are you not a wee bit old for a comfort blanket?" Blithe asked.

"Look, you don't need to be like that. I know you're tough. Most people wouldnae go to school if they had half the shit that you have to deal with. I wouldnae."

Blithe turned slightly red.

"D'ye have a girlfriend?"

"You know I don't."

"I know you don't have a girlfriend at school, but that doesn't mean there's not one somewhere."

Jamie laughed. "No, I don't have a girlfriend,' he paused, "Well, apart from the mother of my child and my wife in Motherwell with the twins. I'm thirty, but I've got this disease where my bottom half ages first, that's really why I've got the limp."

Blithe turned to face him, he'd also reddened.

"Shut up."

"You're the one with the stupid questions."

He rose and sat beside her on the bed. She let her head fall to his shoulder.

"What are you going to do?" he asked.

Blithe hadn't considered that she had any choice. She didn't fancy changing school; this ran the risk of being just as bad but further away from the sanctuary of home.

"Wait till summer, only a few weeks till study leave."

"And then sixth year. Do you think that will be any better? It probably will be, but what if it's not?"

Blithe shrugged.

"I could leave and go to college."

Jamie looked sceptical. "My mum doesn't like that – she wouldn't let me do that."

"Just as well she's your mum and not mine."

"Well, I don't like the idea. You wouldnae get the same support, you'd probably have less time to do the work, less time with your teacher."

Blithe looked up at him, enjoying his concern. He kissed the top of her head. She sat up and kissed him properly on the lips.

The dressing gown sleeve slipped down her arm, the ball of her shoulder pressed against the palm of his hand. His hand followed the cold of her shoulder blades, down to the warm small of her back.

Jamie gently arched her backwards, keeping his hand at the small of her back. He splayed his fingers and tried to lift her with one arm.

Blithe arched her back. "Can you stop that? It's really uncomfortable."

Jamie let his arm relax.

"Sorry. I like the curve of your back; it fits my hand."

"Cheers." Blithe said, "I like yer..."

"No. You don't have to think of anything..."

"I like yer teeth."

"My teeth? Yer joking. My teeth are too big!"

"No! When yer head was smaller, your teeth seemed bigger but, these days, they fit yer face, you've just not noticed. Or did ye sand them down? Whatever yev done, you've got nice teeth. Did they not used to stick out a bit?"

Blithe really wanted to compliment his grin but didn't want to stray into romance.

Whenever he smiled, however he smiled or laughed, his rounded brows would arch over his eyes. When he tried to suppress a grin, his eyes twinkled with the effort.

They had vaguely known each other since the age of eleven. Jamie only had a very dim awareness of Blithe. When unprovoked she stayed quiet, fading into the background of every classroom, speaking only when she was spoken to.

By contrast Blithe remembered Jamie from an earlier age – that boy in her year who came back after the summer holidays unable to walk properly. Before then she'd often thought that he was full of himself, when he played the violin, she could recognize the skill but found herself anticipating mistakes, maybe even wishing for them.

She recalled her first impressions of Jamie. For a long time, both he and Robbie were marked down in her estimation for failing to stand out within their group of friends. The group in question weren't funny, they took no risks and observed outsiders with silent superiority. The only thing that marked Jamie out, aside from his injury, was his ability to sing.

She'd been forced along with her year to see the school band perform and Jamie was among the singers. She'd resented the sheer presumption that they would all be happy to be taken from their classrooms and made to listen. It seemed so odd to assume that someone would want to listen to you. If they'd tried to get her to perform, not that they ever did, she might have enjoyed the rehearsal, she might have enjoyed the process, but the performance would have been out of the question.

She could just about picture him years ago, singing a folk song. Those around her had sniggered. She wondered if the musicians detected it or if they were above everyone else, so far up their backsides, they wouldn't care as she would care. The twelve-year-old with the large teeth carried on singing. Each piece was met with applause, and the performers exchanged glances, relieved and a little embarrassed. Blithe had wondered how they got away with it.

They lay comfortably squashed together, side by side in the single bed. Jamie held her hand, examining her wrist and the threads of sapphire beneath the pure skin. He traced his finger along the stream to her elbow. She rolled onto her side, raising her head to look down at him. She ran her finger along his top lip with the same hazy fascination as he had traced along her arm.

"I can feel stubble – like a nettle." She looked closely. "But I can't see it. Do you have an invisible moustache?"

Jamie ran his finger above his lip and nodded. Blithe rolled onto her back and stared up at the ceiling. The windows in the flat above were open and 'Queen Bitch' could clearly be heard;

"She's so swishy in her satin and tat

In her frock coat and bipperty-bopperty hat

Oh God, I could do better than that.'

"Are folk ever going to stop going on about David Bowie? It's been four fucking months."

Jamie smiled to himself.

"Have you stopped singing?" Blithe asked. "Shame to have a good voice and not use it."

"I do, just not at school. Never at school. Whatever the music department does is embarrassing, it would be recorded and then it would be there to embarrass me forever. But I'll have to provide vocals next year, for Advanced Higher, if I pass this year."

"You'll have no bother passing."

There was a note of bitterness in her voice.

"I know that you weren't thinking that it would be there forever, when you recorded Robbie."

"It's true though,' she said. "Stream it and it could stay there forever. Or might not and how would you ken? Unless ye look obsessively. Though, it seems a shame to let that stop you doing things. You should still take risks."

"Like I said, I plan to next year – they'll get some suit in to hear me and everything. That's funny coming from you though, you don't take risks."

"But I don't want that kind of attention. I want to be listened to, but I'll wait till I leave school."

"But if you don't try... Are you trying to be invisible?"

Blithe rolled again onto her back. She felt uncomfortable, as though Jamie had been trying to prize something away from her before she was ready.

Jamie observed her out of the corner of his eye. He picked up his phone and unlocked it.

"The thing is, about singing...I actually think Robbie's a better singer than me,' he said, "I honestly do. I'd get told to stand up straight, head up, connect and I didn't want to do it that way. I stopped wanting to perform, it became, introverted and that's no good. We've all got different ideas about what makes a good voice, but I wouldn't mind sounding like Tom Waites."

"I don't know who that is."

"He sings like he's got a throatful of rusty nuts and bolts."

"And you *want* to sing like that?"

"Well it's not for everyone. What about Shane MacGowan from the Pogues?"

Blithe rolled back onto her side to face him.

"The guy with the teeth, no, without the teeth? My mum used to listen to him."

Jamie nodded eagerly. "His voice has character. Do you know what I mean? It's better than eyes closed, emotional discharge, warbling...those voices that all try to sound the same."

"Oh aye, better than singing that sounds like there's a rock-hard jobbie and it's never coming out."

A look of panic flashed across his face. "Did I ever...?"

Blithe laughed loudly until the bed frame shook and, still sniggering, she replied.

"No. Your singing never sounded like constipation. That's a shame, that's the kind of singing that everyone likes. Gets you on Britain's Got Talent."

Jamie's face was suddenly lit up by the light from his phone, his lips pursed as he typed into it and waited without blinking. Suddenly, the gentle cascade of a piano danced round. Jamie glanced at her out of the corner of his eye and simply explained.

"That is Shane MacGowan singing but, if it had been like a boy band it would have been shite. But it's not. It isn't hitting the notes that makes a voice special."

"Helps though."

Jamie nodded. Blithe listened to what seemed a waltz, and a slurring voice singing, 'Summer in Siam'. No longer needing his hand to type, Jamie reached across her lap to hold her hand.

"Jamie?"

"Mm?"

"Have you just put on make-out music?"

"No!" he gave a defensive jolt.

"Ye fucking have."

"No! No, it was just an example of what I was saying, it wasn't to...it wasn't for mood."

He sat up, trailing off and Blithe grinned.

"But you've gone bright red. I swear I don't know anyone who blushes as much as you."

She smiled at his embarrassment, how he hung his head like a child awaiting a telling off. She leaned forward and brought her forehead against his.

"Stop freaking out!"

* * *

Jim picked his nose and rubbed his dirty finger into his stubble. He dusted his face down before completing the process over the t-shirt that tightly covered his round belly.

He was sorting out the chippie for the night ahead. He surveyed the kitchen, the grease showing up in the dingy afternoon light. He made his way outside and up the concrete steps to the flat above the cafe. The flat was half storeroom, half grotty living space, for when he needed to crash out. Boxes of crisps, drinks crates and discarded boxes lined the bare walls of peeling woodchip. Two mismatching sofas, an office chair, a dusty TV, and a nest of plywood tables barely filled the wide space. It was only partially carpeted and what carpet there was, was so thin it felt like walking on concrete. An empty space, where a cooker had once been, indicated a shared kitchen and living space.

Jim was aware that his son, Aldo, used it from time to time. He fetched a few boxes that he'd taken from the Cash and Carry and lifted them to the top of the stairs, went back down, and returned with another load. The door into the flat was open, and he heard a cough and paused to listen out.

He followed the noise through the flat, heard another grunt and followed the sound to the sofa at the far end of the room, stepping over an old plate, smeared with the remains of yesterday's tomato sauce. The sofa was usually covered in sheets, carrier bags and junk. Most of this was now on the floor, though the snoring shape beneath the dust sheet had contorted itself around a few bags. Jim knew that from time to time people slept there, but no one else was in the flat to his knowledge.

A hand poked out – on closer examination it was clear that a sleeping body was facing the wall, a mass of black hair visible behind the hand.

Jim was too tired to be angry. He guessed that this was one of his son's friends. He gave the old sofa a kick. The head turned, and the hand clasped the sheets protectively.

"Donnie. You supposed to be here?'"

"Shit, shit sorry. Fuck."

Jim hadn't turned on the light in the hall. He was in two minds as to what to do.

"What time where you meant to be starting wi' me?" He demanded.

Donnie tumbled out of the sheets, fully clothed and bleary. He rubbed his head and tried to think.

"Were ye on the night?"

Donnie nodded. He wouldn't have stayed if that wasn't the case. He often stayed in the flat above and had not been discovered until now. He stank. He had slept in the clothes he had worn for both cleaning and cooking and even Jim, whose sense of smell was poor, recoiled.

"Fuckn' get yerself cleaned up then. Yer no coming down reek'n like that."

Donnie nodded and checked that his holdall was still at the foot of sofa. He hurried to the toilet, washed under his arms and sprayed his body with antiperspirant. When the first cloud settled, he sprayed himself a second time.

He ran down the stairs, not yet sure how serious his crime was. It was three o'clock, his shift wasn't due to start till five. He didn't keep track of the hours he worked and only had a rough idea.

Jim stood at the bottom of the steps smoking and glanced up at him suspiciously. Donnie felt the silence, and Jim waited threateningly in the vacuum. At last, he ventured.

"Do you want me to start in the kitchen?"

Jim nodded, the threat was cast off, and he moved aside for Donnie to begin.

Still anticipating punishment, Donnie cleaned the cafe floor and then the kitchen, trying to move with the efficiency of a machine. He found that moving in this way was a barrier to experiencing the here and now, a meditation taking him away from both body and mind.

Jim stood in the back doorway, reading the Daily Record. He ignored Donnie until he saw that he'd finished mopping the kitchen floor.

"Yer gonnae have to do that again."

"How?"

"Because next you'll do the surfaces, get all the shit af them and it'll need doing again. Ye mop the floor last, did yer maw no tell ye how to clean a kitchen?"

"Ye should have telt me before..."

"Aye well... Yer no down to be working the now."

Jim drifted upstairs. Donnie's eyes were heavy, he was so cold that his hands shook and his knuckles glowed bone white. Soon the fryers would be switched on and the red glow would burn off the chill. His empty stomach craved something hot and stodgy. He tried to move quickly to keep warm, wiping down the surfaces of crumbs, foil, and strips of cling film. Donnie carried the bits in his bare hands to the overflowing bins splattered with hardened condiments. He heaved the full bin bag out and hurried out the back doors without tying it. At the same moment, Jim rounded the corner and, in order to avoid him, Donnie dropped the bin liner. The rubbish burst out and in an instant the wind spread its contents from the backdoor.

Donnie's hands were still shaking, and he stood for a few seconds, not sure whether to seal the bag or try to re-stuff what was getting away. Jim punched him squarely on the shoulder, snatched up the bag and headed over the potholed car park to the main bins.

"Fucks sake, you clean that up NOW. Yer fucking useless Donnie, dinnae ken yer arse fae yer elbow."

Donnie rushed inside, grabbed another bin liner and with a fumbling hand struggled to open it from the ripped perforation. Jim marched back, beginning to gather up the cans and rubbish that were blowing around the car park.

Donnie could feel where the fist had impacted just below his shoulder, but it was easy for him to dismiss; he couldn't get upset about things like that anymore. In less than an hour, the fryers would be switched on, but the rush of the night ahead seemed far away.

Having cleaned up the rubbish, Jim gave Donnie a poke of cold chips and an energy drink for which Donnie was embarrassingly grateful, not realising that without these things, he really would have been useless.

Jim had once said something to him about putting him 'on the books' if that was what he wanted. Donnie did not see that an official contract would help him, he could see more benefit to not declaring his work. He hadn't declared his unemployment, and even if he did, the money wouldn't come for a while. He couldn't face going to the job centre. He didn't believe anyone there really wanted to help him and feared the strings that would be attached to any benefit he was eventually given. They would slot him into the right process and keep dragging him back to the next hoop or simple test. He saw no pride in that. There was no pride in working for Aldo's dad, but at least he found the job through being someone's friend and therefore, through his worth as a human being.

Jim assumed that Donnie was signed on at the job centre and that the threat of being convicted as a fraudster would ensure his secrecy. He assumed they both benefitted from the deception – it wouldn't be the first time he had been in this position. Jim paid him cash in hand, rounding up or down to the nearest tenner.

Donnie powered through the first half of his shift on sugar and caffeine. There was a TV mounted in the corner of the cafe which distracted him until customers rolled in fresh from the pub. At 1.10, Aldo turned up, helped himself to some chips and a roll and sausage and headed upstairs with a few cans.

Jim went upstairs for a quick beer, leaving Donnie to finish up. He gave his son the keys and left half an hour later without saying anything to Donnie.

Jack Viney, another ex-colleague from the pub, made his way through and up to the flat above. At 2.00, Donnie was alone downstairs and exhausted. He had a continual ringing in his ears and had to check several times to ensure that everything was turned off. He couldn't trust himself.

He locked the doors and mounted the concrete steps he could only feel in the pitch black, following the light above.

As he stumbled into the flat, he nodded to Jack. Jack was a big guy. His belly hung over his belt as though his legs had been squeezed, inflating a barrel chest in the process.

Music played through a smart phone plugged into the wall. Donnie flopped back onto the sofa and closed his eyes. The sound quality and the music itself were bad but the sound drowned out the ringing in his ears.

"Yer dad's alright," Jack remarked to Aldo.

Donnie opened his eyes, faintly curious.

"Aye he is." Aldo replied between puffs. "See, what you and I do, isnae his business."

Jack noticed that Donnie was listening and explained.

"Jim walked in on me when I was doing a line. Said nothing, just carried on."

"Well...Yer a fucking adult." Aldo nodded.

"Aye but, if we got found out, in his business."

"Youse are wi me." Aldo explained. "See, dad found Donnie on the sofa the day. He thought he was alone, practically shat himself, but as long as he works, shows up on time, disnae matter."

Jack wrinkled up his nose and turned to Donnie.

"Man, ye should get a shower. No offence but."

All the horrible jobs seemed to linger within his clothes; grease and damp and vinegar permeated the fibres.

Donnie heaved himself off the sofa and shuffled over to a plastic bag to grab another t-shirt. It had also been worn but was the better of the two.

He tried to be quick, but Jack saw him, or saw what little there was to see when Donnie was sideways on. He observed the curves and shadows of his exposed ribs before they were concealed beneath the t shirt.

Aldo stood up, chucked a blister pack at Donnie, and went out for a piss. As Donnie furtively shoved the pack into the back pocket of his trousers, Jack leaned forward and whispered.

"Ye ken he's ripping ye aff?"

The fear of being ripped off had been floating round Donnie's head before Jack articulated it.

"You gave him a fifteen quid for the score yesterday– is that right?"

Donnie nodded.

"Get it cheaper online man, much cheaper."

"Ma phone got nicked and now, I've got this shitty brick that cannae do much more than receive calls."

Donnie pulled an old phone out of his pocket. Jack examined it with amusement.

"Fuck man. That's an antique. Seriously, is that last century?"

"It's ten year old so... Could you sort me out?"

Jack shook his head. "Already been done for dealing once. Sorry but. Could ye no just get another phone? How much is Jim paying ye?"

Donnie did a quick calculation and added on an extra pound and fifty.

"£8.00 an hour."

Jack raised an eyebrow. The toilet flushed, but Aldo did not materialise. Instead, he called out from the bathroom.

"Donnie, can you come here a wee minute?"

With a rush of something like panic, Donnie snapped to attention. His body fought movement; aching tremors ran through his limbs as circulation brought them back to half-life. He sloped off after Aldo like an obedient old dog.

The bathroom door was ajar, the voice disembodied behind it.

"I'll just grab you a t shirt."

He entered the bare bathroom with his head down, trusting weakly without wondering. Then came the slap. A heavy curtain of cold water clapped the breath from his body. His eyes clenched shut. Laughter. He heard Jack running through, more laughter. His eyes stung, running with cold water and a large concentration of lemon washing up liquid. Bubbles popped in his ears. He stood still and dripping, arms out and frozen. Donnie tried to open his eyes, but the soap stung. A towel was pushed into his hands, which smelled used and felt damp, but he dabbed it against his stinging eyes. He heard the tap run but still he didn't wonder why and stayed obediently still for a second bucket of cold water to be emptied over his head – no washing up liquid this time. He cleared his eyes – now free of soap.

"The water will come through the ceiling!" Jack shouted, "If you dinnae clear it up, it'll come through the roof and fuck your dad's electrics!"

"Fuck!" Aldo stopped laughing.

Donnie pulled his t shirt off and watched numbly, his teeth chattering as both of his t-shirts were used to mop the floor, balled up like paper towels, stamped on to increase their absorbency. He stood shivering, welded to the spot to drip dry. Jack was down on his hands and knees, dabbing Donnie's t-shirt over the huge wet patch on the bathroom floor. He smiled and Donnie smiled back through chattering teeth. He tried to enjoy the joke, until he couldn't stand it anymore, enduring cold to the cusp of pain. He scurried through to the living room and curled up on the sofa, warming himself against the cushions.

Once curled up, he thought about drying one of his t-shirts out for the following day. He did not consider asking to borrow one, he felt no entitlement and no rage. He had almost no feelings at all but for a sense of shrinkage, he'd reduced himself to this puny body that would not warm up. He felt a simple sadness at being so cold, wet, and skinny. He thought about hanging the t-shirts up to dry, but he couldn't move. All night, shivering, he pictured them in the place where they were to lie all night, balled up rags on the bathroom floor.

CHAPTER 7

Jamie walked into Queen's Park from the south side and made his way slowly past the entrance to the Victorian glasshouse, along the path and into the trees. He'd asked Blithe to meet him there because he couldn't walk her home. Her agreement had been so flat and disinterested that he didn't expect to see her. He still didn't have her number, so he walked alongside her after school and hissed his request without directly looking at her. Blithe played along well. She didn't seem to care when he asked her to come to his bit of town. There had been irritation in the agreement that made him think it might have been sarcasm.

Blithe came into the park from the west side. She stayed in the shade under the oaks and chestnut trees, keeping to a gentler path that slowly inclined up past the rose garden to where the grass grew long, and the road below couldn't be heard.

They faced one another on the pathway, relieved, as expressionless as they could manage. Blithe followed him down the grassy slope towards the trees, squelching the last of the bluebells. The long grass glowed where the evening light reached through the trees.

They caught a faint whiff of cigarette smoke as a fellow unseen conspirator walked the path behind them.

Jamie seemed to slowly skid to the ground – the weak leg stretched out, dragging into the turf and the other folded beneath him.

"Sorry about having to come here."

Lying down, Blithe stared up through the veins of light in the foliage. Jamie cast a shadow; she felt his fingers running through her hair. He sat up with his elbow resting on the knee he'd drawn up.

He opened his bag and unwrapped a sandwich from tissue and cling film. The mayonnaise had merged with the bread completely. Jamie offered a half to Blithe, who recoiled.

"Should you not have eaten that at lunchtime?"

"I forgot. I'll still eat it though. It looks like party bag cake, stuck to the napkin."

"Is that a kind of a cake?"

"No! The best bit of a party – the party bag with the balloons and the shitty wee games. You'd always have crushed cake at the bottom. I'd still eat it – and the icing glued to the tissue, the whole thing. I've probably eaten the equivalent of an entire tissue."

Blithe sniffed. "Well, I didn't go to that many parties. I cannae mind eating crushed cake. Anyway, how come I had to come all the way out here?"

"I've a study timetable," he explained. "My mum thinks I'm not doing enough and she's got the next month timetabled for me. One hour's revision before tea, my dad's working at home so, I'm stuck with it."

"Oh aye, I forgot that yer mums a teacher," she replied absently.

"I'll be able to see you home Wednesday and Thursday."

"Why?"

"Ye might still be getting shit Wednesday and Thursday."

"Aye and I'll be getting it the rest of the week."

"Could you not get the bus on those other days?"

Blithe sighed and let her arm drape round her head, guarding her hair from being stroked. He rested his hand on the curve of her elbow and noted her furrowed brow.

"Do you want to walk with me?" she asked.

"Aye."

"Well then... Stop treating it like something else, like yer walking the dog."

Jamie flopped on his back. Fearing a serious discussion, he took a sudden interest in the canopy overhead.

"Because that's what it feels like..." she muttered.

"I've told Robbie to see a doctor but I dinnae think he will. Am I a shite friend? I haven't said anything about you, but it's not like he loved you, he just pretended."

"I know," Blithe agreed but it still irked her to hear it.

Jamie detected this in her voice and quickly added.

"You should still be flattered, but his family are really close, closer than my family and he would have let you in on that."

Blithe sat up; now it was her turn to observe him from above.

"He let you in?" she repeated.

"Aye. He invited me round to the house. His dad wanted to talk to me and I mean, talk to me properly, he was asking me questions about school and where I lived and that."

Blithe narrowed her eyes. "Sounds nosy."

"His dad was the first of his family to leave Iran and he went to study in Glasgow. A couple of years later, his family came to London so his sister could go to university. When the whole family come up to Glasgow, to see the city and meet Helen, Robbie's mum, it all went wrong. They hated Helen. They lived in some shitty tenement that was probably marked for demolition, they're..."

"Bunch of snobs?" volunteered Blithe.

"No. They didn't like to see the family coming down to living in a pissy tenement. They wanted to see their kids doing alright fur themselves."

"They sound like a bunch of snobs."

Jamie shook his head. "I've met his aunt, she's not a snob. I was properly introduced to her a couple of years ago. She said that she'd heard a lot about me. I didn't know what to say to that, so I said, 'likewise." Like I say stuff like that. See what I mean? I would never introduce Robbie to my aunt. My parents wouldnae expect me to, but Robbie's family is not like that. If you're a close friend of Robbie's, you're a friend of the family. You're let into the family."

Blithe rolled onto her side and let her arm rest against Jamie's chest.

"They must really have hated Glasgow,' she smiled. "You don't know though, yer only hearing what one side wants ye to ken."

Jamie caressed the arm that rested against him and supported her wrist, as though it was bone china.

"Maybe it was his mum then. She doesn't take any shit. Robbie told me that you were like her, actually."

Jamie gave a guilty smile. Blithe grimaced, she wondered, as he had, whether there was something slightly perverted about that. He pulled her by the arm, dragging her across him. She buried her face in his shirt.

"But even though I was let in, I've never seen him emotional before. Compared to me he's always controlled. Even when he's angry, disappointed, or hurt he just deals with it. So what you got from him, that's rare."

This made Blithe squirm.

"You've watched it then?"

He gave a sigh. "No".

Silence descended. Jamie stared upwards, absentmindedly strumming her arm.

"I was always, always being told to control myself,' he said, "Till that wound me up as much as whatever had wound me up to begin with and I broke things."

He adjusted his head to look at Blithe, her face still and listening.

"Usually my own stuff. I can remember looking at drawings I'd made that I'd ripped up or picking up the pieces of a model I'd smashed. My parents left me alone to clean up and learn the hard way and I did, I think. Robbie never had that problem to solve, that's why he's in the mess he's in. The stupid things that take over yer mind, he never let things blow up till they felt like that. If something was unfair or wrong it would get to me, not him. Whatever it was, he never obsessed, he was able to think of other things when he needed to. Now he can't and, to be honest, you should learn that in childhood, no now. The first time I met him, I was on the verge of a tantrum and he was all composed, I was cutting across the playfield in first year and a football hit me on the head. I was 100% sure someone had meant to do it. So, I planted myself down and put my head between my knees, just squatting. It was the kind of tearful sulk I used to do all the time; I was like that. Anyway, it was Robbie who came over and asked if I was okay. Obviously, I told him to fuck off. He tried to be reasonable but I didnae let him speak, I told that he could have broken my neck. And he, all calm, says he didnae kick it and maybe I should go to the nurse. I tell him I'm not going to the nurse and then he says it would be good if I could move because I'm still on the pitch. I was about to run off but then the ball gets kicked at me again and this time it definitely is deliberate, it's slammed down on my head from above and I run off snivelling because the second kick hurt more than the first. I'd laugh if I saw that now, how could you not?"

Blithe nodded.

"I think we became friends because we balanced each other out. Sometimes I almost wanted to electrocute him, just to get a rise, you know?"

"Thing is," Blithe murmured, "I never wanted him calming me down. I'd rather go off and have a fucking good go. That's better than calming down." She considered and then added, "Most of the time."

"Aye, but ye say things ye regret."

"I tell ye, there's a lot of people I regret *not* telling to fuck off. Anyway, who's even listening to me."

"I was. When you asked me if the accident had taken years off my life."

"Shut it!" she paused and then raised her head from his chest to look him in the eye. "I'm sorry about that."

Jamie grinned. "I'm going to have to be heading back." he gently gathered her hair at the nape of her neck. He tilted her head up and looked her in the eye.

"What about you?" he asked. "Don't you have to study?"

"My mum trusts me to get on with it. She's got plenty of other worries without worrying about whether or not I've been studying."

"Would she not pressure you that bit more, if she had less to worry about?"

"Probably," she conceded. "I still think she trusts me more than your mum trusts you."

Jamie gave her a dig in the ribs but Blithe didn't laugh, instead she seized up and so he stopped and clasped her to him.

"What are you wanting to do when you leave school?" he asked.

"I'll try and join the police."

Jamie laughed. Blithe glared back.

"Not sure whether to leave it for a year or not. How is that funny?"

"It's just, authority, you know? You'd have to do what the government told you to do. Would you arrest me if the government told you to?"

"Aye. If that was my job. What do you want to do?"

"No idea. I'll maybe become an activist, see if you arrest me."

Blithe narrowed her eyes.

"I don't think the police give much of a shit about activists. Can ye imagine? Police on their way to a suspected Al Qaeda cell until they get a call, no wait, it's the fucking vegan activists. Smash! Into the greenhouse, Hands up! Or we'll rub sausages in yer faces!"

Jamie nodded. "But do you not want to go somewhere else,

live somewhere else just for a wee while?"

"Of course, but if my mum's alone and gets sick, then I can't."

"You cannae think like that."

"I don't mean as her carer – I'm not thinking like that. What if the council make her move to a one bed place and I don't have a home to go back to?"

"Scotland got rid of the bedroom tax though. They can't move someone just like that."

Blithe didn't want to argue but she did not share his faith.

"With the lift and everything. If we lose a family home because I've fucked off then what? We were supposed to be getting a refurb, but that was cancelled. Is that because they want to bring the flats down? That's what we ask ourselves, we willnae get a straight answer. I ken what yer saying, it's not happened yet so don't worry. Na. The things that I see happening... It is what it is. Shit does happen. All the time. Maybe when I finish school we can ask to be re-housed. I don't know. Everything's getting worse."

Jamie stroked her cheek.

"You can't think like that. My parents are worried about their debts but I won't hang about to help."

Blithe rolled off him and sat up with renewed energy, mustered for the purposes of going home. She didn't want to argue with him, but his situation was very different from hers.

"No, I do think like that."

"Well you shouldnae." He replied just as simply.

Blithe narrowed her eyes. "Your mum and dad own their home, right? So, you don't sit waiting for the rules to change, for when they think yer mums fit for work, and when she actually is. It stresses us out, when mum's worried, she eats, when she eats, she becomes sick, when she becomes sick, she can't work, when she can't work, she gets depressed and round and round it fucking goes. You don't choose that. You guys have choice. We don't."

Jamie nodded solemnly. "Does yer mum know you think like that?"

"No. She'd want me to think like you. She'd like me to think I've got the world at my feet but you know, she's never really tried to make me believe that, and I think that's because she widnae be very convincing."

* * *

Blithe was exhausted when she finally arrived home. Even with the extra comfort of the borrowed shoes, her feet ached.

While Jamie's meal was being prepared, Blithe was completing the last trudge up the hill. Even then, she didn't take the lift when she finally reached home, but clumped up the stairwell.

Donnie heard her key in the door and pounced before she'd had time to put her school bag down.

"Where's mum?" He demanded.

"Why? Why d'ye need her?"

Donnie ignored her.

"She's no answering her phone. Fucks sake. Why does she even have a phone?"

Blithe dropped her bag in her room and trailed after Donnie, who was marching between the living room and kitchen with pent up energy.

"Oh." Blithe remembered, "She's got the doctors after work. That'll be why her phone is switched off."

"Why's she at the doctors?"

"Irregular heartbeat and her breathing's bad..."

Donnie snorted dismissively.

"That Paki bastard will just be on at her to lose weight again."

Blithe's mouth dropped open.

"What the fuck!"

"What?"

"Do you know how much of an arsehole you sound when you

say things like that?"

Donnie seemed genuinely baffled. "What? He's a bastard and he's a Paki. I'm no saying he's a bastard because he's a Paki. Dinnae be giving me all that PC shite."

"If ye really think he's a bastard what does it matter where he's from? Practically every doctor she's ever seen has been on at her to lose weight. D'ye no understand that? A five-year-old could."

"I can say what I think in my ain house."

"Oh, on you go then! Let's hear how much yer brains have turned to shit!"

Donnie sneered and turned away into the living room, while Blithe stormed into her bedroom. She turned on her laptop, took her water bottle and textbooks out of her bag and arranged them on the bedside table. She would read while her laptop loaded. There would be plenty of time, as she usually had to re-start it.

Donnie had been reasonable once. Away from school at least, he had been in focus with the world around him and in tune with those he shared it with. Four years before, they might have been together in the lounge playing Guitar Hero. They'd want to watch the same films, request the same food and laugh at the same jokes. Now he was, as Jamie observed, nothing like her and she didn't want to love the person he had become. Instead, she wanted to keep moving further away from him.

Lynne returned from the doctors one hour later. The doctor had not been happy with either her weight or her blood sugar levels, but was concerned that focusing too heavily on these things made her anxious and was, therefore, counterproductive. She'd agreed, relieved and said.

"I ken what yer going to say, what you always say."

"Well, it's good that we agree. But we need to try something else. Perhaps you should try to get active with a group of people. Not the gym necessarily, gentle exercise in a more sociable environment."

Lynne agreed readily, but honestly feared being forced to befriend a group purely because, like her, they had trouble getting out and making friends. Weight loss, improved diet, social life, and confidence seemed far away; a version of herself that existed in a kinder parallel world. She was provided with a few leaflets at the reception desk and promised herself that she would keep trying until she found something she enjoyed. That alone felt like moving in the right direction, but that would pass, and the looming prospect of the first attempt or the first meeting would terrify her.

She arrived home to silence, her children locked away behind their bedroom doors and a pile of foul smelling washing dumped in the kitchen.

When Donnie eventually emerged into the living room, she was shocked at the sight of him. His t-shirt hung off him, the stretched collar exposed his ribs. The thin fabric fell in folds against the notches of his bones. She did not ask him where he had been and what he had been doing but, after a silence, he volunteered the information.

"I've been volunteering. I got a trial shift at the chippie, the one run by Aldo's dad."

"Which is it? Trial or volunteering?"

"Volunteering, but there'll be work at the end of it."

"Can ye not claim for housing?"

Donnie mocked the question with a tut and a shake of the head. It was meant for her to see, perhaps to remind her that she couldn't discipline him. Whether or not this was true, she did not fear him. She waited while he eyed her angrily. She repeated the question.

"Fucks sake!" He exploded, "I'm no here half the fucking time, why should I be paying ye housing?"

"Because we need it," she explained calmly. "I cannae afford to miss out, I don't know about you."

He'd wanted to ask her for money, but he could not bring himself to do so.

Donnie did not sleep until the morning. After midnight, he lay awake for many hours, passing out some time after four. He came to life around lunchtime, but returned to bed twice where he sat up, drinking mug after mug of warm diluting juice which he pressed against his clammy hands.

He had another bath and left for his shift at 3.30. As he walked, a headache quickly set in, the sun seemed to burn into the back of his head. It wasn't particularly hot, he walked past plenty of people wearing coats. He felt better in other ways. He was clean and had managed to consume a simple but substantial meal with minimal digestive discomfort. As his day began, the school day ended.

On the road ahead, he could see the start of the approaching army, dressed in his old school uniform. He looked out for his sister. In his mind, they had not really fallen out. Then he saw her. If she had not been staring so vacantly ahead, she would have seen him across the road. At that moment, a scrawny girl with dingy blond hair walked alongside her and shouldered her towards a bus shelter. Blithe didn't even give the girl the satisfaction of stumbling. She seemed to have prepared herself, and stopped dead, planting herself firmly at just the right time, her eyes fixed resolutely ahead. The drizzle became heavy rain, but Donnie stayed where he was. He barely felt it. Without even a hoodie to protect her from the rain, the scrawny girl ran away across the road. Donnie let her go. If it had been a guy, he would have had to threaten him. While he hesitated, he saw the tall boy with the limp catching up with Blithe, keeping to her side, shielding her in case anyone should try to shove her again. They did not talk, he did not touch her, but they clearly understood each other. Like police after a riot, they walked to the same beat.

Donnie did not want Blithe to see him. A small shop selling electronic equipment provided a convenient place to duck into.

From the doorway, he watched the pupils pass and his sister scurrying away. He waited until all the pupils had vanished from sight before carrying on, ensuring life happened in his absence.

Robbie waited on the main road outside the school, hoping for company on the way home. With his rucksack firm against his back, his coat zipped up to his nose and his hood hanging low over his eyebrows, he was an accidental spy hurrying through the gates.

He saw Jamie ahead and expected him to head for home, but Jamie turned instead, in the opposite direction, though he had no hood or umbrella. The rain pelted down, but he made his way without hesitation, head down, marching into the wind and the rain. Robbie looked around; everyone would be getting the bus if they had the change. The crowds dispersed quickly in weather like this and so there was no cause for Jamie to be with her now, the only thing that would befall Blithe was a soaking.

The rain against his hood sounded a reassuring beat. He felt insulated, as it had a long way to go before it would soak in. He considered running after Jamie and confronting him, instead he watched the figures melting into the distance through sheets of rain before he turned and made his way alone.

* * *

When Jamie and Blithe cautiously entered the flat, they listened out for a few seconds. When they were sure they were alone, Blithe went straight to the bathroom to brush away the frizz from her wet hair. Jamie went into her room, dropped his wet blazer by the door and waited anxiously on her bed with his bag on his lap.

Blithe meanwhile took a towel to her hair, brushed it a second time and hurried into her room, suddenly worried that he might find something incriminating. She cast her eyes around; no pants on the floor, no old bras hanging out of drawers and with some relief she plonked herself down on the bed beside him.

His floppy hair clung as one mass against his head, his nose and cheeks shone pink. He tried to push away the hair from his face but swept strands like rats' tails across his brow. Blithe grinned. Realising his appearance was comical, Jamie suddenly shook his head backwards and forwards before tossing the hair from his eyes.

Blithe squinted, unimpressed and so he knew that whatever he'd done, he didn't look quite so funny.

Jamie delved into his bag and produced a small plastic cellophane bag from a pouch.

"What's that?"

Jamie replied in a hesitant monotone, "To... cheer you up... after the other day."

"Do I need cheering up?"

Jamie dithered and suddenly thrust the bag at her.

It was a pirate birthday party bag that had waited for many years at the bottom of a utility drawer, where it had become sticky and crumpled.

She glanced up at him before delving in, reassured that he did not look mischievous, only nervous.

The bag contained a chalky old balloon, some kind of whistle, a yo-yo and a slice of cake wrapped in two pieces of kitchen roll.

"I had to scavenge around a bit. It's not birthday cake, it's ginger loaf."

Jamie waited for the verdict and laughed nervously.

"It's just a silly wee thing. It's stupid, a stupid wee thing." Blithe stared at the objects now lined up on the bed.

"No, no. It's not stupid. What's this?" She held up the whistle. "It's a kazoo."

Jamie took the kazoo and blew into it. The sound of whirring acceleration burst from the small piece of metal, and he tilted his head, satisfied with the sound.

"I thought, how can ye be miserable with a party bag? Ye ought to remember when there was nothing to worry about, apart from the balloon popping or the cake getting crushed."

"I'm not sure that stuff ever bothered me. I was bothered by stink bombs in the park and when I had to go to my dad's, and I couldn't be arsed to."

"Aye true – that wasn't all that bothered me. I freaked out if the cat hadn't come in."

"Do you still have the cat?"

"Aye. A fat old ginger tom called Christopher. Not Chris, always Christopher. He looks like a Christopher."

Blithe carefully refilled the bag and felt its satisfying weight, designed for a hand smaller than her own.

"Forget all the junk," he said. "Just eat the cake."

There was such sweet anxiety in his voice. Yes, presented in any other way it was junk, but the act of bringing it together made it special. Of all the ugly knick-knacks she'd ever amassed, she held in her hand the junk supreme.

"It's not junk," she murmured.

The first kiss of the day was assured now. He knew it, she knew it.

Blithe's hair smelled like incense and damp clothes. Not nice, not bad. Her hair was chilly and damp, but her cheeks were warm. His palm cushioned her fist and cupped it protectively.

She felt his wet cuffs and looked carefully into the rosy, clammy face. She carefully untucked his shirt. No sooner was it free than he pulled it over his head. She moved backwards, positioning herself on her pillows as he dragged his bare arms out of the tight sleeves and cast the shirt to the floor. She pulled her shirt over her head and threw it down where it lay crumpled beside his.

He watched her carefully, observing her posture, her knees drawn up high, another line of defence. He was not frightened. They understood each other.

She suddenly pulled up the covers and slipped beneath them, vanishing entirely. Snake-like, she slid her tights and skirt off, nudging them to the foot of the bed where they fell in a muffled thud. After some moments, she emerged and resumed sitting cross-legged on her pillows. Unobserved, Jamie had taken off his trousers and wet socks but sat in exactly the same position. They were mirroring one another, sitting on either side of a single bed, trying not to laugh, trying to pretend they were now familiar with being familiar. Jamie noted the silver star shorts and black bra only fleetingly, he was more struck by her transformation. Her wet clothes had shrouded her into the defensive dark figure and having cast them off, she glowed, bolt upright on the pillow.

Blithe prevented herself from laughing by looking away from his smile to his hands lightly clasped together, long white fingers with clean nails. She barely noticed the scar on his knee, but he was still a waif, his body pale and hairless. As his windswept complexion reddened, he finally laughed and stretched out over the bed towards her.

She wrapped them both in her sheets, for a while they lay beneath the covers, legs coiled round legs as the chills faded away, feet rubbing together.

Now warmed, Jamie sat upright on her bed, looking out of the window he was cast in silhouette, his drying hair sticking up from where he had been lying down. His bare chest lean and lithe but strong to the touch.

"Are you enjoying the view or is there something happening out there?" Blithe asked.

"Nothing happening."

The downpour eased to a burr. Two complete rainbows, one behind the other, faded to the south, to cloud and hill. He peered into the distance, to a spot on the horizon forged by glaciers, where the city stopped, somewhere he had never been, a place never arrived at, driven around and always in the distance. A secure place of no consequence.

She watched as his arms developed goose-pimples. He threw

himself down on the bed, stroked her head clumsily and smiled at what he had done, and what her eyes reflected back at him. He sat up again and turned to the window to write.

'I was here.'

Blithe reclaimed the duvet and, grabbing two corners, wore it like a cloak. She sat up behind him, resting her chin on his shoulder. She cast the duvet over her head and in the dark, she clung against him until she had to roll round and away from his arms.

He took care, when he fell on her he pulled away a little, so the tips of their noses touched. Though she seemed so delicate beneath him, he gave hungry kisses, pulling away to look at her until their tongues moved together in a rhythm that didn't want to be broken.

She unclipped her bra. He drew his hands through her hair and slid her bra from her arms. He tried to glance at her breasts before his hands covered them, shielding more than feeling. He kissed them with careful reverence before returning to her mouth.

She rolled over and sat up astride him. She looked carefully at the boy with his head on her pillow staring up at her with fear at last appearing in his wide eyes. He held out his arms, wanting her back. She turned behind her and saw his bare legs in the gloom, her eyes picked out the lack of symmetry. She looked back at him and wanted to laugh, you would think from the panic on his face, that he had some pulsating tumour rather than just scarring and a bit of wasting.

She patted his leg reassuringly and fell forward into his outstretched arms.

The rain hit against the window with a soothing tap, the wind groaned from far away. Within her bones, she felt safe.

From the small of her back he pulled her tightly against him, just to feel the delicate curve. He felt her ribs against him - her soft belly tight against his.

The wind and rain rose and fell, rose, and fell. Footsteps

hurrying outside, glass smashing into a bottle bank, car horn protesting and engines struggling then exploding. So much fuss and struggle out there.

Lying side by side the loose limbs wriggled together. Her thumbs slid under the elastic of his shorts. He quickly slid them off and lay down over her slowly, examining her face, afraid he would see shock now that her black pants with the silver stars were the only piece of clothing worn between them.

Using her hands and feet she felt the length of him, an uninterrupted swathe of skin.

"Should we be doing this?"

He'd been asking himself this question but had no answer. He worried she'd ask it and, since he had no answer, it was better coming from him. Blithe heard but didn't think she needed to answer. Instead, she squeezed her body against his and gave a sigh. A lovely deep sigh.

In an instant he rolled on top of her, his hands pinning hers, for a second the whites of her eyes seemed to expand and she tensed. Pushing at his shoulders she was aware, for the first time, how powerless she was beneath him. She gave him a dig in the ribs. He giggled, a gurgling laugh that sounded so odd and out of place that she could only laugh too.

He had to ask the question. If he'd been in any doubt of the answer, he wouldn't have asked it and he heard himself, despite mental rehearsal exclaim.

"Can-I-shall-I?"

She nodded and rolled over, rested her head on his chest, closed her eyes and breathed him in. From where he lay, her eyes staring back looked huge. Both enthralled at being viewed in such a tender and bewildered way. When he stood up, she was at first inclined to drag him back and keep him there. From her warm position of safety, she watched him pad over to his blazer, while her legs kicked around the surface he'd vacated.

Glowing white in the gloom he crouched to search his pockets. His vulnerability was clear as he threw a quick glance over his shoulder, knowing he was being watched.

He found the condom in his wallet when he checked it a second time. He moved over to sit on the edge of her bed. This was the first time he'd ever needed to use one. For practice, it had been simple but now the need was desperate, he felt the pressure of being watched. When it was on and finally looked right, it felt uncomfortable. He rolled it off and re-applied it. It was comfortable but he worried that in re-applying, it was now inside out – or had it been before?

Blithe lay on her back chewing a smile, not because he was taking a while but because she'd seen him cross the room and decided that erections were funny. She now glanced at the long white body hunched at the end of her bed.

She rolled over. A smile spread across her face that she would not want him to see. She tried to stop smiling and looked up at the ceiling and then back at the figure still hunched at the end of her bed. She burrowed down into the sheets.

It had occurred to her that he had walked with her, hoping to be repaid in one way or another. Her intuition had offered some reassurance, but the fact remained, he kept following her, all the time pretending it was an obligation not a choice. She had not pursued him in any way.

The taunt that she would fuck anything, was flung at her often enough, but it hadn't taken hold enough to make her defensive. Only now she wondered whether he believed it. Was that why he was here now? Five minutes ago, she'd wanted him so much it hindered her breathing, but those feelings had quelled. She had the right to change her mind.

She sat up, pulling the covers over her chest protectively. He looked over his shoulder fearfully, and she regretted what she was going to have to say.

"Actually... Can we not?"

His eyes momentarily widened with outrage. His mouth clamped shut. She wore a rictus, tense smile.

"It's just... my mum'll be back soon."

Her shoulders were hunched, her arms tight across her chest though it wasn't cold. In that pose, he couldn't believe he would be welcome again in her arms. The strange, slightly smug smile on her face suggested she was laughing at his expense. There was nothing for Jamie to do but gather up his clothes.

"Don't be..." she began. "It's not you."

"It's alright."

He was beside her, but his voice was far away. He pulled his shorts and shirt from the pile of clothes and then pulled on the wet trousers and socks with a grimace. His clothes were beside her but he went to great lengths to avoid looking her in the eye.

Blithe tried again,

"See... She could come home any second."

Entirely unconvinced, Jamie nodded and picked up his bag.

"I'd better be getting on anyway."

He looked at her properly. He wanted to know whether he had done something wrong, if he had taken too long, if there was something wrong with his body. He could ask but thought that if an answer came it wouldn't be honest, just painful.

Blithe didn't see him to the door. Alone, he found the lobby eerily silent. He walked slowly past the lift and opened the heavy doors into the back stairs. He paused and sat on the steps. He was in a cold unwelcoming world compared to where he had been ten minutes ago.

The memory made him shiver. He hadn't felt naked but, in a delayed reaction, he recalled feeling it. He stood up and dropped a copper coin down the stairwell, not moving until he heard it slam onto the tiles on the ground floor. Jamie sorrowfully descended the stairs, though his limp clearly earned him a place in the lift. It seemed necessary to sneak out.

CHAPTER 8

As long as she wasn't singled out, taunts didn't usually bother Blithe. When sex entered the collective conscious around her, the taunts mutated and became harder to ignore. Louder, deeper, and more confident in their ability to humiliate, they informed her that she was a whore or too hideous to find anyone who would pump her. She had ignored taunts for years, so routinely thrown out by voices who were only ever heard to give out abuse. It *was* meaningless and she had tried to silence it by being silent. Only now it mattered. Those words weren't meaningless if they meant something to Jamie.

She did not consider that he wouldn't walk her home again, she only planned what she would say when he did. Theirs needn't be a serious in-depth discussion. She wanted sex but she didn't want to be used. She could not trust someone sexually when they pretended not to be with her. Surely these were the sentiments of any self-respecting human being?

Blithe spent her lunchtimes in the school library. Students were not allowed to eat and drink there so Blithe hid behind large books. Using her lap as a plate, she ripped up her sandwiches into small mouth-sized pieces that wouldn't prevent her talking if she suddenly needed to.

She sat at a small table in the poetry and classics section and often thumbed through books if an author or title jumped out at her. Often an upright hardback concealed the sight of her head down on the table. She almost managed a snooze and nearly dribbled on the table.

She left the library just before the lunchtime bell and went to the toilet, knowing there would be no queues. It wasn't that she had suddenly become timid, but toilets presented too many possibilities to those who wished to see her humiliated. While sitting on the toilet, there was the possibility of missiles sailing over into the cubicle, puddles to be pushed into. It was better to wait till everyone else had gone.

She washed her hands as the bell sounded. As she made her way out, she saw Jamie walking towards her. As he approached, she looked through him, knowing he would look through her. Once, in the same situation, Jamie had smiled at her, but she hadn't noticed. As far as she had been concerned, she wasn't allowed to look at him during the school day. He drew level, she glanced up, but he didn't look back.

She made her way to English and waited outside the locked classroom. As a group of girls gathered, Blithe turned to the wall. She never used to daydream before but now did so increasingly, no longer anticipating interaction. When she did get the chance, she mentally rehearsed what she would say to Jamie.

"I don't want to feel used."

No.

"You pretend not to be with me until we're walking home. What's that all about?"

No.

"Are you going to tell Robbie?"

No. She would go on the attack if she needed to but that wasn't how she wanted to start. She recalled the look on his face as he stood by her bed, unable to ask for an explanation, lost and humiliated.

She glanced over her shoulder. Robbie kept his distance behind her, talking to Josh, the boy who had told him he could do much better. She noticed that Josh was a lot taller than Robbie. Robbie could still pass for fourteen, but he was losing the wholesome, rosy look. Robbie seemed to become aware that Blithe was staring, though he did not react strongly, he nonetheless managed a look of revulsion.

"Blithe, do you think Codey's trying to get into Maddie's pants?"

Blithe glanced up at a group of girls, including Josie and Leanne. It was Daisy Frazer who had asked the question, the only one of the group keeping a straight face. Blithe liked her directness.

Josie shook her head as both a prompt and an appeal not to encourage this. Blithe didn't want to comply, a smile spread across her face, and she replied decisively.

"Definitely."

"See?" said Daisy, "Blithe would ken. She's been attacking Blithe for weeks, desperate to get her head into Maddie's pants."

"Shut up. That's rank!" Screeched Josie, but a frantic bat at her side warned her that Mr Farrell was coming.

Blithe could have pointed out that, whatever else they were, Connor and Cody were together, but that would have spoilt the fun.

"She'd be her slave, for her she'd agree to wear just a dog collar." Hissed Daisy, and giggles burst out.

"Okay." Mr Farrell muttered. "Be sensible girls, be sensible..."

"Why'd you lock the door sir? No one else does." Demanded Leanne.

"Because years ago, a pupil set fire to some papers, does that answer your question?"

"Was that Blithe's brother, sir?"

"No. I don't believe it was. Settle down."

* * *

Codey didn't pursue violence for the sake of violence, and she was not seeking it at all when she left the school. Easy to miss in the herd of pupils, she traipsed towards the gates with her mouth open, as though muttering to herself about the injustice of the events she left behind. She leaned far forward, as if carrying a heavy weight. Her hair was no longer golden as it had been when she was cute, but lay lank until the wind caught it and lifted sections like sheets of cobwebs.

Behind her, Leanne dashed through the crowds with excited skips. She caught up, clutched at Codey's arm and giggled, but Codey only nodded sulkily. Leanne abruptly straightened up and spoke rapidly. At first Codey ignored her, then she screwed up her face as she struggled to catch the words with the grounds so busy. Leanne became very serious. Even as her mouth formed the words, she was visibly outraged. Codey's pace slowed, her mouth set to a line, and she stopped abruptly in her tracks. Their roles reversed, she grabbed Leanne's arm and held her steady while she demanded more information. She pointed as she spoke and then with a final jab, a gesture like a starting gun, she released Leanne and marched away.

Leanne gave her a head start of five paces and then followed. Codey marched and would not look back or look anyone in the eye until she hurled her fist into the face of the girl who had humiliated her.

The sea of pupils moved around and parted for her, not because of who she was, but purely by the way she moved.

She feared she was being laughed at, but she did not look to check. She knew a lot of them were too cowardly to laugh in her face, but she would have preferred for everyone to drop their masks, even if the result was that they all laughed at her. It would be better than deception.

She decided she would floor the brittle boy; it didn't matter if he broke his leg a second time; or was it a third? She'd say she bumped into him on her way to Blithe, she could make this a convincing lie and bump into him in just the right way. He fell very easily.

She knew Connor would be getting his bike. He must have stopped for a smoke, or she would have seen him by now. She didn't want him near, she wouldn't like to see him watching her critically, he might try to stop her. Codey passed through the gates and broke into a run.

Blithe had a hippy rucksack, leather patchwork in bright primary colours, the kind of bag Codey's gran had owned. Codey saw Blithe just before she rounded the corner. She nodded to herself, satisfied that teachers would not have a view of the scene and cars on the main road would not be able to stop. Codey slowed to a jog, letting Blithe abandon the safety of the school. She turned the corner and cried out after her.

"Hey! You!"

Blithe didn't turn around; Codey gritted her teeth. Blithe knew never to turn around or to run in situations like this. Codey had her own rules to abide by, which included calling out a warning.

"Blithe! You get yer arse here! Ye don't want me to come to you."

The warning had now been given but even with her name called Blithe didn't turn around. Codey began to run and she saw, perhaps as her footsteps sounded, Blithe's own steps quickening.

"You fuck'n look at me! Don't walk away fae me!"

Blithe knew she didn't have change for the bus but searched her pockets. It took willpower not to look behind her. She hoped Jamie would soon be jogging along at her side but it was clear by the speed and regularity of the footsteps behind her, that they could not have been made by him.

A fist landed a hammer blow on the top of Blithe's head. Blithe threw up her hands as her bag was yanked from her shoulder, spinning her round to face her attacker.

"What the fuck have you been saying about me?"

Codey shoved her with both hands, forcing her backwards.

"Saying that I've been sucking up to Maddie?"

Codey shoved her again with a punch below each shoulder.

When Blithe stumbled, she pushed again, sending Blithe backwards onto the pavement below.

"You talk about me like that again I'll smash yer face right in."

Blithe kept to the ground, her palms grazed and burnt against the pavement. Codey knelt on the ground and reached out for Blithe's black ponytail. She jerked it back, tightened her grip on the leash while she said what she needed to say.

"I'm no a fucking lezzy."

Codey let go of Blithe's hair and gave her a quick slap across the face. It was not done with full force, only to show that she was in command.

Blithe's stoicism vanished as she slapped her back across the face. She dived forward, straightening unsteadily, shaking with anger.

"See how you make pals? Ye'd be better aff sniffing arses down the kennels! Dinnae care but fuck off and die!"

Codey's face became cold and gritted, her emotion burned down to ruthlessness. Across three lanes of heavy traffic, Robbie and Jamie watched.

Jamie had put his hand over his mouth when Codey grabbed Blithe's hair. He now balanced on the kerb, head darting back and forth, tipping forward to cross but not committing to the dash he was poised to make. Robbie knew how Jamie felt, he'd noticed the wide eyes soaking up the scene, unable to blink. He'd gasped before he'd had time to cover his mouth.

"She's stoked it man," Robbie said regrettably. "This is going to be about something else, there's something else going on here. You cannae keep helping her. She's got to help herself. Come on."

Jamie didn't move.

"There's loads of people about. She'll be okay."

A van drew up and blocked the view across the road. Jamie turned to his friend.

Robbie tried again. "Come on. Don't get involved."

That wasn't the instruction Jamie wanted, and his long noise twitched, like a dog's muzzle before it snarls.

Without Robbie he would have crossed the road by now, deflected the aggression in some way and shared what was to come. With him there, he might still have been able to do this, but over lunch he'd declared that he wasn't going to walk Blithe anymore, that he had to study and these walks had gone on long enough. When he said it, he had meant it. Now he realised he hadn't meant it at all.

"We treated her well man, come on."

Jamie could only sneer to, and at, himself.

Blithe ran towards the bus stop, and Codey marched after her, confident that running was an unnecessary effort. Blithe turned and saw Daisy tearing up the street towards them. Codey was only five paces away from Blithe and advanced towards her with her arms out as though to declare that she had no weapons, professing confusion that she should run from her.

"Codey! Codey!"

Daisy called her name like an ineffectual teacher only to be shrugged away.

"She wasnae even talking to us!" Daisy shouted.

Blithe turned to sit down at the bus shelter. When she cast her eyes across the street, she saw Jamie walking up the hill with Robbie.

It was too late to avoid her. He looked away because looking back felt wrong, but he paused in his tracks, swallowing his act of cowardice. He turned back just as a bus drew up on the other side of the road, blocking his view.

"Don't get involved!" Robbie could no longer hide his exasperation. "Studying's harder when ye'v had yer head kicked in. You are the worst person to deal with this kind of thing, ye'v no clue, you'll fall down like a house of fucking cards!"

Jamie sighed.

"I've done nothing. All that time walking her, and I've done nothing and now I'm watching, and doing fuck all."

"Well... I'm sure you gave good cuddles."

Robbie spoke wearily but he hit the target.

"What d'ye mean?" Jamie demanded.

"Well, what else are ye doing? What else can you do?"

"Oh get tae fuck! Robbie, even when you're not being a miserable bastard, ye can still be a cunt."

"I didn't make you do anything!" Robbie cried. "I didn't stop you crossing that road and ending up with a broken nose. I said what I thought, so kill me. Can you not think for yourself?"

The bus pulled away and revealed Codey turning back towards home and Daisy, shaking her head, walking in the opposite direction. Blithe was gone.

Seething, Jamie made his way up the hill. Robbie jogged after him.

Blithe had stuck her hand out for the bus though she had no money. If she cared enough about where the bus was going, she would have seen that it was out of service. Just as the bus slowed Codey had caught her up and in a rapid, cat-like movement, drew her nails across Blithe's cheek. Blithe covered her injured face too late, it felt like a burn and would hurt later. She slowly removed her hand as the bus drew up and the door opened. She'd stumbled up the steps and didn't notice that the cab door was swinging on its hinge.

Codey had placed a foot on the first step, nodded to the driver and demanded, "Where yis going?"

"Bus depot pal."

"Can I still get a half intae town?"

Horns sounded behind them. The bus was using space another needed and blocking it from moving over but the driver ignored it and seemed to think.

"Right, ye want tae..." He took out a laminated sheet from a compartment by the door.

"Aye, ye'll be wanted tae..." Only now did he look at her.

"Get tae fuck. Get the fuck off my bus." He shooed her with the laminated sheet. "Aye on ye go."

Codey slowly stepped away and Blithe looked at the driver, fearful that this also applied to her. She couldn't see that the welts on her face had risen red and angry, nor did she know that the driver had seen the swipe that made them.

"Not you pal. You stay here the now."

Codey had given the doors a kick and then kicked out again at the side of the bus as it pulled away. The cab door swung backwards and forwards.

"Aye the doors fucked. Cannae send it out when it's like that. Are ye okay pal?"

Blithe didn't want to cry, but if she were going to, she would rather it have been when she walked home alone. She hung her head. She felt the nail marks sting as the tears ran over them. Her nose and throat were full, and she gasped for air.

The driver glanced in the mirror.

"The lassies are just as bad ehh? Every bit as bad. No, I've been there, we've aye been there. I'm taking us back tae the depot in town, so you just tell me when ye want aff."

Blithe nodded.

"Aye but... I've no change," she said at last.

"The till's nae working so I couldnae take it off ye if ye had it. Don't you worry pal. Even if we get ye tae the depot we can still get ye hame. I shouldnae huv passengers though, I'm probably no insured or some shite. Ye okay now?"

Blithe wiped her eyes and stared out. She didn't want to leave the bus, even as it carried her further away from home. She was ashamed of herself. For years, she had coped well on her own. It occurred to her that men seem to needlessly intervene, forcing their assistance upon women, who must then accept it gratefully or else be viewed as arrogant and ungrateful. Blithe had become used to Jamie's help, forgetting that she hadn't needed it in the first place. This is what men do, she thought, they drain confidence and then fuck off. This was what Blithe's dad had done to her mum; he'd made her pregnant, he'd made her dependant, and then fucked off.

At least Jamie had only left her crying on a bus. Unlike her mother, she could easily dust herself down and resume. Crying in a cold, comfortless little space, she hated that she wanted him.

She recalled the look on his face when he saw her across the road. He was a bystander in mourning, she'd give him that. That wasn't to say he felt it deeply, just that he had a sense of occasion. He hadn't needed to know that she was okay. He cared, but not enough.

"Did she just get ye on the face, hen?"

Blithe tried to smile through her tears and nodded her head. She tried to distract herself by looking out of the window. The bus slowed to the lights and, at that moment, she saw her brother.

"Ma, braer. That's ma braer!"

"You want'n off here?"

She nodded and wiped her eyes. She wanted to thank the driver, but she was too full of snot. She looked back with red eyes, smiled, and nodded. The driver smiled back.

"Nae bother. You take care of yerself eh?"

When Donnie saw his sister running towards him, his first thought was that something had happened to their mum. Blithe tore towards him, her face crumpled and as she neared, he saw the three red lines on her face. She stopped abruptly, to stop herself crashing into his arms, remembering that she didn't want his comfort, it wasn't right.

"What happened to ye?"

He peered into her swollen face. He hadn't seen her like this in years and years. The words were formulated but she was unable to voice them, so he pulled her into an embrace.

"D'ye want to go hame?"

She nodded.

"Then I'll get us hame."

With an arm around her shoulder, he led her to a bus stop. There was no one else waiting in the shelter. She sat down, and he stood by her, a hand on her trembling shoulder. When the bus arrived, they boarded together and ran upstairs to hide at the back.

Blithe took a few deep breaths.

"Oh, it's stupid," she said. "This bitch attacked me as I was leaving. I don't know why I'm being such a fanny about it."

She sniffed and tried to smile.

"What about yer man there, that tall lad? Was he no about the day?"

Blithe stiffened and looked down at her lap, she nodded to herself and then she struggled to keep the tears at bay. Blithe rarely cried but once she started, she found it difficult to stop. She tried to control herself and said, with some effort.

"No. He'd already got what he wanted."

Donnie said nothing. He saw her to the flats and for the second time that day, Donnie began the long walk into town, a walk he'd been about to complete when his sister ran into him.

* * *

Though Donnie couldn't smash the face of a girl, he believed he needed to do something. Whatever he decided, he would not consult Blithe. He had no obligation, and she had no need to know. He knew he was dealing with a girl when he saw the scratches and accepted that there was little he could do about her, whoever she was.

If he had one role in life, it was to look after his sister. He had a right to intervene should anyone take advantage of her. She might have been capable of fighting back but that was no longer enough.

* * *

After working until 2am, Donnie staggered to the flat above the chippie, fell on the sofa again and fell asleep almost instantly.

He awoke at eight, feeling half dead. He had the last couple of Valium from the score Aldo had given him two days before, drank some water and lay down for another few hours until he was ready to present himself to the world on the walk home.

When he eventually made his way home, he felt warmed rather than intoxicated. Halfway there, he decided he would risk skipping the train fare and so he did, choosing his carriage and position carefully, avoiding the ticket collector and hopping off close to home.

Once home, he stayed in the shower for a long time, phasing out until he suddenly came to, sliding down to a kneeling position as the shower pressure weakened and he realised he was cold and shivering. Even then, it was an effort to step out of the bath. He put on a fresh set of clothes and dumped everything else inside the washing machine.

He consumed crisps and biscuits and then moved on to toast and margarine. He did not feel well after this binge; it gave him heartburn and a sensation that his stomach was being stretched beyond its limits. He remembered what Jack had said about Aldo ripping him off and decided to visit an old school friend, hoping he could sort him out instead. He only had five pounds.

At 2.30 he got ready to leave; his hands shaking as he zipped up his coat. He felt a little weak at the knees but he was ready as ever he was.

It took him half an hour to reach his friend's flat. It was on the ground floor of a long, three-story block. A dank, cave-like opening in this line of concrete led to the doors and a communal garden. He knocked and listened out. He heard what sounded like an action film. He knocked again and heard a few footsteps; the entertainment was silenced but no one came to the door. He called out.

"It's just Donnie, Donnie Shearer. Wondering if you could do us a wee favour?"

The door stayed shut. Pursuing such a small amount of money would have been pathetic. An elderly man shuffled past, newspaper under one arm, and a bag of groceries in the other. He gave Donnie a look, indicating with a tut that he knew what the 'wee favour' was. Donnie responded with a louder tut and walked back down the path.

He felt uneasy to be heading back to his old school, to see the kids grown while he'd stayed the same. Yesterday's toe-rags would now be intimidating.

He didn't go into the school grounds. He knew the side road from where they'd spill out but rather than wait on the corner of that road, he crossed over and walked towards the bus stop.

He lit a roll-up and paced backwards and forwards as the swarm spilled out and the pavement filled. Donnie messaged Blithe.

Donnie: Near school. You coming out now?

He waited for a reply, still pacing nervously as his roll-up reduced to a soggy stump. He would not pester her. He didn't want her to know that he had nothing better to do.

Blithe's phone had been switched off. The marks on her face had been noticed and she was sitting again in the nurse's room refusing to name her attacker.

Meanwhile, keeping his eyes on the pupils making their way home, Donnie seized upon a familiar figure. There were few pupils taller than Jamie. Donnie watched him closely as he rounded the corner. He recognised the strange gait but beyond a means of identification, thought no more of it. Jamie turned left and made his way up the hill; the road inclined upwards and he took this at an agonisingly slow and steady pace. Donnie flicked the end of the fag away and watched Jamie from the other side of the road. He smiled to himself when, far up ahead, he saw Jamie cross over to the same side before he vanished from sight.

Donnie was by now conscious of fitting the description of pervert hanging around outside a school. Though cleaner than he had been in a long time, his stubble felt itchy around his neck and on his upper lip. He did not formulate a plan but decided to follow, unconcerned as to whether his pursuit should have a purpose. He quickly caught up with Jamie, still moving at that steady pace. He maintained a distance of twenty feet. Jamie did not look over his shoulder, did not think he had anything to fear and so Donnie moved a little closer, almost halving the distance between them.

He estimated that Jamie was as tall as he was, thereabouts. His black Vans seemed to be fairly new, his uniform was tidy and fitted him well, though his trousers seemed a bit wide for his skinny legs. His schoolbag was sturdy canvas, practical and clean. There was nothing dingy about this boy. Boys like this get away with everything; these kinds of boys don't get caught.

Blithe, in contrast, had not escaped unscathed. Donnie was still shocked at the state of her and clenched his jaw as he recalled it. Hers did not seem to be a momentary low; he recalled it as an erosion, a weakening and that frightened him. He hadn't succeeded in reclaiming self-worth, why should she?

Jamie turned off the main road and headed down to the lower-level station. He made his way down as the train pulled in, increasing his speed as he clattered down the steps. If Donnie could have seen his face, he would have seen that he found hurrying down the steps uncomfortable. Jamie arrived on the platform as the doors opened, sat down, pulled his phone from his pocket, and began scrolling through it. He didn't see Donnie clatter down the steps, run across the platform and jump into the carriage.

Rather than taking a seat, Donnie stayed by the doors and stared through the glass partition into the carriage where he could eye Jamie, sat in the middle, still staring at his phone. Donnie watched him smile and then scroll further down. After a few minutes, Jamie rose, still looking at his phone. He headed to the doors on the other side of the carriage as the train slowly ground to a halt.

Jamie pocketed his phone as he stepped off the train; he didn't glance up until he had to manoeuvre among the small crowd converging towards the steps. At that moment he saw Donnie.

Innocent people, Donnie thought, are not so easily startled. He should have been able to look him in the eye. "Aye," Donnie thought. "Ye werenae that feart the other day, but ye are now."

He smiled as Jamie tried to hurry. It was still easy to outpace him, and they left the station awning side by side. Jamie couldn't ignore him now. Donnie turned to Jamie and grinned.

"Hiya. You no walking Blithe the day?"

Jamie nodded to Donnie nervously. "Uh, no."

"See. I though ye were looking after her. Was I wrang about that?"

Jamie didn't know where to look, how to shrug, how to move.

"Was I wrong?" Donnie repeated.

"She looks after herself pretty well."

"Is that right?"

"Well, she's a lot tougher than me."

"Nae doubt."

They approached the entrance to an alley. If Jamie took it, he would be home in ten minutes. If he didn't, he'd follow the main road until the intersection and then almost double back on himself. Condemned to a long and awkward walk with Donnie Shearer, he turned down to the alley, hoping to see Donnie make his way alone and disappear down the main road.

He took the turn. Donnie stayed at his side. As Jamie's heart sank, it continued to beat fast and steady, to the march of the inevitable.

"Nae doubt." Donnie said again, "She's tougher than you, ye snobby cunt. Naething to say? Just gonnae fucking ignore me now?"

Jamie kept his eyes straight ahead. He could stop, where they could still be seen, before vanishing into the shadows of the alley.

"Is she alright?" Jamie asked.

"What the fuck? Why would she not be? D'ye ken something?"

"Look," Jamie sighed. "I'm just on my way home."

"Aye, she was on her way home an' a' yesterday. Ye ken when tae fuck off ehhh? You choose yer time very fucking well."

Jamie walked on, trying to ignore him. He could see the street at the other end of the alley.

"You gonnae fucking answer me?"

Donnie grabbed a fistful of Jamie's collar and pulled him closer.

"I've not done anything wrong." Jamie tried to pull away, but Donnie kept a tight hold.

"Ye sure about that? See, my idea of wrong and your idea of wrong might no be the same. See, I saw her yesterday, I saw the scratches all down her face. Did ye no see that? Were ye too busy keeping well out of the way, aye, we were, ye slippy bastard."

"I didn't do that to her!"

Donnie looked over his shoulder and grinned to no one. He turned back, pulling Jamie towards him, bringing their faces close together.

"Are you fucking stupid?"

Jamie didn't understand and exclaimed, "I didn't do that! Did she tell you that I hurt her?"

"No. That was a stupid wee lassie... Oh, but I ken what you did by the way and if you ever try that shit with her again, I will punch yer teeth intae yer face."

Jamie pulled away but Donnie barred his way.

"Yer no better than her."

Jamie frowned. "Never said I was..."

"Aye, ye didnae say it. Ye fucking think it but. Ye act like ye are."

"I've a lot of time for yer sister."

This was the truth but it was not what Donnie heard, he heard something like a brag.

"That fucking right?"

Jamie didn't understand how he provoked this reaction. He

was unprepared when Donnie stepped up and smashed his forehead into his. Jamie had never been malkied before and, as he fell back against the concrete wall, he allowed himself to fall to the ground completely.

"That fucking right?" Donnie roared.

As Jamie touched his swelling forehead, Donnie dealt him a kick in his ribs. Jamie tried to curl up but failed to protect the fingers of his left hand, exposed on the ground for Donnie to stamp on.

Donnie wanted to hear something from him; the silence unnerved him. He thought of his sister.

She had been so self-contained; she had never sought attention for the sake of it. Not so long ago she had performed perfect backflips and, when landing perfectly, hadn't looked around to see who had seen; she did not look for praise. Never. He could see her, like Degas's ballerina. In his haze he forgot that it was three years since she'd back flipped on the grass, her needs were not the same but still he kicked out at Jamie, aiming for his stomach and the hands that tried to protect it, for robbing her of that poise and certainty, angry that it might never come back.

He heard the noise as he'd intended. Like a cough as his stomach lurched, and then a gasp.

Donnie was certain that Jamie had used Blithe because he considered her in some way deficient. She was, like her brother, deficient but not sympathetic, for how would they garner sympathy? They still lived in the only home they'd ever known – they'd never had to flee it, they'd never experienced racism, had no special education needs and a mum who was ill, but not in a way that counted; her ill-health was a just a drag. Innocence and vulnerability fade quickly, extinguishing assistance and opportunity. All he had now were dismissive cursory glances that seemed to say that he was all he was ever going to be. It seemed insane to Donnie, that he was such a familiar sight, and yet so utterly alone.

At that moment it seemed to be people like Jamie, clean skinned, wide-eyed boys who do well, the people who would laugh at his exam results and laugher harder if he moaned about what came after. "What do you expect ye dozy bastard?"

And he had to be in some way responsible but Blithe wasn't. What happened to him should not happen to her. It was all over for him; he was an adult and knew not to blame others.

He kicked again and saw a flinch, a fresh terror, a whimper. Jamie had managed some stoicism when he first curled up but now he wondered when it would end. He no longer really felt the blows – they did not scare him. What scared him was not knowing what would come next, not knowing when it would end.

Donnie was familiar with this stage and could not resist playing with it.

He began to walk away down the alley. No one was coming, and he turned around. Jamie was just about to stand up. He froze when Donnie turned back, his hands on the ground, poised to stand, almost on his hands and knees. Donnie stayed still and observed that he could terrify just by looking. He felt he had a right to enjoy it. He was dealing out justice.

Jamie's terror turned to despair as Donnie would not walk on, would not signify that it was over. Still on his knees, Jamie leant back and gave only a slow, sorrowful, shake of the head; he couldn't reason with this animal. This gesture was provocation and Donnie ran towards him. Jamie had time only to slink further backwards, arms out protectively.

Donnie was not an animal. He saw the fear as he ran towards him; the image imprinted itself on this memory. It was the last thing he saw before he closed his eyes and took the leap necessary to land a kick to the face. This image, when it came back to him, was clear enough to remind him that this boy was the same age as his sister, a boy horrified at the creature charging towards him. No matter how afraid, he would not cry out, he would not use words as, in his frightened eyes, Donnie was less than human.

Another moment and Donnie saw Jamie lying on his side, his creased face briefly exposed before he covered it entirely with his hands.

Donnie walked back towards the train station. He did not look back.

* * *

Jamie heard his moans perfectly through his ringing ears. Not wanting to lie in a pissy alley, he sat up against the concrete panels of the fence. It felt as though a dentist had done a hash job of numbing his lip. He felt rashes of pins and needles spread around his jaw. The real pain sparked when he tried to move his mouth. He glanced down and saw blood dripping onto his white shirt. He watched the drops falling; he didn't try to stop or staunch them, but was simply mesmerized that they came from him. The blistered fingers of his left hand did not seem to register the ground beneath him as well as those of the right.

He leaned forward, felt the pain in his ribs and then fell back again, just for a moment, to keep the pain still while he thought about what to do. He closed his eyes and took gulps of air until it proved uncomfortable. Then, from a couple of yards away, he heard someone snort and the click of a peddle.

He was afraid once again; desperately afraid that it still wasn't over. He covered his face as the bike rounded the corner of the alley. The brakes screeched and then a familiar voice seemed to marvel at the sight before him.

"Fuuuck…"

He parted his fingers and saw Connor standing over him. He watched as he calmly dismounted and leant his bike up against the wall.

"Are ye okay?"

Jamie smiled and felt another strange sensation as his lip stretched. With the hand that had not been stamped on he made the sign for 'okay'.

Connor leaned forward for a proper look.

"Aye, I just passed Donnie Shearer. He has got tae be losing it eh?"

Jamie wasn't sure whether to agree or ignore.

"Can ye stand up like?"

Jamie began to stand, aching now in the small of his back. Connor pulled him up by the hand and slowly walked him down the alley. He stumbled onto the street where rows of semis faced the road, separated by low pebble-dash walls.

Jamie sat down and tried to see where the blood was coming from. At each tap of his face, he examined his fingers.

"I'm gonnae get ye a taxi," Connor announced.

Connor started to head towards the end of the road. Jamie stood up to protest.

"I'm no gonnae fuck off, I've ma bike back there. Sit down."

Jamie no longer doubted him and watched him walk down the road to the corner. There, he stayed by the main road, craning his head, using gestures to hail which often turned to frustration.

Jamie's levels of adrenaline were fading. He stood up slowly and began to walk down towards the corner. As he walked, he tasted blood pooling in his mouth. A drop fell and landed on a shirt button with precision. He paused halfway down the road, though his legs had entirely escaped the assault.

Connor was still failing to hail a taxi. He turned and saw Jamie staggering towards him.

"I telt you to stay there! Sit down man!"

Jamie was almost on the corner now, but here the hedges grew over the top of walls, leaving little space to park his arse. Connor marched over,

"Gie me yer blazer."

He held out his hand ready to receive it. Jamie eased it off and handed it over, as Connor dropped his own grey hoodie on the wall next to him. He put on the blazer with a business-like shrug of the shoulders, straightening out the sleeves before he returned to try and hail a taxi.

"Ye know… isss no far." Jamie lisped; he began to shiver though it was not especially cold.

"How not?" Connor demanded. "How would you not take a taxi, when yev someone to pay at the other end? It's nae bother, two minutes out of their way, if that. No man. Taxi."

Jamie accepted this, though as his dad had a final interview, he was not certain that he would have someone to pay at the other end.

Connor turned back from the road and watched Jamie dabbing the blood.

"See, that's going too far. I wid never go that far. Fucks sake."

Jamie looked up, not sure he was being spoken to. He found the experience of being looked after by Connor slightly surreal.

"Honest I widnae. Codey widnae either. What happened the other day, that's the furthest she'd ever go. I heard about it after, fae her first and then I heard what folk were saying."

He leaned into the road, trying to distinguish cars from taxis.

"Ye cannae huv folk walking all ower ye. Ye have to stand up for yerself. That's what she's about man, that's what I'm about an' aw. Stand up fur yerself…" Connor glanced again at Jamie and added, "He should be sectioned man!"

Jamie's expression barely changed, but Connor took enough from it to bounce the rhythm of conversation.

"I cannae blame Codey fur being fucked off but… She called her a brown-noser, or said she wanted to eat Maddie out or something, I dinnae ken. Ye canna say stuff like that tae Codey or about Codey. Naething wrong with being fucked off. When she's yer friend then she's a fucking good friend. She's good to me like."

He sniggered to himself.

"See after I sprayed that, ye ken, that thing about Blithe on the wall, I tell you I had a spectacular fuck. Spectacular."

"Tha' wss you?"

"I'm no fair but I'm balanced, balanced to perfection on the saddle of the bike, Codey's holding it but it's still shoogly as fuck. Then, she's on the handlebars and I pedal us away, still shoogly as fuck but, later behind the bakery..." He grinned.

Jamie stared at Connor, apparently stupefied, but this was partly down to his swelling lip.

"Look." Connor said. "If you're that bothered about location, location, location, you're no doing it right. I was going at it till she got splinters in her arse cheeks."

"I can walk." Jamie stood up.

"Wait now, a taxi's coming. Better no huv its light on."

Connor waved frantically and the taxi indicated to pull in. Connor looked back with a grin and bounced up to the passenger door.

"Will ye take ma pal back there? Just around the corner. See him? Will that be alright? Aw cheers."

He nodded back at Jamie, removed the blazer and handed it back. Jamie picked it up with his right hand, it being the cleaner of the two, and stumbled into the back of the taxi. Connor leaned in.

"Right now. See if ma bikes been lifted, I'll fucking kill you."

Again, Jamie only stared back. Connor grinned.

"No! I'll no kill ye, ye fanny. Alright?"

He slammed the door shut and chapped on the window as the engine started.

Jamie sat up straight to see his reflection in the rear-view mirror. He went quickly from shock to fascination. His hair covered his forehead and much of his eyes but there was something wrong with his mouth, under all that blood it seemed lopsided. The driver eyed him carefully.

"Ye alright?"

Jamie nodded but now in the comfort of the taxi, away from Connor, he was shaken up. He wanted to be at home. He'd seen the blood on his face, already dry and dark, the skin beneath white and waxy.

"Let's get you home, son."

It was a journey far too short to be worth it in normal circumstances, in barely a minute the driver turned into his street. Taxis normally stopped in the middle of the road as parking outside was never easy. The driver on this occasion parallel parked before asking where Jamie lived. He feebly indicated the house with the red door.

The driver turned slowly in his seat and addressed him as a child. "Will someone be in?"

"Maybe."

The driver nodded. "You stay there just a wee minute."

He seemed to toddle across the road, adopting a more military gait as he made his way up the path. Jamie stayed in the car, prepared to be compliant, as he didn't want to have to think or make a decision. He was willing to hand all planning over to the taxi driver simply because he looked and sounded a little bit like his granddad.

He had not expected to see his mum for a few hours, but she answered the door. She glanced over towards the cab and then, as the driver gestured calm, she dashed inside in a panic. The driver slowly walked back towards the cab. He started the engine as Jamie's mum dashed out of the house, coat halfway on, the strap of her bag in her fist.

He turned away from the window as she ran across the road. He was relieved and emotional at the sight of her but wanted to feel this in the smallest of doses. When she slid in the back beside him, he smelt the familiar perfume and her old leather coat, but he remained staring blankly ahead.

"Aye. He needs to get seen," she said breathlessly.

Watching his home disappear before he'd been inside, Jamie felt wretched.

"Where are we going?"

"A & E."

He scrunched up his eyes. "We'll be waiting hours! No! Can I not wash my face?"

The swelling muffled his voice.

"No, you need to be checked out."

She tried to put her arm around him, but he stiffened stubbornly.

"Aye", the driver added. "Yer mum's right son. Best tae get checked out."

"What happened?" she asked, the effort of staying calm fraying her voice. "Where did they get you?"

He glanced to his left where his mum waited, one arm on his shoulder, the other stretched from her lap to his knee. He stared tearfully ahead again and tapped his forehead with a priestly gesture, touched his chin with his forefinger, his stomach with both hands and then held up his sore hand before letting it flop into his lap.

His mum ran her finger along his jaw and then lightly tapped his swollen lip.

"Thanks for doing this," she said to the driver. "I got a lift back today. I was planning to work late but changed my mind when I got offered a lift, I was going to work from home. Literally I'd just arrived when you knocked. Do you have to do these runs a lot?"

"Aye, not normally at this time of day though. Hopefully, you'll not have so long to wait."

Hours were spent in waiting rooms. Every so often, Jamie remembered that his mum sat at his side, waiting for a change and a chance to mother. Eating, drinking, and talking hurt, so there was nothing for her to give.

"Do you know who it was?"

He shook his head.

"Do you know why? Did they take anything from you?"

Another shake of the head.

"Do you really not know? Don't you have some idea?"

This time, only a sigh. All his little aches massed together over the hours had left him pining for comfort. But he wouldn't sit up close to her, wouldn't touch her hand; his job was to endure it.

He was seen by the nurses within the first hour, seen by a doctor another hour later. The greatest damage occurred to two of his bottom teeth and he was sickened to feel them wobble. He was reassured that they wouldn't fall out, though follow-ups would be needed. While they'd waited for the x-ray, his mum mentioned, in a low voice, that his dad's final interview had been successful.

When Stephen met them at the hospital, Jamie had gotten used to being sore and his father stared at him openly, almost rudely, before exchanging glances with Suzannah and giving a regrettable shake of his head. Jamie did not offer his dad congratulations. A false congratulations would hang in the air, any enthusiastic follow up would be too obviously false.

They walked through the hospital car park in silence. It was the quiet, empty stage of evening and Jamie felt hollowed out. He folded himself into the back seat of the car, wanting to recline and close his eyes.

"Does it hurt?"

He glanced up. His dad addressed him from the driver mirror, a reflection waiting for a reply.

Jamie shook his head.

"Aches though," Suzannah added.

"Aye. That must have been scary."

Jamie nodded again. Suzannah smiled at Stephen sympathetically.

"Wait till we get back, eh? We're both desperate to get home."

Stephen nodded and started the engine. Suzannah turned in the front seat and smiled at Jamie reassuringly. He only looked back at her, and she re-adjusted herself as the car turned from the car park.

He wondered what Blithe would say if she saw him now. He imagined her passing him in the corridor at school. She'd avoided looking at him at school, but now she would have to. She would be triumphant. He couldn't really blame her if she did. Had she wanted this to be done to him? Specifically requested that he be 'Seen to?'

He glanced down at his hands. One hand with long white fingers, the other with grazed knuckles and a forefinger discoloured, the nail turning purple. This finger still had a peculiar numbing charge, as though it had sustained an electric burn.

He looked out at the darkening streets and the rain now falling, glittering like sequins on the road, so reflective he could barely see where the reflection of the traffic lights joined the real. It all seemed to blur into one as sorrow curdled with guilt. His stomach lurched and his eyes stung. He needed to stop the thoughts that would lecture him, only he didn't have the will. He stared out, hand over his aching mouth. The circling thoughts were right; he deserved every bruise that was to bloom.

Suzannah turned her head and saw Jamie huddled. She stretched out her arm to rub his shoulder. He stared fixedly out of the window.

When the smell of home finally greeted him, warm and protective, he didn't follow his parents into the kitchen. He needed to wash away the hospital smell and fall into bed.

He slowly mounted the stairs. Downstairs, the kettle boiled as routine. Krissie waited at the top of the stairs.

"What happened?" she asked.

It was not his injuries that alarmed her, she looked for those first and was unimpressed, she imagined a lot worse. When she looked at him properly, it was his face that shocked her.

"You look like crap!"

"Oh, fuck *off* Krissie!"

She knew he didn't mean it; they might even apologise to each other later. His voice gave it away, a voice strained to its limits as he stumbled into the bathroom and slammed the door. She let him go, hoping to have him on her own later, away from their parents when he might tell the truth.

Jamie locked the bathroom door and turned on the shower over the bath. There, his hurry ended. He leant heavily against the door with his eyes clenched shut, pinching the bridge of his nose. For a little while he was able to hold himself together in a knot of sharp elbows. He took a little while to undress, freeing his arms slowly. The bathroom was full of steam when he finally stepped under the shower. The warm jets striking his sore lip and grazed face, stung with a constricting pain. He glanced down at the water flowing round his ankles, the colour of rosé wine. He did not care to examine where on his body the blood came from. The water soon ran clear, while the hiss of the shower smothered the sounds he wished he wasn't making.

CHAPTER 9

Blithe sat on her bed and made a third attempt to blow up a red balloon. The balloon's rich red colour dissolved as it finally gave way to the force of her lungs. She tied the end and batted it to the foot of her bed. It looked so happy but out-of-place; it needed to be gone. The kazoo would go too, attached to the balloon it would parachute to another place, to be swept up by the wind and then away by a city sweeper. She wanted to watch it sail away ceremoniously. However, the window did not open fully and so the balloon popped as she attempted to squeeze it out. The kazoo fell down the side of her bed.

The party bag had been in the kitchen bin for a few minutes before a change of heart saw it saved and placed in the thingummy drawer, with the elastic bands and broken pencils.

The scratches on her face were beginning to fade. She told her mother that she'd run into an overhanging branch.

She reluctantly put on the shoes that Jamie had lent her. It was the last day before study leave; in five hours she wouldn't need them. She walked as fast as she could on her way to school and as she crossed over the main road, she heard a bike bump up the kerb behind her. A second later she felt the wheel strike against her heel.

"Does yer psycho brother have a hit list?"

Blithe stopped to let the bike overtake her. It didn't.

"Ye deaf?" Connor demanded.

"Ask him. I dinnae ken."

Blithe resumed her fast pace and Connor wheeled along

behind her.

"He went for Jamie Gilchrist, split his head wide open."

Blithe nodded.

"Did ye ken that? So he telt ye?"

Blithe was tired of this and shot him a warning glance.

"See?" Connor continued. "He'll no be at school the day, pure guaranteed."

"Right…" She muttered, unconvinced.

"Don't call me a liar, bitch."

She could not have called him a liar. She looked for Jamie and couldn't find him. It wasn't so much his absence that verified what Connor said, it was that she was left alone, able to eat her lunch in the light of day, attention drifted over her.

Connor cycled past her on the way home, lifting both hands off the handlebars to better mime spurting blood.

"Split right open, man! Wide open!"

She stood still, watching as he cycled off after the crowd who would normally have made her their business. Connor never quite kept pace. He cycled ahead, veered back, sped away, came back. He seemed to be able to take off whenever he wanted to, when the mood took him; he would wheel away, as carefree as a bird.

Blithe stepped into the lift, breathing in the fusty metallic air as the doors closed. She closed her eyes as she sailed up but started crossly when the lift stopped before her floor. She levelled her rolling eyes as her mum walked into the lift.

Lynne grinned and gave her daughter a friendly nudge.

"Oh yev caught me! Yev caught me!"

Blithe followed the trajectory of the nudging arm with narrowed eyes and asked icily.

"Are you having an affair?"

Lynne chuckled. "Am I no single? No, I was power walking. Did better than you though eh? Made it up to the fourth floor."

Ordinarily, Blithe would have been supportive but she was

weary and worried.

"Aye, but I've already walked miles."

Lynne nodded. "Aye, but there's more of me to drag."

The lift doors opened. Blithe let her mum go ahead and watched her rake around in her handbag for the keys she'd had in her hand minutes before.

As soon as the door opened, the sound of gunfire echoed down the hall from Donnie's bedroom. Lynne hung up her coat and bag and walked to the kitchen. Blithe marched to his bedroom but stopped outside, head bowed as though her eyes could burn through the door.

She considered whether to knock or just to burst in. She hammered on the door with her fist. Firing ceased. Heavy footsteps approached.

She burst in suddenly, hoping to smack him in the face with the door, but only his hand felt the impact as he reached for the handle.

"Fucks sake!"

She pounced after him as he bounced back.

"Did you beat up Jamie Gilchrist?"

"Who?"

"The boy that was here! Ye gave him a fag! Did ye smash his face in?"

Donnie's face stiffened. "Is that what he telt ye?"

"No! Wasnae at school the day. Everyone's saying someone fucked him up, and some folk have been saying it was you!"

Donnie stared through her. Blithe slapped his arm; he recoiled from her and slunk away to sit on his bed.

"Did you or did you not?" she demanded.

Donnie scowled back. "He's an arsehole. After the other day, he proved himself tae be 100% pure cunt, if yer that much of a cunt, shit needs to happen to you. Do you not remember the state ye were in?"

She knew there was no way, in any circumstances, that Jamie

would be asking for it. She wanted to run forward and slap her brother around the face. Lynne appeared in the doorway.

"What's going on?"

"None of yer business!" snapped Blithe without turning around.

"Ma flat, ma business! What's all this about?"

Donnie and Blithe exchanged glances. He waited for the accusations, and she waited for his excuses. Under Blithe's fierce glare, Donnie spoke.

"Folk at school have been telling Blithe that I beat up some twat in her year."

"Smashed his face in," Blithe added bitterly.

"On no!" Lynne sighed. "No, come on now Blithe, away wi' me."

Blithe focused firmly on her brother. She did not see her mother's outstretched hand, waiting for her own. Lynne tried again.

"No. It'll be someone that looks like him, out making trouble. Just blethering wee lassies. Don't you listen!"

Blithe took a step towards her brother, keeping her scratching hands firmly down at her sides.

"Someone did. No exactly a hard man. No exactly tough. Mind that boy in my year, who was in the wheelchair at the end of second year? Crutches the beginning of third? Mind him do ye?"

A slight jerk of Donnie's head indicated a nod.

"And then," Blithe continued, "He was back on crutches a couple of years ago. Mind that as well?"

Donnie shook his head emphatically.

"No? Aye well, ye werenae really going to school at that point so no, ye widnae mind him then. He's changed a bit, no that much though. I'm still surprised ye didnae recognise him."

She studied his pale face and slowly began to nod triumphantly.

"That's right. Ye beat up the disabled, ye useless dozy bastard!"

Donnie's eyes hollowed as his face drained. He rocked forward and then back, and gave a laugh so forced it must have hurt, a drawn out wheeze, before he managed to say:

"He was walking okay when I seen him!"

"Aye. Was."

He laughed again, another wheeze, as though clearing his lungs of grit.

"Nae luck! Well, if he was that fucked already, how come you couldnae dae it? Could ye no just prod him if he goes down that easy?"

"He'll call the police! That'll be you sorted! Beating up the disabled, ye fucking eejit!"

Blithe shouted to banish the grinning troll in front of her, to make her brother ashamed once again. She felt her mother grab her hand and let herself be led away.

Lynne was equally disturbed by the spectacle and was relieved when Blithe finally let herself be led from the room. Once they were both in the kitchen, Lynne closed the door calmly and leaned back against it with a sigh.

"No, Blithe. He's just winding ye up!"

Blithe stared into her mum's hopeful eyes. She could tell that Lynne had had a good day and Blithe wanted to allow for the possibility that she might be right, but she could not lie.

"No," Blithe said softly.

"It's a rumour. I keep seeing boys that look like Donnie fae behind. No, calm down, eh?"

Blithe stared back sorrowfully and shook her head.

"He's my son!" Lynne exclaimed "He's no perfect, but he's no like that. No. Is it a friend of yours that got jumped?"

Blithe finally averted her eyes and replied, "I've no got any friends."

"No? How was school?"

Blithe pulled a sour face and shrugged, as much to say, *how do you expect after what I've just told you.*

"Yer back late. Where have ye been if yev no been with pals?"

"Pollockshaws Library. Revising. Ye can ask Katie if ye don't believe me. She was working there today."

Lynne believed her and was glad to know her daughter cared about her education. It was some comfort to close their conversation with. They were not in silence for long. The kitchen door was thrown open violently, shoving Lynne forward in the process. Donnie's state had changed in a small space of time. His leering grin had gone.

"Ye still talking about me?"

Lynne steadied herself against the kitchen side and hung her head.

"We've no been gone two minutes."

"Aye but we have." Blithe added, "Mums been defending you, so leave her alone."

Donnie shook his head, his lips parting as he muttered silently to himself.

"He disnae deserve to have ye go'n schizo. Mind what ye said tae me?"

Blithe looked at him in blank askance as his expression changed. He took a threatening step towards her and said, in a low whisper of suppressed rage.

"You ken what ye said."

"No. I cannae mind. What did I say?"

Donnie glanced regretfully at his mum, but Blithe was so certain that she had no hand in this that he had to put her right.

"Ye said that he got what he wanted fae you. Then he fucked off and I found ye."

Blithe had forgotten that she'd said those words, couldn't understand why she'd used them – unless to shut him up. Words like that have a kind of finality.

"Aye. So? What do you think this is? D'ye think that I've got some kind of honour that you need to protect? You don't sort things out for me, don't you dare sort things out for me. All you dae is fuck things up. I'd say sort yerself out but ye'd fuck that up too."

"Blithe!" Lynne steadied herself with both hands and spoke slowly. "Now...Donnie, ye didn't?"

Donnie cursed himself for not lying consistently.

"Oh. I had words with him. I gave him a scare, that's all."

Lynne nodded.

"A scare?" Blithe laughed, "We'll get to see it, he'll have been caught on CCTV."

"No," Lynne shook her head, "Blithe that's enough."

"Oh, he will." She jerked her head in Donnie's direction, "He's not very bright."

"Enough! It's all blethers. All nonsense! A boy disnae turn up at school and folk throw around accusations, start stirring everything up when the boy is probably just off with the cold."

Blithe was ready to give up.

"Well. I don't know,' she said, "I've not seen him. I heard there was a lot of blood. He's not at school. That's it. If it's bad, you'll have the police beating on the door. Just saying."

Lynne's heart began to thump, she suddenly felt dizzy and had to carefully guide herself through to the living room where she slowly collapsed into her chair. She opened her mouth wide to receive gulps of air. Despite her efforts, she seemed to have a throatful of frayed rope, her demanding lungs effectively sucking her airways shut.

She thought she heard Donnie. "Ye alright ma?"

She heaved her feet up on the coffee table, tilted her head right back and told herself not to panic, panic only made it worse. She stared at the ceiling and the grip around her airway loosened. She turned her head towards the kitchen and saw her children watching her from the doorway. Much as she didn't want them to be concerned, she would have welcomed anyone who might understand the terror she had just experienced. She had repeatedly told them that it was all her in head, and she feared that they didn't believe it *felt* real. It felt like drowning. She could see that Blithe was weighing up the spectacle without any sympathy. Donnie at least looked guilty and came towards her.

"Can I get ye anything?" he asked.

"Would ye... get down, the chippie, grab three suppers. I dinnae, want to cook... the night. Can we all... can we all just calm down ehh?"

Blithe was certain that her mum was putting it on. She stood, arms folded, in the doorway. As far as she was concerned, everything she saw, from Donnie's concern to her mums near collapse, was a performance.

"Just get two," she called. "I'm alright. I'll get myself something later."

"Why?" Lynne asked, "Where are ye going?"

"I'm gonnae return some shoes."

"How long will ye be?"

"Back before eight I think," and with a voice intended to provoke, Blithe demanded, "Is that a problem?"

"No."

Blithe made her way through the lounge to the hallway.

"Blithe, hen?"

"What?"

"Don't you talk to me like that. Understand?"

Blithe nodded.

She made her way through to her bedroom, grabbed the shoes, dusted them down and put them in her school bag along with her physics books. She changed out of her uniform into jeans and a blue shirt. A simple outfit, but one she knew suited her. She marched out of the flat without saying goodbye.

Lynne was grateful to her for going and letting her have Donnie all to herself. She didn't particularly want to eat, where her stomach and chest had tightened her entire trunk ached. She was able to put this discomfort to the back of her mind, enough that she could focus on her son.

He looked awful. He wore a shabby white t-shirt, and she could see lots of little cuts peppering his arm, like insect bites. These marks didn't seem to heal properly, leaving putty pink spots that threatened to permanently scar. Never in all his adolescence had he been so skinny and greasy but that was a minor part of what screamed out at her. His eyes frightened her, yellowy whites with dark lines, worse than bags, as though he had forged them by clutching his eyes shut. He was far too young for them. His lips had drained and become faded and dry, yet she still wanted to stoke his brow and embrace him.

"Ye gonnae tell me? Should I be feart?"

"No. I'm no like that. Na. That's no me."

"Ye said ye scared him. Look, I don't want to keep asking questions. Yer sister's away, so you tell me, and I'll listen."

"I did scare him." Donnie said slowly, "He said something about Blithe, sort a' sneering thing, like, like he'd had her. Ye know?"

Lynne nodded, rolled her eyes, and adjusted herself in her chair.

"How lads can be."

"Aye, ye ken."

"I do. On ye go."

Donnie stared at the floor for a while and said simply.

"So, I thumped him. I didnae mean to hurt him. I just wanted to wipe the smug look af his face, that's all. Just one punch, I didnae see any blood and I went home, just went off on ma way. I don't think anything will come o' it."

Lynne nodded.

"I believe ye son, I believe ye, but it's not up to you to go pushing yer way into yer sister's life. Not fur ye to do. I ken yer pals might no agree but that's not how I raised ye."

Donnie nodded.

"I ken," he said. "I'll no do it again, not after all this. Do you want me to go and grab the suppers?"

Lynne stood up stiffly. Donnie followed her through to the hall where she went through her bag and pulled out a twenty-pound note.

"That's fur three days shopping and tonight's dinner. Right?"

* * *

Blithe had been on his street before. It was only six weeks ago, but it felt like an earlier life. She and Robbie had spent most of Saturday together and on the way home they'd passed Jamie's street. After messaging Jamie, Robbie suggested that they stop and wait for him. Blithe waited with him for a while, having nothing better to do. She had turned to see Jamie walking down his path, and that had been her cue to depart. She'd not expected to like him and with a quick kiss, she'd skipped away.

Coming back to that spot reminded her that it could be soothing to sit and talk to Robbie. He'd thought everything she said was funny. He'd been desperate to look after her, and that was incredibly irritating when it wasn't necessary. He arrogantly assumed that he could solve all her problems.

She hoped Jamie's house would be easy to identify. The pathway he'd walked down had been somewhere in the middle, but in a street of close terraces this still presented four possibilities. She knew she needed to select a door or else loiter until she had to make her way home.

She had already walked far that day and hadn't eaten much. Her feet ached within the old grey shoes and made her sorry to return the comfy ones. As she built up the courage to try a door, she noticed a fat marmalade cat pushing his body up against the wall. He tiptoed along against the pebbledash in order to treat himself to a cat massage. Blithe whistled but the cat only watched her, content with a rocky rub, so she made her way over and knelt down to stroke it. The cat stayed to let her rub it between the ears.

This was Christopher and, as had been promised, he was friendly, his sandpaper tongue gave her a quick lick on the back of her hand. This was an unfamiliar sensation to Blithe and she grinned. She sat cross-legged on the pavement, hoping the cat would sit on her lap. Christopher only walked around her, considered her, pressed himself against her back and purred. On his second rotation, he stopped and nuzzled his head against her hand.

"Hey Christopher. Where do you live, eh? Gonnae show me where ye live? Where are ye getting fed fatso?"

When she stood up, Christopher scurried further up the road and began to walk up a path. Blithe followed, almost to the door, until she heard a yapping and saw through frosted glass what appeared to be an angry Jack Russell.

Blithe looked back at the cat, rubbing himself against the gate. "Bastard!"

She ran back down the path, sending Christopher scurrying.

He sped to a house two doors down with a red door. Blithe cautiously followed and saw the cat waiting expectantly on the front step. She approached.

If he answered the door, she would see his face. She couldn't comment on the damage, no matter how bad; she would thrust the shoes at him, say nothing and go. That was the plan, made up a second before she chapped the door.

Christopher sat up straight, waiting patiently for her knocks to be answered. Her heart seemed to stop, as footsteps marched her way. Girl and cat exchanged conspiratorial glances.

The door was opened by Suzanna Gilchrist.

Christopher slipped past her ankles into the house. Blithe hesitated.

So, this was his mother. Blithe didn't see any of Jamie in her. Her face seemed so severe, harsh jaw and high cheekbones. She looked like a drawing of a teacher, with short black hair and black rimmed glasses.

"Is Krissie in?"

Suzannah gave a harassed sigh. "Ah. Hang on a wee minute. Come in."

Blithe stepped inside. The smell of bolognese awakened a gnawing hunger. It did not escape Suzanna's notice that Blithe inhaled very deeply.

"We're just having dinner; I'll just see if she's finished."

Suzanna made her way to the back of the house where the rest of the family were eating. She intended to leave Blithe waiting in the cluttered hallway, but Blithe unthinkingly followed her, gazing around as she passed the staircase, stepping over shoes, noting family photographs and curiosities. As she inhaled, she reflected that her mum would never forget to get a friend's name before leading them through the house.

Suzanna glanced over her shoulder, surprised that the girl followed her.

Stephen had moved away from the kitchen table as he began the clear up. Jamie was taking his time with what seemed to him to be lasagne slop, more sauce than substance, custom made for someone who had been kicked in the teeth. He guarded his mouth between bites to hide his swollen lip. Krissie was just finishing up, she hadn't heard the exchange at the door and did not expect friends to just turn up. She faced the corridor as her mum walked down it.

Krissie noticed that someone was coming to join them, she frowned and straightened up to see. Jamie had his back to them and continued to eat slowly and carefully. His was so engaged in this that Krissie's desperate efforts to get his attention failed. She seemed about to hiss, when he recognised the warning on her face, just as his mum stepped into the kitchen.

Jamie twisted round. He saw the top of Blithe's head, her long silky black hair worn down and then her flushed face, tired and beautiful. He could not conceive of anything more terrifying. He returned to face his plate, while Krissie waited in vain for any kind of message.

"Oh, good, you've just finished." Suzanna said to Krissie.

"I just stopped by to drop off the shoes ye leant me." Blithe explained, holding out the bag.

Krissie froze for a second.

"Oh! Oh right. I'd forgot about that."

Stephen scraped the last of the lasagne into a bowl and asked.

"Krissie, has your friend eaten?"

When Stephen turned, he was surprised to see a girl older than his daughter. He'd thought the voice familiar, but was confronted by a stranger.

Krissie looked back at Blithe as much to say, that question was for you.

"No but... it's fine."

"Sure? I thought we were eating late."

Stephen looked closely at her and laughed to see her quandary. Blithe saw a resemblance to his son and grinned back awkwardly.

"Aye. It smells great but I should really head back."

"Well...It's only a small portion mind. Jamie's still eating. Taking his time."

He nodded towards his son who made a greater effort to cover his mouth.

Stephen assumed he was shy.

"Ach, she'll have seen worse," he said dismissively and then he turned back to Blithe. "Sure? Can you not message home, save them a job?"

"Okay, ta."

Suzanna indicated Stephen's vacant chair while seating herself opposite. She looked tired, the kind of tired that comes on the heels of frenzy.

Blithe had never spoken to Krissie before. She considered herself lucky to have remembered her name.

Stephen placed the bowl and cutlery down in front of her. She began to eat, and silence descended, she felt her presence to be an intrusion. Jamie wouldn't look at her and she wouldn't look at him. For all she knew, he was contemplating standing up and ordering her out. If he pulled his mum to one side, would it be wise to make a run for it? He *could* do these things he wouldn't; he was too still, too meditative and, she also knew, too kind.

In the uncomfortable silence, Blithe was sure that Suzanna was on to her. Krissie said nothing and tucked the shoes behind the table, out of view of her mum.

Suzannah turned to Jamie and gestured to his jaw.

"How does it feel now?"

Jamie made an ambivalent noise and hunched his shoulders.

Suzannah turned her attention back to the visitor. She felt she had to talk to her, since her daughter wouldn't.

"Have you had to come far?"

"It's no bother. Half hour walk."

Suzannah nodded. "Could you not have dropped those off at school? Save you all the bother of walking all the way here."

Blithe froze, as though ensnared.

"Sue." Stephen cautioned, "She didnae expected the Spanish Inquisition."

Blithe looked at Stephen gratefully, still with his back to everyone, now engaged in making coffee; that too was starting to smell lovely.

"Thanks. This is really nice by the way. I wasnae expecting to get fed."

"Oh, it's nae trouble." Stephen replied, "Would probably get chucked out otherwise."

Suzanna observed Blithe as she resumed the shovelling of lasagne. She'd give herself indigestion.

"What year are you in?"

"Fifth."

"Oh, so you're in Jamie's year?"

Blithe nodded, Jamie didn't react.

"Ah of course, so you're on study leave too? So, it's nose to the grindstone? When's your first exam?"

Blithe swallowed.

"A couple of weeks. English. I'm alright with English, I don't know why I took Physics though. I used to be good at it but... I made a mistake in taking it."

Suzanne's face became kind.

"That's just how it goes. Do you know what you want to do when you leave school?"

Blithe nodded eagerly.

"Join the police."

Suzanne's eyes widened for a second, but she nodded.

"Aye, well. A job for life."

"Well, unless I get killed but... that would still make it for life."

Jamie made a grunt, muffled by his hand.

"Well... that's one way of thinking about it." Suzannah reflected.

Blithe looked at Jamie properly for a few seconds. His hand stayed over his mouth, his hair over his forehead. From what she could see, his nose was a little swollen and red but there was nothing there to alarm her.

Suzanna noticed this.

"Not looking his best but you've seen worse, eh? I'd say he's ready to present himself in public."

Blithe smiled and nodded. Jamie ignored them both. There was another uncomfortable silence.

"Is anyone in your family in the police?" Suzannah asked.

Blithe shook her head.

"No. I'm always being told about people who've been fu... sorted out by the police, you know what I mean? Well, that's what they say."

Suzanne nodded.

"But if it's only people like that that join the police then, then we're all fucked..." Blithe checked herself. "Sorry."

"Well, I've never had any issues with the police force,' said Suzannah. "I think you've probably just heard a lot of horror stories."

"Aye but, you get the odd arsehole."

Having already tolerated a bit of swearing, Suzannah, in teacher mode, cleared her throat.

"Of course, that's the way in all walks of life though."

Blithe nodded.

"I've met a few bad ones, a lot of decent ones too but. I want to be the one that tells them what to do. I want to do the ball busting. Otherwise, there's no point."

Blithe wouldn't talk like this if she weren't very nervous. Nerves can affect a person in much the same way as alcohol, but unlike alcohol, where your self-awareness is diminished, she heard her nonsense with enhanced clarity.

"Discipline isn't easy," Suzannah remarked.

"No. But it must help to not, like, care if someone likes you. I don't care about fitting in, it's never bothered me all that much."

"Well... isn't it natural to want those you respect, to like you?"

Blithe considered this as she swallowed the last mouthful.

"No. I don't think so."

It did not seem necessary to Blithe. She was used to people having no discernible feelings whatsoever towards her.

Suzannah grinned. "Well. I think that attitude may put you at a great advantage. I'm sure you'll do very well."

Krissie had been looking very uncomfortable. She kept an eye on her brother for signs of anger or distress. So little of his face was visible it wasn't easy, even when they could have exchanged glances, he made sure they didn't. Krissie concluded that some threat lay behind it all and she had, in all innocence, played along. She took a deep breath.

"Shall we go up to my room?"

Blithe didn't even look startled.

"Sure," she rose from her chair and nodded towards Suzannah.

"It was nice to meet you."

Suzannah smiled, "Aye, you too, good luck next week."

"Aye, nice meeting you," Stephen called.

As Krissie led Blithe through the house, she wondered if intimidation was at work. It seemed that Blithe had invaded their home with all the ease of a gang leader and accepted their food as though she had a right to receive it.

Since his attack, Jamie had been withdrawn, he'd hardly moaned. He wasn't accepting sympathy and seemed almost angry when it was expressed. Suzannah had suggested to Krissie that it was down to masochism; he'd had enough of being delicate. It was an explanation that Krissie had accepted, until now.

Blithe moved slowly behind Krissie, to better take in her surroundings. The house was cluttered and dusty, the hallway and stairs designed when people were smaller. Black and white photos of old familiar scenes, wedding pictures and more recent portraits. Some reminded Blithe that their families were not so different. The small figures on the west coast beach could have been her and Donnie at Tighnabruaich ten years ago. Donnie had also been photographed, like the wee boy in the picture, helping his baby sister to walk and, like him, milk teeth had gleamed in the proud little grin.

She followed Krissie into her room and closed the door behind her. It was only a small room with a single bed, but it impressed Blithe. The shelves were neatly arranged and clear of tat; there was a huge poster of a female guitarist on the wall. Krissie's room had been designed and arranged, whereas Blithe's had evolved slowly over the course of her life. She was jolted when Krissie suddenly demanded.

"Can you tell your brother to leave him alone?"

Her voice had shaken but, having got that off her chest, Krissie wore a determined expression. Blithe was now incensed.

"I did!"

"Wh... What did he say?"

"Not much. For your information he wasnae all that clued up on who Jamie is, or what it is that he's supposed to have done."

"What has he done?"

"He hasn't told you?" Blithe feigned surprise. "Well, if he's no telt you then it's none of yer business."

Krissie nodded her head. "I was worried. What's wrong with that?"

Blithe narrowed her eyes.

"There's nothing wrong with that. I just don't like being told to call him off, when I never called him out. I don't set my brother on people."

Krissie nodded. "Why are you here then?"

"I wanted to know what happened. I heard that he'd been cut wide open, and then I was told that it was just a wee knock to the head."

"I think it's somewhere in the middle."

Blithe nodded. "It normally is, isn't it? But he's okay?"

Slow footsteps mounted the stairs.

"I think so. They checked him out and that."

"I didn't come to stare or anything." Blithe said quietly, 'I wouldnae do that. Can I go in and see him?"

Krissie was taken aback.

"Aye, sure, not up to me."

Blithe smiled at her, sheepishly but sweetly.

"I'm serious, I was worried. I've walked for hours today, seriously I could show you the blisters. You seem like a nice girl. Honestly, if you ever see my brother hanging around, trying anything on with you or Jamie, you tell me, and I'd report him myself. Okay?"

Krissie nodded, but she didn't trust her words one ounce.

"Cheers, Krissie."

Blithe smiled again, this time with the patronising smile an older girl gives a younger.

Blithe backed out awkwardly and closed the door. She could hear the parents talking downstairs and breathed a sigh of relief. She heard movement from the room opposite but stood frozen at the top of the stairs, staring down at the front door. She pursed her lips, walked to his room, and knocked lightly on the door.

Krissie waited behind her bedroom door, listening out for her steps on the stairs or raised voices from her brother's room. Instead, she heard Blithe's voice, now gentle, ask.

"Alright if I come in?"

She heard her brother murmur something and his door quickly opened and closed.

Jamie did not look up as Blithe entered. He sat on the edge of his bed, phone in hand, scrolling through messages he'd already read.

Blithe lent back against his bedroom door. As with Donnie, the older brother had the bigger bedroom though the double bed left only a small amount of room. A music stand stood partially folded by the window, by the bedside there was a chipped chest of drawers on which a pile of textbooks teetered. A variety of colourful speakers with LED lights were positioned around his room like square baubles.

"Are you okay?" she asked.

He nodded.

"Have you told the police?"

His eyes stared fixedly at the screen on his phone.

"No."

"Will ye?"

Jamie shrugged.

"If yer going to get him done, can ye say it's about drugs. Say ye found him shooting up in a supermarket toilet, and he flipped out."

Jamie put his phone down on the bed beside him and glanced

up at her for a moment, mystified.

"Why?"

"Because. If you don't make it about drugs then, he'll just be punished. With drugs, he might get some sympathy or else the punishment just makes everything worse; you go in for assault and ye get sucked into a sharknado of shit."

A slight smile formed briefly on Jamie's lips.

"I've not said anything," he said. "Connor was there just after, he didnae see anything but he might say something. I've not."

"No? What about yer family? Have ye not told them?"

"No. I said he was about my height, skinny with brown hair."

"Donnie's got black hair."

"Aye."

Blithe leant against the door.

"Was that a mistake?"

"No."

"Are you going to go back to the police?"

"No."

These one-word answers were starting to annoy Blithe, and she reached for the door handle behind her.

"You're telling the truth?" she asked. "Yer no just saying that so I'll fuck off?"

Jamie shook his head.

"See, I don't understand why you would do that. You know him, he's not in a gang, he's not even got real pals. You keep schtum, why?"

With his index finger, Jamie meekly drew a circle in the air, as though to orient the flitting point.

Blithe waited impatiently, Jamie cleared his throat.

Blithe could see that his chin was red, the cut to his lip was now peeling – which seemed to just about account for the many twitches of his mouth. He looked up at her in spite of it, trying to iron out the twitches and keep his lips still.

"Ohhh..."

He was almost there.

"You," he said at last.

She waited for more, but he continued to stare at her and repeated.

"You."

"I've nothing to do with him."

Jamie shook his head.

"Seriously, I'm no involved. I didnae get him to do this."

Jamie rubbed his hand along his jaw.

"How did he know then?"

"About what?"

Again, she willed him to spit it out.

"About what Codey did to you?" he asked.

She waited for him to name his crime, but he couldn't. Instead, he kept his eyes on her, unashamed as they began to glaze.

"He was the first person I saw,' Blithe explained. "He went back home with me, made sure I was alright. He asked where you were. You can guess what I said, I said ye ignored me, ye walked right past. I didnae say a lot, it's not like I blamed you. But you clearly did not give a fuck."

"I... I do. I'm sorry."

Blithe laughed from sheer exasperation before looking back at his tragic face. He bowed his head, and she was at once terrified that he was quietly crying, but with a sniff he raised his head. He looked up at her with such a determined focus, his mouth set serious and contrite. His eyes shone; his face coloured by the struggle. The reality of Robbie in tears had not affected her as much.

"Are you okay?"

He closed his eyes.

"Come here."

Then she stepped forward, her arms came to rest around his shoulders. His forehead rested at the arch between her ribs. He'd been fighting tears but as soon as her arms were about him, he stopped fighting and simply breathed in the sweet, spicy smell of her. Relief came to him in every deep breath, the tears were no longer there to be fought.

Blithe stared down and wanted to run her fingers through his brown hair but no, that would be to go back as though nothing had happened.

Then he looked up at her, his chin still resting against her belly. He looked up at her fondly, gratitude sparkling in his eyes. Without thinking, she stroked his hair away from his forehead and as she did so she saw a bruise.

"What did he do? Just what I can see?"

"He kicked me in the mouth."

"Let's see."

Jamie released her and leaned back on his bed.

"I don't know if you'll be able to see it. Wobbly front bottom."

"Dirty bastard."

Jamie smiled and opened his mouth. Blithe leant forward and ran her finger along the ridge of his bottom set of teeth until he jerked his head away.

"Careful. I don't want them falling out."

This was the worst of it, harm had come to that perfect set of teeth.

"That fucking bastard! You might not want to make his life hard, but I fucking will. He should have knocked his own teeth out – they're rotten anyway, no great loss, you've good teeth. He'll get it for this."

"Oh don't. It's not permanent, I hope. You have to live with him."

"Depends how much I make him suffer. He can skulk off to one of his other dens for all I give a fuck. Don't you worry about me."

Jamie looked at the fading scratches on her cheek and gestured towards it.

"You can barely see it now,' he said.

"It'll be gone by the weekend."

"I'm still sorry."

"Shut up. It'll set you off again."

He shrugged, "So what if it does? I'm still sorry."

Blithe nodded.

"I'm away home now. Don't worry about seeing me down the stairs."

"Before you go, how did you know where I lived?"

Blithe smiled a broad childish smile.

"Christopher."

"Ah, that sly bastard. Would have been easier if you'd messaged me. I think I can give you my number now, if you want it."

"Aye, jot it down."

"Jot it down? If you don't want it, just say."

"No, I'll take it, I just didn't take my phone with me."

Jamie looked sceptical.

"I always take my phone with me."

"Well", said Blithe, lifting her arms from her sides, "I didn't. You can search me."

Jamie made his way over to his bedside chest, where his textbooks and notebooks were piled. He scribbled his number down at the bottom of a page in his jotter. He carefully ripped it out and handed it to her.

"Seriously, don't feel you have to take it."

"I'm taking it because I want to, seriously. I'll message you in the morning and you'll ken that it's me because I'll say, '*I fucking told you so*', right?"

She took it, stepping away from him hastily. She paused as if trying to remember something. Too much of what she wanted to say could not be said. Instead, she nodded curtly and left his room. He heard her scuttle down the stairs and then watched from the window as she marched away with ease. If it were a film, she would look over her shoulder, but it wasn't, and she didn't.

CHAPTER 10

Robbie grudgingly joined his family at the dinner table. The lights were low; the wine had already been poured. A dish of herbs, mutton, and kidney beans steamed. They had a small, underused dining room, but they were trying to make better use of it now.

His parents, Saeed and Helen, were concerned that the recent upset could impact on Robbie's exam performance. They had decided to remove all the pressure they could and come together as a family at dinner time. It did not come easily; they were all busy and tended to grab food during the week. So far, their efforts hadn't really proved worthwhile.

Saeed started cooking as soon as he came home and now, hours later, served it out.

Saeed and Helen would invariably focus on Robbie, but after a while of not getting anything back, they would end up talking to each other about things that did not matter to Robbie. They would realise that Robbie either sat bored at the table or shovelled his food, not sitting back in his chair until his plate was clean, whereupon he showed no renewed interest in what was being said. He only wanted to be excused.

Helen slowly stirred her food, considering appropriate conversation starters.

"How's Jamie?" she asked.

"Don't know. I've not seen him and he's not been replying to my messages."

Helen glanced at her son, having detected a little bit of animation in his voice.

"That is unusual." Saeed remarked, "He talks a lot."

"Absolutely," Helen agreed. "What have ye done?"

Robbie smiled a guilty smile. "Well, I do feel a bit..." He paused before lingering over the next word, "responsible."

"How so?" Saeed asked.

Robbie coloured. "Well. I asked him to walk...her. You know, her."

Saeed nodded but Helen was baffled. "Why?"

Robbie shuffled defensively.

"She was going to get beaten up!"

"Oh, Robbie! Let her get beaten up."

Robbie grinned. "Well that has happened... I don't know what it was about, but it has happened. Nothing too bad."

Helen leaned forward across the table and pulled at his cuff.

"Don't think about it. Close the door on the whole thing and stay out. It can't have been sensible to put Jamie into that situation. He's so suggestible."

"Oh, then you're really not going to like what happened next."

"I don't think I will."

Robbie smiled and sat back in his chair. He was not the victim in the story he was about to tell, he was once again the wise voice and Jamie, the victim. That felt better.

"He walked her much further than I asked him to. He took it too far, that's not my fault."

Saeed chewed his meat with a thoughtful look on his face.

"This is chivalry. Though I don't think being that chivalrous is wise, not here and not during exams. Involving yourself unnecessarily in messy disputes doesn't tend to end well at any time. I'm not saying you did anything wrong. I think... yes, close that door now."

"I have. I only ever meant it as a total one-off and even then, just until she was left alone."

"Try something more modern next time." Saeed added, "Let the lady fight her own dragons, don't send in your knight."

Saeed laughed at his own joke and continued.

"But from what you have said, she perhaps invites this aggression. If so, there is really nothing you can do."

Robbie nodded. "That's what I think. When it all started, when people started to have a go at her, I wanted to do something because…when we were going out, I would have jumped in, I could have been there. I don't feel anything now, I don't really care what happens to her but… I never wanted revenge."

"Good," Helen added emphatically.

"But, as I said, Jamie kept walking her because he's always thinking she's about to get attacked."

Helen frowned. "He has quite an obvious limp. Maybe not the best person to be doing that."

"He still limps, he walked her to stop her getting attacked, what does she go and do? She gets her brother to beat up him."

Robbie sat back, waiting for the reaction.

"Is he okay?" Helen asked.

"I don't know. He won't reply to my messages! I asked him to walk her only once, weeks ago! Just once and he has been walking her, like, over a mile home, with his limp. It's not my fault."

"No, no, it's not." Helen added hastily.

Saeed nodded. "Still, I can understand why he may not wish to speak to you. He might not blame you. I think it is more likely that his pride will be hurt."

"You know what that's like." Helen reminded him. Robbie nodded dismissively.

"Do you know how bad it was?" she asked.

"Bad enough that he missed the last day before exam leave. Mind when Suzannah wouldn't let him take the day off and he was sick all over the toilet bowl. Remember that?"

He checked himself for being inappropriate.

"Sorry, but if she's let him off this close to exams it has to be bad."

Helen agreed. "Well he's delicate, isn't he? Mentally too."

"Mentally?"

"Well, he's quite a sensitive soul. I'll maybe send Suzannah a message, I'll not mention you but, just say that I hope he's okay."

"If he's still off tomorrow, I'll drop by and see him."

Helen nodded. "What I can't understand though is the cycle of violence. Stoking it and then trying to come over all needy."

"No." Robbie said, "She wasn't needy."

"No? You have two nice boys with the best of intentions, getting hurt in one way or another. How can she not feel bad? And will she learn from any of this? I suppose if it was a serious beating, Jamie'll have called the police, but then he'll be to blame for grassing her brother up, and then the whole thing starts all over again."

"And you wonder why I'm depressed," Robbie muttered.

"No," Saeed smiled, "She thinks the worst of young women. Your mother is at the larvae stage of mother-in-law."

"That's sexist," Helen pointed at her husband with her fork.

"Well, I don't know." Saeed conceded. "These girls exist, and I often see girls and boys acting with a very staged kind of aggression."

He turned to Helen. "You seem to have a very clear idea of this particular girl. Tell me, when you look at this picture, do you see her getting on with our son and his friends?"

"People deceive when it suits them. Perhaps there are problems at home..."

Robbie thought for a while.

"She was convincing", he said. "She was convincingly nice."

* * *

When Blithe arrived home, the dingy sky was lit with cobalt blue, burnt at the edges by the setting sun. She made her way up the back stairs, passing in and out of sinister shadows, as some floors were lit and some were not. The fire doors contained sound within the stairwell and the dull thud of her footsteps bounced around her. She was exhausted when she reached her floor but found herself staring numbly at her front door. She didn't go inside; instead Blithe let her bag slip off her shoulders and decided to make herself at home in the lobby. If her mum or brother came out, she hoped the sight of her would make them feel guilty. The neighbours could think what they liked. Blithe sat with her back to the wall and dragged her bag onto her lap. She pulled her textbooks out, fished around for a pencil and started to read, underlining passages as she went. Blithe studied silently in the lobby for an hour. It was chilly but no one disturbed her. Only when her backside began to ache did she finally make her way inside, pushing the key into the lock between two fingers so it wouldn't rattle and then turning it slowly.

She opened the door just enough to squeeze through. Her mum's door was first on the right and regular snores sounded from within. Blithe felt almost parental knowing that whatever happened next, her mum would be safe from it, having finally lulled herself to sleep. The living room and kitchen were in darkness, some chips had been left for her on the side, but they were now stone cold. She downed a glass of water in the kitchen and made her way back out into the hallway.

Donnie's door was at the end of the hall and she approached it slowly, still able to pick out the sound of her mother snoring.

She expected to hear something from her brother's room – light emitted from the base of the doorframe but there was no sound. She knocked on the door and heard the springs of the bed ping but then nothing. She knocked again, heard the sound of a body sliding down to the floor, and knocked louder, forgetting her mother for a moment.

"Awright..." he called.

Hearing him, Blithe walked in and found Donnie slumped beside his bed, his head tilted back against the mattress and his legs stretched out across the bedroom floor. His dead eyes tried to focus on her as he stared open-mouthed.

"I went to see him," she announced.

She stepped forward. Donnie followed her with his eyes, still gormless, unaware that his mouth had fallen open.

"Who?"

"The boy whose teeth ye kicked in."

Donnie's eyes stayed on her, unwavering and now, a little unnerving. A silly grin spread across his face, and he gave a laugh that was as empty and dead as his eyes. It was a laugh that no healthy person could emit.

"He went to hospital. Did you ken that?"

He grunted and looked away. His eyes fell on a lighter that lay beside him on the floor, he picked it up and began sparking it.

"Stop that!" Blithe snapped.

He looked at her, again opened mouthed.

"What?"

"Put the lighter down! He went to hospital, lost a bottom tooth, fractured his jaw and his knee..."

"I didnae touch his knee!"

"Maybe not but he's back on crutches, his knee was healing fae another accident, it wouldnae have taken much, just falling on it would do it."

"Didnae touch his knee." Donnie repeated, but he sounded confused and nipped at the loose skin around his nails.

A cold cup of tea lay on the floor. He raised it to his lips with a shaking hand, the milky film wrinkling. When he finally got it to his mouth, his hand continued to shake, and cold drops of weak tea ran down his arm and onto the carpet. Donnie was oblivious to it.

"The police will be on to you. Actually, I was surprised to find you here. I thought you'd have been taken in by now. Oh well. Not yet. Ye get another night of freedom, another night to do fuck all."

Blithe cast her eyes around the room. It was so bare. Two

band posters from three years ago, curling at the edges, a small chest of drawers, an old TV, a wooden clothes hanger instead of a wardrobe, a digital alarm clock that gave the wrong time and various empty aerosols lined up on the windowsill. The cream carpet was stained with ink, ash, and scorch marks. She carefully closed the door, confident that he would digest everything she had said very slowly throughout the night.

She returned to her room, kicked her shoes off in different directions and, fumbling, put her phone on charge. Before Blithe flopped onto the bed, she felt the piece of paper with Jamie's number on it. She took it out of her jeans pocket.

She was tired down to her bones and let her clothes fall into a heap. She didn't even extricate her nightclothes from beneath the covers. She climbed into bed. She enjoyed the sensation of her naked body between the sheets. She placed her hands over her stomach before letting them glided over her skin, smooth as a shadow.

The front door closed with a slam. She ceased enjoying her body and curled up like the fronds of a fern. As she did so, she drew her sheets around her. She listened out, long after there was nothing to hear. If he were a threat, she would have felt safer without him. Strangely, she did not.

He was gone because she had manipulated fact to fiction. She'd tried to see some spark in that vacant face but there was nothing. She could have said anything, and he wouldn't have flinched or questioned her. She'd said all she could to stoke fear, only now did she realise it hadn't been slow to sink in, the fear had hit him all at once. Now it was too late to take it back. Sleep was a long time coming.

* * *

Donnie's legs shook, even standing still in the lift. He been sitting down too long to feel anything other than stiff and so jiggled his limbs. It was dark now and he knew that, as he walked through town, the night was revving up nicely.

He walked towards the city, his racing mind seized at anything that would distract him, anything that would turn the fear off for just a moment. It wasn't long before he was walking through crowds where everyone was having a good time, the smell of aftershave and perfume wafted like cigarette smoke. One funny look attracted more funny looks. Once he looked over his shoulder towards a group of men outside a pub, all with a pint in one hand and a fag in the other. As he suspected, they were all looking straight at him. He gestured with his hands and shouted.

"What ye fucking looking at?"

The men sneered and said nothing. Donnie carried on.

Forty minutes later, he arrived at the chippie. He glanced through the window, but he didn't know the girl who was working there. She looked about thirteen. He snuck round the back. No lights shone from the flat upstairs, nonetheless he went up to the flat to knock but heard nothing. He stood, exhausted in the dark. He leant back against the rail and stared into the cracked car park below, so dark it seemed as smooth as a pool. A car drove past the shop front, it screeched, and someone screamed. Then he heard the muted sounds of a drunk, confused, and resentful; his departing crew cheering at finally seeing the back of him.

Donnie heard all of this in the inky dark and did not move. He would not go home, and with that resolve he found energy as he scuttled down the concrete steps. He was in total darkness but didn't stop, his only guide the crunching gravel until the streetlights lit him up again.

He wasn't angry but he powered himself by adopting the guise of anger. He leant forward, flexing his shoulders as though to ram his way through passers-by; a young man unhinged. His steps stamped the ground. He cleared his dry throat and by this innocent act, appeared to be announcing himself to the empty street, indignant to any who tried to sleep.

He had taken six blue pills after dinner on the condition, self-imposed, that he would stay in. Going out under the influence was dangerous; it could lead to be being tanked-up around strangers, inclined to say crazy angry things that he could not recall the following day. A sequence of events reduced to one insignificant scene in his head that no amount of mental strain could contextualise.

He had not planned to make the trip; he had not thought it would be required. He was unaware that he had taken Etizolam and so it seemed to Donnie that the Valium had deserted him, since the former can wear off quickly. He could be wrapped up, slowed down, and protected, instead, he was adrift in intense fear, confusion, and nausea. Only a chemical could cure him, it was not as though he could calm himself, he had no counsel to give, and his body didn't listen to thoughts.

He knew that if the police came for him and certainly, if the boy got worse, he wouldn't have another chance to escape. He would be stuck inside, his brain pickled in reality. He wanted to plunge into relative bliss until the punishment clamped him. Nothing else would motivate him, law and order would stop the fun eventually and then time alone would take care of the problem of dependency. There was nothing on the other side of the problem once solved, nothing hopeful, just the end. Donnie could not conceive of recovery as something hopeful. The end as a notion, was comforting. The world we're all meant to ascend in our various ways seemed cruel to Donnie, from the bottom the structure seemed to incline away from him. The mechanics of work programmes, searches on Universal Jobsmatch and all of the associated bodies of the world of work, did not accept him into their workings smoothly. He'd tried, but if his mum couldn't navigate it successfully, he couldn't see how he possibly could. Her CV did not represent her, it only registered her as belonging to the great needy demographic. Being taught for the millionth time how to write a CV when he had nothing to put on it, led to only one place. It leads you to waiting for a mini-bus on a frozen street, waiting to be shipped out to some factory with a bunch of people who don't speak English. He'd not had the clarity to cry for months now.

His foot dragged against the ground and he stumbled, his march fading to foot dragging, even to toe dragging. Once this dimming energy was extinguished, he would be able to fall asleep anywhere, on a bench or in a doorway.

Eventually, he found himself outside Aldo's flat on the edge of Dennistoun. A corner where high tenements were stacked and inadequate street lighting was brushed by the warning lights of cranes towering on the skyline.

Aldo lived on the fourth floor of a tenement; it took a little while for Donnie to remember the number. He buzzed and half expected to hear an angry stranger but instead quickly heard Aldo's voice.

"Hello?"

"Aldo? It's Don. Just Don, can I come up?"

Donnie ran his fingers over his short hair and noticed a cold sweat on his forehead. A sound like the burst of an electric shock rang out and the door into the tenement finally gave. He stepped into bright light and the smell of old concrete and dusty paint, his nausea increased but he approached the stairs steadily, ready to grasp the rail on his way up, staring straight ahead, taking aim at what he needed.

While Aldo had been very quick to answer the buzzer, he was very slow to answer his front door. Donnie had to knock twice. The catch of the door was lifted and as the door swung open, Aldo was already walking towards the living room. No one greeted him and Donnie followed him through. Aldo only acknowledged him once he reclaimed his fag from the empty can on the arm of the sofa and sat back down.

"Were you on the night?" he asked suspiciously.

"No. Night off. I had tae get out of ma flat man. Ma sisters become a wee cow."

Aldo wasn't alone. Jack Viney sat in the middle of the second sofa, halfway through rolling a joint. Both sofas faced a huge TV mounted on the wall, but the screen had been paused. Jack looked up and nodded towards Donnie. Piles of DVDs, games, and consoles were stacked all over the room. A glass topped coffee table between the sofas was covered in empty cans and overflowing ashtrays, some sticky glasses were stacked under the coffee table. Their windows were covered by white office blinds. The smoke was so thick, you could draw in the air.

Donnie unfolded a chair and positioned it between them, since neither budged from their central positions on either sofa.

"Aye," Donnie continued, "I had to get out. I couldnae stay there, ma wee sister was coming at me, right in ma face."

Jack lit his joint, look a puff, sat back, and surveyed Donnie as he slowly exhaled.

"How old's yer sister?"

Donnie had to think for a bit. "Uhhh...almost seventeen."

"Aye well then. They turn intae cows, it had to happen eventually. Starts about eleven, by fifteen, ma sister was pure evil."

"She's threatening me! Threatening tae get the polis on me."

"You got a criminal record?" Aldo asked.

"No! No yet! She's fucking wanting me tae get one but!"

"What fur?"

Donnie groaned through gritted teeth.

"This fuckn'... fanny, this boy she was seeing."

"You mean her boyfriend?" Jack smiled.

"Aye. So far up himself, he could poke his snotters out fae the inside. I sorted him out. Just a wee bit though, I kicked him in the face but, no hard like. Turns out the boy's no just a massive fanny, he's also a delicate wee lamb."

Jack and Aldo exchanged glances.

"She thought he was a fanny," Donnie continued, "He fucked her, fucked off, and left her to get beat up. She was bawling about it, and I had to take her home, she was in that much of a state. So, I sorted him out, a warning, ye know? Don't-you-ever-try-that-shit-again. She flips out because, suddenly, he's a good guy again. A good guy that's going to call the polis on me."

Aldo grinned. "Are ye bricking it?"

Donnie nodded.

"When did ye sort him out?" Jack asked.

"Days ago, like three days ago."

Jack considered. "If they're going to get ye, tends to be sooner no later. If yer no lifted by th'morra, you'll probably be okay. Did he ken ye?"

Donnie nodded.

"Aye well then, definitely. If he kens who ye are and where ye live, well then, widnae worry that much. Gie it a few days, don't do anything stupid, but I would have thought that you'll have got away wi' it. Still bricking it?"

Donnie grudgingly nodded. "Ma fucking sister but. That's no right!"

"D'ye need me to sort ye out?" Aldo asked.

Donnie nodded. "I've no got a lot on me. That's the only thing."

Jack blew a smoke ring. Aldo rose from the sofa.

"I'm paid in the next couple of days..." Donnie continued

"I ken." Aldo muttered, "Ma dad pays ye."

He slouched out of the room.

Donnie shook his head at Jack. "I'm no getting involved in ma sister's shit again. She can sort it out for herself."

"Aye, mibbe avoid her, if she's like that."

As Aldo returned with a blister pack, Jack nodded towards Donnie. "He's still bricking it."

The score in Aldo's hand was Donnie's, not because they

couldn't say no to him, but because he was a charity case. If they'd believed him capable of conniving against them, sounding intelligent, or just credible then they wouldn't have tolerated him. He let himself be laughed at.

"Aye. I'm shitting myself," he said.

Aldo flicked the blister pack across the room, taking Donnie by surprise.

The strip hit his hands but however much he tried to catch; the pills bounced off his fingertips. They landed just under the coffee table. Donnie knelt down and fished them out.

"Will I get ye a pill dispenser?" Aldo asked, "Gran had one. I can pop them fur ye, put them in for the week."

"Cheers,' said Donnie kneeling by the table. "I wasnae expect ye to throw them at me. I'll sort ye out when I get paid."

Donnie sat down again and glanced up at the frozen screen, waiting for it to resume.

"Ye got a new phone yet Donnie?" Jack asked.

"Naw." Aldo answered for him, "He's still got his Gran's old one."

"It's my mum's old phone." Donnie explained. "Ma other one got dropped."

He shuffled on his backside towards the coffee table and fished the last of his tobacco out of his tracksuit pocket ready to roll.

"You still got that other phone?" Aldo asked Jack. "He'd be able to help us out a bit. He's not far from Kennishead, but he needs a better phone. See, he cannae download anything on what he's got."

Jack sniffed. "Have ye spoke to him about it like?"

Aldo looked back towards Donnie and nodded. This was a lie; he hadn't spoken to him about it. Donnie didn't correct him.

"See, cannae sell fae ma dads, dinnae want to sell fae here." Aldo explained. "No want'n loads of folk coming in at weird times. It's better to sell away fae the city centre."

Donnie would agree to help him, whatever it was, he would agree.

"You wanting a drink?" Aldo asked him.

"Aye cheers."

While Aldo disappeared into the kitchen, Jack leant forward and asked, "Is the chippie no paying ye?"

Donnie pretended he hadn't heard, but from the pursing of his lips, Jack knew that he had.

"Or is Aldo just fleecing ye?"

"Fuck off!" Aldo shouted from the doorway, making his way back, carrying a litre bottle of coke. He dumped it down on the coffee table and demanded, "Are ye gonnae gie him the phone then?"

"Aye okay, ye can have the phone," Jack agreed.

"Cool." Aldo turned to Donnie. "Wee bit extra cash willnae be bad eh?"

Donnie grinned and nodded. Jack continued to stare into the ceiling, slowly blowing smoke rings before asking.

"Ye ken what it is that we're asking ye to do Donnie?"

"I'll be a delivery man, that's no bother." Donnie muttered. "Ye ken I live with a mum?"

"That was what I was expecting. She wise tae ye?"

"She trusts me."

"Sure? Aye well. We ken a few folk up yer way, no that many. Keep yer head down but, to be honest, we're too wee, too small fry fur it tae be an issue but trust me, you do not want to compete with some of the guys around there. We supply to folk we ken, we're not punting, if ye try to build custom ye'll sail out yer ain window and end up as mush. So, don't go looking, ye understand? Wait fae a call fae us. We get Diazepam and Methadone and weed. It's no a lot but."

Aldo nodded. "Fur wur pensions."

Jack scoffed. "Not fucking thinking about my pension!"

Donnie popped four blue pills out onto his hand. He clasped them in a clammy grip, the sweat from his palms coating them steadily.

"I was thinking about giving up the pub." Jack murmured to

himself. "I cannae really be arsed wi' it. It's just cover but it's paying me fuck all."

Aldo shook his head, mindful of bitter experience. "No again. I widnae risk it again man."

Jack inhaled deeply and suddenly coughed through laughter. "Aye. You just fucked up. I'd not mouth off like you. What was it ye got? Six months in?"

Aldo nodded, clearly rattled as he stared into his ash tray, planning responses he'd never give. He smiled ruefully at Donnie, whose existence reminded him that there was a worse place to be.

When Aldo went back into the kitchen, Donnie emptied the pills into his mouth. They tasted warm and salty from where they'd been in his hand.

Aldo returned with three tumblers.

"Help yerself," he said. "Just gie me thirty on pay day."

Donnie gave him a thumbs up.

"Better drink a lot of that vodka if yer giving him thirty," Jack muttered.

Donnie leant back on the floor as Jack poured the vodka out. Now that Donnie was leaning back, Jack noticed that his t-shirt creased on the line of his ribs.

"Fuck that!" he exploded, "Eat some fucking food."

Aldo decided that he couldn't be arsed to watch the rest of his film. Instead, they turned off the lights while he and Jack played a racing game on the big screen. Donnie drank his vodka neat, his eyes heavy as he lay mesmerised by the candy pinks, purples and yellows flashing all over the room. He smiled right on cue, as the players sparred and crowed.

They forgot Donnie was there, lying flat on the floor soaking it all up. His mind wrapped tightly in cotton wool. As Jack loaded another game, Aldo moved off his sofa to sit beside him, freeing a cushioned space for Donnie. Donnie peeled his body from the floor, arms like matchsticks, legs like lead against the pull of the lovely floor.

While Aldo and Jack finished off their session, Donnie fell into the warm space vacated by Aldo's arse, so warm he pressed himself into it and closed his eyes, still seeing the flashing lights. Limbs loosened, muscles surrendered, he was enfolded in a warm wave of fatigue and carried away.

* * *

Aldo was annoyed to see Donnie still lying there, at ten thirty the following morning, but not so much that he would wake him and kick him out. Aldo ate his cereal standing up in the kitchen, downed a pint of sickly diluting juice and had a shower. Once dressed, he scribbled Donnie a note, he left this by the front door and hurried out.

'Shut the door properly on yer way out. I'll bring the phone round tonight.'

Donnie lay still, the silence absolute, save the slamming of doors echoing around the close. The warm space around his body rapidly cooling.

CHAPTER 11

Head down, Robbie marched down the empty school corridors with his hands out, ready to ram against the fire doors. The ram was hardly needed, the doors gave easily. He raised his head as they swung behind him and took a deep breath of the cool midday air. Now free, he slowed his pace, treading noiselessly on the empty asphalt. He turned on his phone to type a message while he walked through the main gates.

Robbie: Biology exam done. Can I come over?

He wasn't sure how the exam had gone, he couldn't remember specific questions, struggled to recall his answers and yet, he felt good. He headed towards the shops, which also happened to be in both the direction of his home and Jamie's. Ten minutes later, as he approached town, his phone buzzed.

Jamie: Ok.

Robbie had skipped breakfast and now craved sugar. He stopped by the mini supermarket and bought a bag of giant cookies. He didn't like to walk and eat, preferring to stop and properly savour his food, but his stomach seemed to be on the verge of digesting itself. He hadn't seen Jamie since he'd been attacked. He was determined not to show any shock; even if he did want to marvel at the cuts and bruises, he would try not to. It was, he thought, better to accept violence and in doing so, appear immune to the threat of it.

Jamie came to the door rather slowly, almost bear-like in spite of his wiry frame. Craning round the door, he narrowed his eyes as though they were failing him.

"Who else did ye think it would be?" Robbie laughed.

"What?"

Jamie's cut, lopsided mouth ceased pouting, but became tight and unfriendly.

"Never mind. Look though, I've bought sweeties." Robbie raised the bag.

"I've got dodgy teeth," Jamie replied quietly.

Jamie stepped back to allow him to enter. Robbie followed him down the hall towards the kitchen.

"It's just me,' Jamie said as they entered the kitchen. For once, there was no music playing.

Jamie had taken over the kitchen table for his studies. He closed his laptop and stacked his books before sitting down. Robbie sat down opposite him, opened his cookies, and offered them across the table.

"I could cut it up for you."

Jamie shook his head.

"Don't be a miserable bastard."

Jamie gave a smile, very much to himself and said, "Bit hypocritical that."

Robbie took a bite and chewed merrily.

"Least you know the word."

"I do," Jamie replied. "I also know condescending."

Robbie nodded. "Oh, well done. Ye alright?"

"It could be worse."

Robbie smiled encouragingly. "Aye. That'll heal up quickly. What'll happen to Donnie?"

Jamie flinched. "Who said it was Donnie?"

"Everyone."

"Well, I never said it was Donnie."

Robbie drummed his fingers on the kitchen table as he swallowed the last of the biscuit, he was still hungry.

"Are you okay talking about it?"

Jamie nodded but Robbie was unconvinced.

"See when I'm depressed," he said. "I don't like loads of questions, talking might not feel good at the time, but afterwards I don't feel so, so heavy, not so much like a big lump."

"I'm not depressed." Jamie replied coldly.

Beneath a critical eye, something he didn't think Jamie could ever deliver, Robbie struggled.

"Okay, sure."

"I dinnae want to be one of those people who never say they're sad, they're always depressed."

Robbie nodded. "There's a difference."

"I know there's a fucking difference. *I* know."

Robbie sighed. "Are you still fucked off with me because Blithe got scratched up?"

"No."

"Then what? Shall I fuck off with my big biscuits?"

"No." Jamie sagged. "Sorry."

"Because Connor's is the closest anyone's got to an authorised version. He's saying you fucked her, and then Donnie fucked you, in the face." Robbie restrained a laugh. "He kicked you in the face. No-one's saying he raped you." Robbie grinned and took another bite.

"You said rape wasn't funny."

Robbie frowned. "I don't remember saying that."

"No? Well, you did."

"I don't remember saying it, it's true though. So, did you?" Robbie asked.

"What?"

"Did you fuck her?"

Jamie slowly shook his head.

"The V's not for victory."

Robbie nodded. "You catch fewer diseases that way, less than if you go fucking about with skankies."

"You didn't fuck her, did you?" Jamie said sharply.

"No."

"So, how is she a skank?"

Robbie's lips parted, but he was again lost for words and could only blink rapidly as his mental approach changed gear.

"Was she gagging for it?" Jamie pressed.

"No!"

"Well then, she cannae be much of a skank, if she doesnae even fuck her own boyfriend."

Robbie was familiar with these outbursts. It was his ability to stay calm that often ignited them, while Jamie became too wound up to successfully argue. He saw now a rage that Jamie had settled into and found that it was he who was unprepared.

There was so much anger in Jamie, his face red, his eyes sunk and narrowed. His heavy brows enhanced by the bruise on his forehead as the cut on his lip enhanced his sneer.

Robbie took another deep breath. "Got rejected then?"

Robbie stared him out, daring him to respond and say something stupid. The barb was not intended but the cold civility disintegrated. Jamie stood up suddenly, the chair screeched as he rose but before he stumbled over it, he recovered himself, hands steady on the table.

"Fuck off."

Robbie didn't regret it; he was glad to have his answer.

"Oh," he said, making this small word last.

Jamie moved behind him, to the kitchen surface, the cupboard door opened, the tap blasted on and then, as Robbie faced the now empty seat, he could hear glugging.

"It's easy to forget her," Robbie said quietly, "summer's coming and she's not going anywhere we're going. I wasn't planning to visit the bingo hall."

The glass clanked down on the side. Robbie twisted round in his chair.

"I don't like it when you're quiet. If you want me to go, I'll go."

"No. I'm thinking."

"Try doing it out loud. It's not like you're subtle, no offence."

Jamie stared down at the sink, touching the cut on his lip with the tip of his finger, and then running the nail under the flap of dry skin to prise it up. Robbie resisted the urge to tell him that it wouldn't heal if he kept doing that but turned back with a sigh. He noticed that Jamie's phone was face-up on the table. He could see a message bar at the top of the screen. "Fucking told U."

The sender's number had not been saved in the phone. The tap turned on again as Jamie rinsed his glass. While he did this Robbie turned the phone round, memorised the last few digits and turned the phone back around. He checked the number against his own phone to find that the message had indeed come from 'Witch', the name he had assigned her, low down on his list of contacts.

"Oh, let's forget about it," Robbie said. "Are you really that fucked off with me?"

Robbie turned and saw Jamie considering him critically.

Robbie tried to be sympathetic. "That's a sick thing to do though, getting him to do that to you."

Again, Jamie thought. *Again*. He closed his eyes.

"No. She didn't get her brother to do this. Why'd you think that?"

"Her brother's a headcase," Robbie said simply. "He's like that and since he didn't know you, - that's right aye?"

Jamie nodded.

"Aye, so all the information he had on you came from her."

"Well, it could have been a misunderstanding…" Jamie said weakly.

"Oh, come on! Really?"

Jamie sat down opposite him but rather than dragging his chair back under the table, he leaned forward, elbows and arms fanning out across the table so his chin could rest comfortably on his hands.

"I'll give her the benefit of the doubt. That's fair."

"Was that message from her?" Robbie asked coldly.

Jamie's head jerked up slightly and red filtered into his pale, lightly freckled skin.

"Because if it is, that reads like a threat has been carried out."

"That's the only text she ever sent me." Jamie said quietly.

"So, she threatened you? She is gloating – that's definitely what that is."

"No, no, she's not gloating. She's not."

But slumped against the table, barely able to lift his head, Jamie did not sound certain.

"Why? Why are you letting her away with it?"

"I like her."

"What? Why?"

"I like her."

Jamie looked up, his features softening at last.

"Why do you like her? Her brother's just tried to smash yer face in."

"I don't like her brother. I like her," Jamie said simply.

"But she's using her brother to threaten you."

"The other day there, she came here to give me back something that I'd lent her. Really, she just wanted to have a keek at ma face. I gave her my number, I offered it to her, but she said she didn't have her phone and I thought it was an excuse... I thought maybe she didnae really want to take it. She said she did and that when she used it, she'd message and say, 'told you' and I would know it was from her."

"Are you going out?"

"No."

"Just friends?"

Jamie paused. "No exactly."

Robbie processed this news with a business-like nod, but his stomach lurched.

"You know that I can't ever be around her, I can't hear about her from you, if you '*like*' her. She's the thing I would wipe from my memory, the total crushing embarrassment of what she did to me. Why would you go there? Are you that desperate?"

Jamie shook his head.

"No, not that desperate – look, if I was desperate I wouldnae go for Blithe." He grinned, remembering her faltering tone and wrinkled nose as she'd said, "Actually... can we not?" For the first time it was funny.

"Is it just attention then? Someone shows you some attention and then you're all over them?"

Jamie gave a concerned glance and let him continue.

"She's readily available, right there, so you don't have to make any effort to find someone you actually like. She makes you feel better about yourself. I understand that. She's experience, which you'll be grateful for when you meet someone you do like. She'll do for that."

Jamie grinned, even with his head hung down the grin was transformative – the row of neat teeth changing the shape of his long face with a glowing but introverted smile.

Robbie was the more intelligent, demonstrably the more academic, but Jamie consoled himself that looking older equated to being better looking. He also had something else, he'd been in bed with her, never mind what happened afterwards. Her silver star pants were for a short time the only item of clothing worn between them. The more Robbie put him down, the more tempted Jamie was to fill in the detail; *you don't know what you're talking about, I do, I've undressed her*. Tempted yes, but he said nothing, and shook his head.

"Talk!" Robbie exploded. "Don't just shake your head at me!"

"What ye say, it's not true, but you don't want to listen."

"Well, I'm only telling you what it looks like."

"I don't feel better about myself, I feel worse," Jamie said. "I wouldn't use her, it's fucking out of order to say that, I widnae say that to you."

Robbie gritted his teeth.

"So, what are you going to do then? What does she think? Does she think she's finished with you? Was her brother delivering that message, through the medium of face-stamping?"

He was goading him, he knew, but he may as well have been goading himself. Jamie was calm, Robbie seemed to collapse inside like a crushed can. He had been excited; the first exam was out of the way and the day ahead was his. He was so eager to see Jamie, to see his injuries, to talk through what had happened. He had even hoped he might comfort. He swallowed and tried again.

"Do you think that maybe she's telling you one thing but doing and saying something else? You don't know what she said to her brother."

"No."

"But she must have said something to make him do that."

Jamie nodded. "But I deserved it."

Robbie's first instinct was to reach out across the table and shake him.

"You did not! How did you deserve that?"

Jamie would not shout back and replied quietly, "I know I should have helped her."

"How? She's not your girlfriend!"

Jamie had no response other than a grimace.

"You're not friends, she's not your girlfriend. Or is it friends who don't quite get round to fucking?"

"Maybe..."

Robbie had run out of words to shout and leaned across the table; hands raised in surrender.

"I like her." Jamie repeated. "I like her more than anyone I've ever been out with. There you go. I'd be a headcase to tell you that if it wasn't true."

"But you've not managed a relationship of more than six weeks. You're still making do."

"Aye well, that's all you're getting from me."

There was no point in shouting anymore. Robbie tried to be measured and calm, and hoped his voice wouldn't shake in the attempt.

"I can't be friends with you if she's yer girlfriend. I *hate* her. She's a fucking swamp thing and, honestly, she smells like beans and toast, so look out for that, but most of all, she's a fucking atrocious human being! Listen to me! I've come out of it and you, you fucking lemming, are going in! How can you do that?"

"I got to know her..."

"Fuck that! You *think* you know her."

"At least as well as you do." Jamie replied. "When I first walked her, I said, if I were a girl, I would go for you, and she suggested I go for it. She never *ever* slagged you off. Everyone hated her, it would have been so easy to come out with some bullshit about you. But nothing."

"So? She didn't drown any kittens, at least, I don't think she has." Robbie muttered.

"See, there's no one I ken that would drown kittens but the world is hoaching with folk who would lie to get out of the shit. I've lied to get out of trouble, haven't you?"

"Not lately."

Robbie pressed his fist against his mouth, Jamie watched and waited. The tense silence broke when Jamie at last said,

"I'm sorry. She's not my girlfriend but just don't slag her off, don't talk about her like that, no to me."

"That bothers you? Me being insensitive to her? Because you *like* her but not as a friend? So you've had yer tongue down her throat?"

He paused to allow Jamie to deny it, he didn't.

"And you still didn't notice that she tasted like beans?"

"She didn't taste like beans."

Robbie let his head slam, face first, onto the table. The sudden bang made Jamie smile.

"Alright?" Jamie asked the top of Robbie's head.

He'd probably hurt his nose; it couldn't be comfortable pressed against the tabletop. Jamie tilted his head and squinted, knowing he shouldn't laugh, but feeling a nervous urge to do so, until he heard a sniff.

"Robbie? It's alright... We're not going out."

Robbie cushioned his face with folded arms, keeping his head down, he muttered something.

"Look at me," Jamie said, "I cannae hear you like that."

Robbie looked up with streaming eyes.

"You want to."

The drunken rambling after the party was the closest Jamie had ever come to seeing Robbie cry, and he'd put that down to intoxication. Now that his face was tearful and swollen, Robbie looked about ten.

"You should watch it." Robbie said.

"No."

Robbie picked up his phone, his fingers then worked to pull the cables of his headphones from where they'd been tangled within his pocket.

"No!" cried Jamie, "I'll smash yer phone before I watch that. Stop it!"

Robbie began to scroll, Jamie tried to bat his arm, but Robbie lifted his phone and continued his search. Anguish was thrown for a moment over his face as he located the clip.

'Stop it!" Jamie shouted, "I know how I felt when she got punched to the ground. I don't need to see that."

"But you don't know why she got punched. You've not seen it so you can't judge."

"I don't want to judge! Why do I have to judge?"

"Don't judge then but I want you to watch it!"

"Why?"

"If you watch it, I won't rip into her, I promise, until you want me to and you *will* want me to, one day."

Robbie's phone case had a built-in stand but when he turned his phone for Jamie to see, he held his hands out either side, as though waiting to be cuffed. Jamie shook his head.

"I want you to watch it."

Robbie slid his headphones across the table; he did not want to hear it. The sequence began to play. Jamie put one bud to his ear and looked at the screen.

Robbie was of course, the larger image on screen, Blithe was just a stamp in the corner. The recording started as a fairly mundane conversation but Blithe frowned for the task that lay ahead until she, rather brutally, interrupted.

"I think we should stop going out. It's not working."

Jamie feared what was to come and glanced at the tearful figure beyond the screen.

"What... was it something I did?" Robbie had asked.

Blithe wrinkled her nose, as though the answer was to be yes, before replying.

"No, it's just one of those things."

"Are you sure? Can't we talk about this?"

Blithe frowned. "No. I don't want to."

Jamie had imagined his big, snotty, contracting face but the reality was that Robbie's face stiffened and he turned his head to profile, not moving other than the tremor of his chin as he failed to keep control of his mouth.

Blithe rolled her eyes but would not have done so, had he been able to see her. Then, Robbie put his head in his hands. Jamie couldn't catch his words due to a combination of tears and poor sound quality. He focused on Blithe, her face passing through an array of emotions: irritation, concern, frustration and back to irritation. Jamie knew this was not cruelty, she just didn't know how to close the conversation. If ever a face told of the urge to tiptoe away it was Blithe's. He wasn't blind to his friend's distress, though he couldn't make out words, he heard it loud and clear. At last Blithe leaned forward and said.

"Robbie, I'm going now, okay? I'm going. You're a good guy, yer going to be alright."

Jamie closed his eyes and removed the earbud. He stared at Robbie and repeated her words.

"You're a good guy, you're going to be alright."

"Don't laugh at me."

"I'm not," Jamie placed a hand gently over Robbie's. "It's not that bad. It's really not that bad."

Robbie nodded, staring at the hand over his own, the hand still a little scuffed from where it had been stamped on. He would keep his promise not to slag Blithe off, but considered messaging her instead; 'Blithe, Are you sure? Do you know that he still takes his parents in with him when he goes to the doctors? His mum still chooses his clothes.'

As far as he knew, these things were still true, but he wouldn't tell her. He couldn't. Grief would have to find another way out.

* * *

Aldo received a message from his dad, asking if he knew where Donnie was. He then tried to call Donnie's phone, but it rang out. It wasn't unusual for Donnie not to answer, his battery ran down very quickly and if the police had him, he would have handed his phone in at the station. Aldo assumed that Donnie had been arrested. A shame too, he wouldn't be all that useful once he was known to the police.

In a windowless pub, Aldo was finishing off part one of a split shift. The daytime punters only ever came to watch sport or because they knew someone who worked there and so, aside from a few propped up at the bar, all the benches inside and out were empty. Light from the displays, fridges and taps lit up the bar, by contrast, everything on the other side was in gloom. It exacerbated Aldo's headache. It was just a case of idling, waiting for the hour to strike and the first part of his shift to end. He thought about Donnie, asleep on his sofa. He knew that no one in Donnie's family would be able to direct the police to his flat. He didn't think Donnie would ever have talked about him. Arrest seemed less likely, the more he thought about it. If the police were looking for him, they would go to his home, but they wouldn't find him there – not today. Even when he wasn't avoiding arrest, he would not go four miles home, only to have to come all the way back for a shift starting at four.

Aldo wouldn't normally go home between shifts but reluctantly gave in to the nagging fear and marched briskly home. He didn't know what to expect as he mounted the steps of the tenement. It was possible that Donnie was still sleeping at quarter past five.

* * *

He opened his front door cautiously. Once the heavy door boomed shut behind him, he sensed from the silence and the air he breathed, that his flat was empty, his note lying unread. He turned left into the living room and jumped when he saw the figure curled up, facing the back of the sofa, lying just as he had left him. He knew then. He approached and touched the rigid shoulder.

Donnie's mouth seemed to have fallen open, as though his teeth had suddenly become too big for his mouth, as it had sunken and shrivelled with his tightened cheeks.

The blood now pooling inside Donnie's body contained Diazepam, alcohol and Alprazolam. His daily doses of Valium varied in concentration. Some of the substances inside his frail body had been knowingly ingested, others not. Their toxicity had been increased by a chemical reaction as they'd combined. His heart rate had slowed until his heart stopped.

Aldo stood up straight, holding out his hand as though it now carried disease. He walked briskly to the bathroom to wash his hands. He then went into his bedroom, grabbed a carrier bag and gathered up everything he didn't want the police to find; blister packs, hash already chopped into cubes. It all went in the plastic bag, which was then stuffed inside a bin liner. On the mat by the door, there was a pizza menu, and a free newspaper. He balled these up and added them to the bin liner for bulk. He walked down to the back green slowly, listening out for anyone coming out to the staircase. He was fortunate, no one saw him on his way out. He placed the bag behind the bins and placed another full refuse sack on top of it. They would not be collected for days. If the police seized it, he would be angry, but they would not be able to prove that the contents were his.

He would leave the empty bottles and the overflowing ash trays; the living room would be as he found it. He wouldn't get far pretending they'd been sipping tea and talking politics. Aldo walked out of his flat and sat on the first step leading down. From there, he tried to do two things at once, call the police and roll a joint on his lap. He could not recall Donnie's second name, it just went out of his head, nor his exact age. Was he twenty, twenty-one?

The emergency services asked him questions about the body, and so Aldo had to return to the flat and confirmed with exasperation, that the body was indeed stiff and not to come to life again. They seemed to want to keep him talking, asking who else was there, if there was anyone he could call. Aldo wanted to get off the phone and finish rolling the joint.

Once the joint was rolled and lit, Aldo walked down to the ground floor to wedge open the door with a brick. He returned slowly to the same step, once again waiting by his front door, afraid to see the body of what had been his friend. He grimly considered the safety of his drugs downstairs, that maybe he should have triple bagged it. If they checked the history of the address, they might bring the dogs just for the hell of it. He wouldn't be the first to get clobbered by a random sniffer dog.

The paramedics arrived first. If they were there to revive him, Aldo thought, they were wasting their time. He remained on the staircase outside, rehearsing what he was going to say to the police. When the police appeared, it was surprisingly easy, the easiest conversation he'd ever had with them. They could see more clearly than he could, how shaken up he was.

He explained that Donnie had turned up at his flat very late the previous night, already under the influence of Valium or weed. He explained that he'd had too much to drink and had fallen asleep on the sofa. Aldo couldn't say what he'd had to drink or how much because he was in the middle of a gaming session that Donnie would not, in that state, have been able to join in. He told the truth.

His flat now a potential crime scene, Aldo was advised to go elsewhere but he preferred to wait. He stalked the back green, chain smoking and watching the bins.

When he finally went back into the flat hours later, a young police officer was waiting. The body had been taken away and there was a small, partially dried, pool of blood on the sofa. Before he could sit down again, the soiled pillows on the sofa had to be put in bin bags. They gave off a peculiar smell, a tang like iron and acid.

Perhaps it was the relief that it had come to the final formalities, or because he was less preoccupied with the fear that officers might search his home, but Aldo found clarity. He looked around the flat and was suddenly anguished at the thought that he might have left it in the final moments of Donnie's life.

"When did he die? D'ye know that?"

"We'll never be precise about that. It's not possible."

"Aye but, I left in the morning, I walked past him on my way to the kitchen. Was he dead then?"

"He'd been dead for a few hours we think."

"Aye but, was he alive at ten this morning?"

"Listen. It'll go to the Procurator Fiscal but, in my opinion, if he was in the same position when you left as he was when you found him just now, I think it's very possible that he was already dead. But look, I'm not a doctor, that's only logic, you understand. Now, do you have somewhere else to stay? I'm guessing you won't want to be on your own tonight."

"Fucking right. Nae chance though, I'll go round ma dad's."

As he departed, the officer placed a card with a reference number on top of the note that Aldo had written for Donnie.

Alone in the flat and safe from scrutiny, Aldo felt elated for a few seconds. There were no lies to expose, no tracks to cover. He would just have to be careful for a while.

He was about to ring his dad but paused with his finger on the button. He felt a wave a nausea and took a deep breath.

He'd watched Donnie lose weight, he'd watched a physical and mental deterioration. He could have said something to his dad, something in passing, a word of concern but it hadn't even nearly occurred to him. He had not even nearly acted. What he had done consistently, was to laugh, because stupidity combined with a loss of coordination, had been worth laughing at.

* * *

Jamie: Robbie didn't like what I had to say about you.

Blithe: What did you say?

Jamie: That I liked you a lot.

Jamie: Then he made me watch the clip. It's not as bad as I thought it would be.

Blithe: Do you do everything he tells you to do?

Jamie: No.

Jamie: But I feel guilty.

Blithe: You feel guilty for liking me?

Jamie: Aye.

Blithe: Fuck you.

Jamie: He used to be the sanest person I knew. Now, he's always tearful and depressed. I'm not saying it to make you feel guilty, but I don't want to make it worse.

Blithe had nothing to reply now. She knew that she'd been put in her place. It didn't help knowing that he liked her a lot.

Blithe lay in the park, on a lawn between two tight, orderly rows of lime trees. The lime grove stretched neatly up the gentle slope, stretching into the distance until the rows merged. Blithe focused on a point of light, where the branches appeared to finally touch, a star at the end of the forest.

At the foot of the slope, the road curved into the back of Pollok House and the grand entrance leading down into the stately home itself. The only people Blithe could see were a couple out with their grandson. The wee boy was determined to power his way up the road on his scooter while his grandparents toddled after him.

Blithe watched them from the lawn above, thirty yards away. She thought that she must seem a dark presence.She wore black jeans and a pine coloured silky shirt. Her black hair hung down over her shoulders and back. The grass beneath her was verdant and cool, rarely trodden. In the shade of the limes, the dew seemed to last long into the day.

Blithe re-read the message on her phone and lay back on the grass. She pulled her headphones from where they hung against her shoulders, inserted them into her ears, and watched the sky changing over her head. The clouds moved quickly across and with them came a cold wind and the threat of rain.

She was tired but didn't want to go home. Her old, washed-out school bag lay beside her, filled with a couple of textbooks and notepads which hadn't left her bag since she's dropped it into the grass forty minutes before. Even with a cracked screen, she found it better to revise with the internet. She found it hard to sit and read her textbooks. She was anxious but unwilling to admit it.

She had hardly slept the night before and endured the cold because she lacked the energy to get up. A grey squirrel bounded across the lawn towards her and then seemed to shit itself at the sight of her and bolt right back. She smiled sleepily to herself.

The prospect of returning home made lying in the developing drizzle almost pleasant. It was probably safer than going home and telling Donnie that the police were not on to him. She could imagine what he would call her – an evil bitch, a sadistic fucking cow. He would not force his way into her life again, that was as it should be. Her mum would listen, shake her head, and sympathise, but not with her daughter.

She didn't have to tell him the truth. She could claim that it was Jamie who had lied, he who had talked about going to the police only to chicken out. She dismissed this; Donnie would have no trouble believing it, but it would make it very difficult to bring Jamie into the flat again. That was unacceptable.

With a great sigh, she stood up and walked down towards the road, fields either side of her and old oaks all around. It was strange to have come here, so far from home and walked so far into the park. She knew why though, tired as she was. She walked past the path leading to the museum and Burrell Collection, lingering as she saw through the trees, the lawn they'd waited on, the slope he'd rolled down. There, it remained untouched.

Blithe walked sadly under the railway bridge, along by the river and out of the park to face the busy road. A long, winding route stretched ahead of her, dirty cracked pavements, busy roads, and intersections. There was no scenic route from here on in.

She imagined what she would say to her brother. She was angry at feeling any guilt or anxiety on his behalf. She'd over-polished the memory of Jamie's smile; in her mind it had been brighter and neater than it had ever been in reality. Recalling the cut lip and the tooth that wobbled was all she needed to seethe. It helped to hate her brother; it powered her up the hill.

Donnie might have expected his family to act like a gang and follow certain rules; never grass your family up, respect the elder male, no matter how useless he is. This was the message he probably wanted her to understand. He might have subscribed to that mentality by spending too much time sitting round with a lot of other arseholes, bigging themselves up as the alpha male, jealous of each other despite all being the height of shite.

She had worshipped him once, more than she had ever worshipped her dad. He had been a comfort whenever the world was unfamiliar. He was a presence, head and shoulders above her, yet capable of looking her in the eye.

Time and time again, she and Donnie would be taken to a family gathering by their dad. She recalled the discomfort, the fear of being stared at and the feeling of not belonging. Only Donnie could understand this, and while she mumbled and stumbled through crowded, unfamiliar homes and club houses, she had a shield, a hand to hold and lead her. She could tidy herself away behind her brother, away from the enquiring eyes of strangers who seemed to know her. Some sniggered at her politeness, affronted that children should be so formal ('their mum's probably poisoned them towards this side of the family'; 'she's turned the weans against us.''). Then there were others who would be quick to tut, should manners be lacking. For the children who ought never to have existed, it was impossible to win.

When Donnie turned fourteen, Lynne decided that he didn't have to get dragged along to those family gatherings if he didn't want to. She felt that enough damage had been done. For the first time, aged ten, Blithe had gone alone. It was a decision she regretted; she had wanted her brother, like she used to want her mother. She didn't tell him when she came back but she assumed he must have known. She'd simply announced that she'd never go on her own ever again. She didn't tell him that she'd missed him, that's not how siblings talk to each other.

There was a time, a few months later, when she and Donnie were playing Guitar Hero and he received a message from their dad. She remembered how he had looked at her, conspiratorially, cheekily.

"Whose fucking birthday is it this time?" He read on. "Auntie Carmel? Who's that?"

Blithe shrugged. He'd thrown his phone over his shoulder, and they'd resumed their game.

She didn't know if he ever replied but their dad stopped inviting them to family gatherings. Instead, when they needed school uniform, he would take them shopping in town and buy them lunch. These excursions took place about twice a year, but Donnie hadn't come on the last two. He didn't need school uniform anymore, there was no point.

Blithe took the lift up to her flat. Alone, she kept her eyes to the ceiling and imagined the scene, rehearsed the explanation she would give her brother as to why he deserved to be deceived.

The flat was empty. She stumbled in, exhausted after her walk, into silence. Even when her mum stopped off for a take-away, she was always home by six, it was now almost seven. She wandered into the kitchen and saw five pounds left on the side, on top of an envelope on which was written, '*Blithe – For tea.*'

Blithe scowled. She did not want to go out again, but she was hungry. She opened the fridge, and sniffed at the bacon in the food drawer; it had a bluish tinge to it and she put it back. There was also some cheese, half a cucumber and a little bit of very flat cola. There was also a lot of vegetables that her mum bought with the best of intentions but had not got around to preparing. Blithe made herself some diluting juice and turned on the grill to make cheese on toast. She stretched out on the sofa and kicked off her shoes. Shadows started to creep on the streets far below. Heavy evening clouds suspended in the sky, ridged like a flint blade, waiting to stretch and fade into the darkening sky.

Blithe settled down in front of an old sitcom and ate her dry cheese and toast. There was no need to pay attention in order to know what was happening on screen, and she couldn't have done so anyway. She was too uneasy. Her phone had been charging in her bedroom, but she kept it by her side, forever glancing at it until, at eight thirty, she sent her mum a message.

Blithe: Where are you? When will you be back?

A little anxiety nipped at her. She worried that Donnie might have handed himself in at the police station or else been arrested.

Five minutes later credits rolled, Blithe phoned again and heard the computer voice tell her, 'The other person has hung up.' Blithe flicked through the channels, not settling on anything. She generally loved having the living room to herself, but she didn't know what to do and would have been as well watching catch-up on the cracked screen in her bedroom. A text came through from her mum.

Lynne: I'll be late. Get a pal round.

Lynne tended to call, certainly if she were worried. She needed a voice to be fully reassured. Blithe called her but it went straight through to her voicemail, so she sent a text.

Blithe: Is Donnie okay?

She turned over to the news. Nothing sunk in. She sat and chewed her nails, every so often looking out at the darkening skyline. A message finally came through again fifteen minutes later.

Lynne: At the hospital but I'm fine. I'll be home tonight but late. You getting a pal round?

Blithe: Is Donnie OK?

Then nothing again, an unnerving silence.

Blithe: Why are you at the hospital?

Blithe sent this message but a minute was too long to wait for a response. She called her mum yet again, pacing the flat, listing to the ringing. When it diverted to voicemail she called again and then again. Faster and faster, she paced till the neighbours below could hear her. When the call diverted to voicemail for the fourth time, she threw her phone against the wall and shouted.

"I've no pals! Tell me! Answer for fucks sake!"

If the police were at the hospital she'd tell, if he'd overdosed but survived, she'd say something. If he'd been in a fight and was waiting to be taken back to the police station, she'd say.

The TV remained on, an American film from the 80's started up, promising guns and helicopter chases. Blithe turned it off and paced the living room. She wanted to cry, but the tears wouldn't come.

If her mum knew what she was doing to her, she'd stop and answer her phone. She'd underestimated her basic intelligence and concluded that of course, she could distract a teenage girl with the gift of a free house. What use was it on a Thursday during exams?

She was relieved that she hadn't broken her phone when she threw it against the wall. The sturdy old phone had a knack for surviving that the newer, thinner models didn't.

She began a message to Jamie.

Blithe: Can you come over?

But that sounded a little like seduction. She started again.

Blithe: I've a free house tonight– are you about?

Strangely, that seemed to read even more like seduction.

Blithe: Feeling shite. R U free?

She pressed send on gut impulse, as though her hand intervened before she could hesitate a third time. So used to waiting in silence, she was surprised to receive a reply almost instantly.

Jamie: Exam tomorrow at 10.

Blithe sighed and sat down again on the sofa, flicked through the channels before standing up, leaving the TV blaring as she wandered through the house with her phone in her hand.

She peered into Donnie's room. It was just as he had left it - the smell of cheap tobacco, the scorch marks on the carpet, the dingy, mostly bare walls and the windowsill crammed with empty aerosols.

He owned so little and still things were missing, the console he'd kept for years was gone, she'd been too angry to notice that he had been sat in silence. These items had been vanishing gradually. She hung her head and typed the words.

Blithe: Please.

The reply came through as she walked through to the living room.

Jamie: U OK?

Had it been quicker, it might have seemed as though he was there.

Blithe: No.

Jamie: Exam tomorrow. Come over after?

Blithe sat down on the sofa and smiled through gritted teeth. She could tell him that it was alright, go to sleep, be well rested for tomorrow, look after yourself before you think of me. She placed the phone on the coffee table, stretched out over the arm of the sofa, lay her head back and stared up at the ceiling. Her phone buzzed.

Jamie: What's happened?

Blithe stared at it but didn't lift a finger to reply. She hadn't eaten enough but had no appetite, gazing slowly round the room, tired and stunned.

Jamie: Where R U?

Blithe tried to think of something to type back but she was in no hurry – the night stretched ahead of her. She tried her mum again, but it rang out.

* * *

Lynne had turned her phone off. She sat in the chapel at the hospital, a round room filled with pine. She sat in the centre of the room, praying. The minister, a small, matronly figure in an oversized red cardigan, sat opposite. Lynne had been there for hours, not yet ready to leave without her son. She'd seen him, briefly, in the presence of a police officer. She couldn't bring herself to touch him, even if she had been allowed. She'd said goodbye but even as she said it, she thought only of running from the room. Those around her let her take her time, asking repeatedly if there was anyone they could call on her behalf. No, she said, time and time again, believing her insistence protected Blithe. This was not something she wanted to share with her. She could tell her gently. She didn't know how to, not yet, but it would come to her.

When she was ready, she confirmed Donnie's identity and signed him away from living. She had cried then, but it was in sympathy for herself as another person she watched and pitied. She'd cried for the thought of losing a child but had not really cried for her son. Inside the chapel, it was possible to keep the grief from crashing in, it was like a Tardis, once safely inside, it was as though the hospital had vanished around them.

The minister had prayed with her for over an hour. She heard the phone go, saw Lynne switch it to silent and saw that messages were coming in. She knew they were from her daughter.

"You must go home and tell your daughter. Would you like me to come with you?"

Lynne shook her head.

"I could just come with you in the taxi if you like?"

Lynne shook her head, gripped the back of the chair in front of her and then pressed the peak of her praying hands against her forehead.

"Too good of you. That's too good of you."

"No, not at all. Anyone who could see you would offer the same. Would you like me to call a taxi and we can both go?"

"No. No. I must get the bus."

Lynne still could not tell Blithe. She couldn't say it out loud - she could only mutter it to herself. This strange hope that should never have been there, a cruel sense of unreality. He lived too clearly in her mind to be gone like the body in the mortuary was gone.

She prayed as she had never prayed, grinding her teeth in the effort, for a new day to dawn on her breathing son, the worst horror to be swept away before it could hit her in the frontline with its full force.

"He's a lovely looking lad," she said.

Lynne looked up at the minister's soft features. Tears coursed down her cheeks and she let out a sigh to free her voice.

The minister smiled.

"Do you have a picture I could see?"

Lynne picked up her phone, saw the huge number of missed calls but she simply wiped her nose on her sleeve and brought up a photograph that she had taken of the children, two years ago on her birthday.

"Ah, what lovely children you have."

The minister became misty eyed looking at Donnie and Blithe, side by side in the pub restaurant, genuinely smiling, genuinely happy.

"I ken. Ye widnae think to look at me, no a pound of me hanging the right way... No, ye widnae think that ma wains would turn out like that. That beautiful."

"They are. You are too."

"I'm a big fat tank."

Lynne picked up another tissue. Before she wiped her face, she let her face crumple behind it.

"No. I can see where your children get their lovely dark eyes and I see a resemblance. So, if they are beautiful then so are you."

Lynne's face crumpled again.

"Oh, I don't know what to say to her. Oh, how can I tell her?"

The minister leaned over and took Lynne's wet hands in her own.

"What about you? Who's there to look after you?"

"No one."

"Then, for now, let that be me. But you must go home to your daughter. For your daughter."

Blithe stared into the bathroom mirror, eying her reflection as she slowly brushed her teeth. She wore her mum's bobbly old t-shirt, cream coloured with raspberry piping along the seams. It hung off her, almost to her knees, making her appear shrunken and child-like. It had just been washed and was cosier for that. She washed her face slowly with a cheap cucumber scrub, taking her time. She was in no real hurry to get to bed, it was still very early, and she knew she wouldn't sleep.

She stared back at her running mascara and washed her face again, looking back at her dripping rosy face, listening out to the silence in the flat. She abruptly pulled the cord on the bathroom light, and walked along the corridor, faintly lit by the fire alarm, to her room where she remained in the dark.

She sat down shakily on the edge of her bed, looked at her phone and tried her mum once again. She didn't really hold out any hope and still the phone rang out. She knelt on her bed and looked out of the window; the night was very young, and down below a small group huddled under the awning by the main doors. She pressed her forehead against the cold glass. Something awful had happened.

She sent her mum a text.

Blithe: What's going on? I'm scared.

That Lynne ignored this message was confirmation of the worst, but she could not cry for what wasn't yet a certainty. Instead, fear warped her thoughts. She imagined the many ways that Donnie could have died, and in every scenario, she was responsible. She wanted to cry; tears might have slowed down the mania.

Her heart raced, her pulse echoed in her ear when she rested her head on the pillow. When she lay on her back the same pulse seemed to beat away inside her head.

The buzzer sounded, sending her heart racing. Then, suddenly fearing the caller would go away she threw herself out of bed and raced down the hall. She pressed the buzzer to allow them in, before she even knew who they were. Only then did she pick up the receiver.

"Mum? Mum!"

All she heard down the line was the sound of the main doors closing. She kicked the wall with her bare foot. She checked that the front door was locked and that the bolt was drawn. She pressed her face against the spy hole and waited in the dark with her arms wrapped around her.

She had at least hoped that her mum would stagger in and put her out of her misery, let her embrace the new anger, sorrow, or outrage. Though it terrified her witless, she needed to know. She again pressed her eye against the spy hole, she could hear the lift humming on its way up. Her nervous breathing so loud she thought it must be audible from the other side of the door. She took her face away and filled her stiffened, sorry lungs. When she looked back, she saw Jamie take a step back from the door, seeming to fear whatever lay behind it, whatever might come out and get him. He looked from side to side, while shifting fearfully on the spot. Fearing he would run away, she threw the door open with a force that made Jamie take another step back.

She looked sweet and bleary peering at him from the dark, dishevelled in an over-sized t-shirt.

He froze, open mouthed.

"What are you frightened of?" Blithe demanded.

She didn't mean it to come out that way. She wasn't angry

with him, nor disgusted by his obvious nervousness. She wanted to take it back, but suddenly she couldn't form any words. He came towards her, craning his face to her level to better read her. As he came forward, she grabbed him.

He'd been anticipating trouble and was taken by surprise. He looked down at her head, buried in his chest, could feel her arms tightly around him and the raw emotion that needed to break. He put his arms around her and stepped into the dark corridor, letting the light extinguish as the door closed.

In the darkness he held her properly, first running a hand through her long dark hair until it snagged on a knot. His eyes began to adjust to the light from the fire alarm, and he pulled away to look at her face.

"Oh God. Are you alright?"

She tried again to find some words, but nothing came. She burst into sobs.

He pulled her again towards him, his arms crossed over her back.

She could faintly hear through her sobs, the gentle whistling as he shooshed her.

At some point, when Blithe felt that she had been cradled for too long, she began to twist free. He let her go but reached for her hand. She let his grip slip away. Standing alone, no one touching her, she gasped for air and pushed her hair back from her sticky face.

She flicked the light on and shielded her face from the brightness.

In a voice soft and slow, he asked.

"Blithe. What's happened? Blithe. What's wrong?"

She squinted at him. His eyes so wide, his eyebrows, usually curved like questions marks, now formed a furrowed brow.

She walked into the living room and put on a side light by the window. Blithe sat in the middle of the sofa with her hands squeezed tightly between her knees. Jamie slowly followed her through. He did not sit on the sofa beside her, but pushed aside pens and old letters to make a space opposite her on the coffee table. The table was sticky and creaked when he sat on it.

She took a deep breath.

"I... I dinnae ken what's happened."

She drew her hands from the clamp of her knees. Jamie leaned forward and gently held her hands between his own.

"Yer brother?"

Tears still running, Blithe nodded.

"What's he done?"

"Nothing. It's what I've done."

"What have you done?"

Blithe glanced up. He was complicit in this, in a way.

"My mum's no been back. I've been on my own. She's at the hospital but she willnae tell me why. It's something awful."

"How do you know that?"

"I ken ma mum. I was asking her and asking her. I was fucking begging her! She kens, but she ignores me."

"Well, maybe he needs her to help him at the moment. If he's sick, she probably trying to help, maybe help feed him or something. In hospital, it could be anything."

Blithe took a faltering breath.

"Why would she no tell me? If he was sick, she'd tell me. If he were arrested at the hospital, she'd tell me...'

Jamie stroked her forehead.

"But you don't know who's listening."

Blithe reclaimed her hands.

"She kens how to send a text!"

Jamie hung his head for a while.

"Have you had something to eat? You can't think straight if you've not been eating."

"Not much, but that's got nothing to do with it."

Jamie rose and went into the kitchen. Blithe made her way to the bathroom to blow her nose.

This time when she looked in the mirror, a transformation had taken place. Her red eyes sunk in a blotchy mess.

She picked up her phone from her bedroom and noticed, as she walked back into the living room, the smell of toast. Of course. That was the only thing they had to eat. Walking past the kitchen doorway, she could see Jamie grimly inspecting the contents of an old tub of margarine.

Blithe lay again on the sofa, a thin pillow under her arms. Though she seemed settled, the dread remained in her dead stare. Jamie saw it when he set down her toast. He knelt down beside her and placed his palm against her face.

"Maybe he is in trouble," he said, "But maybe after this, it starts to get better. Maybe after this, he'll get some help."

Blithe gave a wry smile.

"You think wrong. Sorry. I ken yer trying to calm me down but he's not a rock star, he's not going to be in and out of rehab. No. In and waiting on the waiting list. Trust me, an assessment, and a very long fucking waiting list."

"You don't know that."

"Aye I do. Half the people in this city are on waiting lists. Look."

She handed her phone over so he could read the messages between her and her mum. She studied his face as he read them, he saw the evasion, and understood.

"Don't panic yet. Just wait. How long's he been gone?"

"Twenty-four hours, but that wouldnae worry me but, we had a fight before he left. I tried to have a fight with him after what he'd done to you."

She looked up and saw again the fading cut on his lip, the shadow that the bruise had become still visible on his face.

"I told him you'd called the police. I telt him that he was about to get lifted."

"Why!? I told you I wouldn't!"

"Tell me he's gotten away with it? I could not be friends with him, could not be pally pally with him after that. Did you expect me to just come back and tell him not to worry about it, say 'It's fine but next time, wear a fucking balaclava.'"

"No. You didnae have to say anything! He could just have waited – found out the long way."

Blithe shook her head. For a second, Jamie looked angry and muttered.

"Well, you're not enjoying it much!"

"I was angry! I was so fucking angry! How else did you expect me to feel?"

She sat up, glaring at him, demanding a reaction.

"I don't know...it wasn't that bad; I didn't break anything."

"That's not the point. I did not expect you to come, but you were the only one I could ask. You're probably the only one with a speck of faith in me. The thing about you... what I like about you, is that... you see the bits of me that I like...the things I like about myself. I embarrass myself...I think I hate...pretty much everyone. So, it's fair enough if folk hate me too...if the feeling is mutual. Then I talk to you, and I'm not embarrassed, apart from when I met your mum. I was shit then."

With the light from the old standard lamp, she could see she was making him blush.

She shook her head. "But I've got so many beefs..."

Jamie smiled, revealing that his teeth could still be neat, his grin still broad.

"I know," he said, "I've a lot more than a speck of faith. More like a..."

"A spoonful?" Blithe volunteered.

"A bag. A big bag."

Keeping her head down, Blithe nodded.

"Thanks."

Jamie could see that she didn't know where to look, or what

else to say. He laughed and sat up, pulling her into his arms, her head dropped bashfully to his shoulder. Blithe smiled a little as they lay back, stretched out flat across the sofa.

"I saw you through the peep hole," she said. "You looked like ye were shitting yerself."

"I was attacked a week ago by the guy that lives here."

Blithe sniffed. "I'll let you away with it."

"And I can't defend myself. I just curl up in a ball, fucking useless."

"Every hard man pretends." Blithe murmured.

"Aye but...you don't need me."

"No," she agreed, "I don't need you. If you hadnae come I'd be lying in my bed, waiting for my mum to come home, and feeling shitty. I didn't need you to walk me back and I'd still be here if you'd not, I widnae have thrown myself in the river. I liked ye doing it though. I wanted ye to. Do you need to be needed or want to be wanted?"

"Both."

Blithe lifted her head, her eyes still wet. She peered at him, trying to extricate the answer.

"Pick one."

"No." Jamie sounded a little hurt. "I disnae matter if you want me or need me. Disnae matter. I'm here."

Blithe narrowed her eyes.

"There's nothing wrong with needing someone" he said. "Do you think that's something to be ashamed of? If I was worried about my wee sister, if she was sick or in trouble, if I was as worried as you, I'd need someone round or to go somewhere. I'd not give a shit about being needy or not being needy."

"You'd be embarrassed if folk knew about us."

"No."

"You fucking would."

Jamie stroked her hair and she remained staring at him with a little flicker of rage.

"No."

"You'd be embarrassed and that's why you did fuck all but watch from across the road when that mad bitch attacked me."

"No. That's not why."

He was so measured that she couldn't maintain any anger. She just waited and said at last.

"I think you are. Embarrassed, ashamed, or whatever it is. Something like that."

Jamie shunted up the sofa to a sitting position.

"Seriously? You don't know?"

Blithe raised an eyebrow.

"My friend. You know what you did, and you know what you did to him... Look, I don't want to talk about this now, not when you're upset."

"But I do."

Her eyes glistened, but her stare demanded an answer so forcefully he had to look away, preparing to protest again that he did not want to have this conversation now. When he glanced back, still she stared him out and he knew he couldn't avoid it.

"He said he wanted to die."

"Doesnae mean he'd do it."

"You didnae get to know him, did you? He does not mess about with words like that. I don't know if he thinks he could do it, but he thinks about doing it. If it were me, I'd probably not mean it, because I'm more like the Boy who cried Wolf. It's the change in him, it's hard to explain unless you know him really well. I knew him on bad days, but I'd never seen him cry before and now he's on the verge a lot. I've been in a similar place after my leg cracked and I could be such a bastard to him, such a surly petulant bastard. He could have thought, being disabled does not entitle you to be a cunt..."

"But he's a fanny and thought it did."

Jamie sighed.

"He knew I'd recover and I know he'll recover; he's my friend and I love him."

Blithe smiled for the first time.

"You love him?"

"Well, I would never say that to him, unless I was completely minced. But I'm not ashamed of it. It's like ye can only say that you love a friend when they're dead, then it's fine. Say it when they're alive and it's weird."

Blithe rested her head against his chest.

"So what about me?"

Jamie didn't say anything. He rubbed her shoulders, as though she was cold.

"You don't know, do you?" she said.

"Well, what do you want me to do?"

"That's not fair." She whispered.

"I know. I'm sorry."

Jamie stood up. "I'll away and get yer duvet."

Jamie walked through to her room. He was still convinced, in spite of the messages, that everything would look better in the morning. Her mum would come home and explain what had happened and all that needed to happen, whatever stupid thing her brother had done and the consequences they faced. To cope, all she needed was to know what she was coping with. He could not conceive of an event that would sink her. Part of him chose not to try.

He walked into her room and took a pause. Not because the room was untidy, he looked around at all the familiar cheap trinkets. The laptop with the cracked screen on the floor by her bed. A thought crossed his mind that perhaps he was wrong to reassure her but what else could he say if he couldn't offer reassurance? So her mum is at the hospital and not answering, some wards don't allow phones. It was strange to torture her own daughter with silence but then she must be a strange woman.

Jamie staggered through with the duvet in his arms.

"You were a while," Blithe observed. "What were ye doing in ma bedroom?"

"Nothing."

Jamie stood over the sofa and cast the duvet into the air above her. It fell in a heap, he quickly flicked it up again from the edges he'd now located. It fell down around her evenly, perfectly.

She made a space for Jamie on the sofa beside her, three feet hung off the back of the arm rest, Jamie's other leg rested on the floor. Blithe curled up on top of him, her head against his chest.

Every so often, he craned to see her face and saw eyes still wide and anxious. So tense she reminded him of a frightened little mouse.

"You should close yer eyes. Your mum'll probably be back soon. Maybe tell her that I've an exam."

"She asked me to get someone round but she never asked me if I'd managed it. She doesnae care. You should probably go home though."

Jamie gave her another squeeze. "I'll leave when your mum gets back."

Jamie checked his phone and turned it onto silent.

"Trains run until midnight."

"Ye sure?"

"I think so."

He was uncertain. He ran his fingers through her hair, but he didn't get far before he was caught on a tangle. He inhaled the sweet smoky smell of her hair in slow deep breaths and gently began to stroke it. The tension he had felt in her shoulders melted and he saw that her face was becoming peaceful.

Lights from the city and moon glowed into the room and she looked so lovely. He felt the regular beat of her breath, warm against her chest and rested his head against hers. He couldn't leave, he didn't even try to move her. Instead, he kept his eyes on her, smoothing her delicate brow, blinking slowly when his eyes grew tired and heavy until it seemed that he would cry if he kept staring. He closed his eyes.

* * *

The key turned in the lock. Lynne pushed the door with her whole body, ensuring it didn't come into contact with the wall. The hallway was slightly illuminated by the side light glowing from the living room. Lynne slowly walked in, treading very carefully on her swollen feet.

She saw her daughter and someone else, framed face-to-face within the folds of the duvet. She saw the foot against the floor, his dark jeans, and trainers. She steadied herself in the doorway, against a sudden rush of cold blood to her head. No empty bottles, no junk food wrappers. Only a plate of toast, discarded on the coffee table.

She didn't want to wake Blithe, but she had to wake the boy and moved slowly towards him. She didn't need to touch him, when she brushed past the coffee table, a plate tipped against the plywood. He woke in stages, the first a gentle waking and then he tightened his grip around her daughter, as though she would fall. Then there was the jolt as he opened his eyes to the unfamiliar and the woman opposite him, with her finger raised to her lips.

He stared back at her in terror. Her sad face tried to smile, her finger remaining at her lips. He took in his surroundings yet again, bewildered, guilty and seeking an exit. He slowly slid from the sofa, trying with great tenderness to ensure that Blithe would not be disturbed, placing another pillow under her head. Standing up now she looked him up and down, taller than she expected from the rather feminine face she'd observed asleep. A bit of a ragamuffin, with his hair far over her eyes, but not so much so that she would not see the wide green eyes beneath, looking back at her, contrite.

Not wanting to wake Blithe, he said nothing. He hazily walked from the living room to the hall. Lynne knelt down by the sofa, unconvinced that her daughter was really so deeply asleep. She tucked the sheets around her. On straightening up she noticed an unfamiliar phone on the table, she picked it up and followed Jamie out. She noticed how he looked at her as he stumbled from the room, checking her again and again with fearful little glances, expecting her to breakdown at any moment. Closing the door to the living room, they stood in the hall by the front door while Jamie patted down his pockets.

She offered him the phone and whispered.

"Now. How are you getting home?"

"What time is it?"

"Gone two."

Not only did the fringe not quite conceal his eyes but she swore she saw the whites of them, he looked up at her in horror, his hand going to his mouth. He hoped that she was joking but his screen came back to life and confirmed it. 2.16am. Over twenty missed calls. He brushed his hair away from his face and stared at his phone, confirming the worst.

Seeing his face more clearly, he had quite a long face with a long nose and a small mouth, drawn in and drained. His skin was lightly freckled, like only a child's can be, which, in spite of his height, he was.

"Ring home. I'll no have ye walking at this time. I ken what yis r' like."

Jamie nodded and made to leave.

"No, stay here while ye call. I want to see that ye get picked up."

Jamie nodded and started to dial. He turned his back to her and walked further down the hall towards Donnie's bedroom. She could hear the squeal from the frightened mother from the other end of the phone and caught the words, "Where are you?" Then only a shrill squeak interrupting the boy as he pleaded. At first, he tried to be quiet but he couldn't be heard.

"I'm sorry, I'm sorry. I fell asleep, no I didn't. I didn't! I've not been drinking, no, not at all, I just fell asleep. I could just get a taxi... No, I'm sorry, I'm really sorry. Stop shouting."

Lynne could hear the despair in his voice.

"Their mum can hear you."

Lynne picked up a bit of post that still waited on the mat, tapped Jamie on the shoulder and pointed to the postcode.

"Do you want the postcode, how about I text it to you? I will! No, I told you, I've not been drinking. Do I sound like I've been drinking? I've not!"

Lynne heard and understood both perfectly. Understood his mother's panic, understood that he was genuinely sorry. It reminded her of her own son. How her own wee boy once pleaded with her that he would be good, really good, if only she would let him get what he wanted.

Once a wistful remembrance, one of the many things she had come to know about children, but now it came with unbearable pain. Unable to bear it any longer, she walked back towards him with her hand out to receive the phone.

The boy seemed to give up his phone in fear, slowly as his mum's voice rattled on unheard. Lynne gripped her keys and nodded the boy towards the front door. He went dutifully, Lynne following with the phone against her shoulder.

"Jamie? Jamie?"

"No, no. I'm Lynne."

Jamie pressed the button for the lift; it was already waiting on their floor.

"I've just come home and found him fast asleep on my sofa – no bottles, no cans. So don't you be too hard on him."

She glanced at Jamie; in the lift's harsh light his eyes seemed to have developed bags. His mother would not be calmed.

"He has an exam tomorrow morning! Did your son not know that? Look, I'm hopping in the car and heading over now, okay?"

Lynne didn't correct her; it would only have made it worse.

"No,' she replied. "I did not know that, but he's still done a good thing by coming all this way."

She imagined the woman down the other end of the phone pulling a face. As it was, all she could now hear was gathering up, and then a sound that may have been the slamming of a car door.

"Aye, he was not here to get pished but to help, you look after him, eh?"

There was no reply.

"You hear me?"

"What? Sorry... sure, I'll look after him, I'll not let him out of my sight after this..."

The doors of the lift opened and they made their way outside, Jamie walking ahead, glancing behind him, not daring to ask for his phone back but clearly alarmed at no longer being in possession of it.

"Okay, bye..."

"No! You be nice to him. Remember..."

But Suzannah had hung up. Lynne stood staring at the phone in her hand. Then she let the phone fall onto the concrete below. They were under the awning by the main entrance, where Blithe had lost her school shoe. Jamie watched as she fell painfully to her knees, letting her head fall so far forward it could easily have slammed against the ground. From her throat came a noise that seemed like a power surge burning through her, a terrible sound but as natural as birdsong. Finally, she threw back her head.

"Oh God!" she screamed. "What am I going to..." She took another gulp of air and another cry escaped her. She crumpled down again.

An angry voice rang out from above them. Jamie scanned the windows, as though that would help. Hope fell through him, like floors falling within a condemned building. He knelt down beside her. She was such a big woman and he was such a weak young man, that helping her rise smoothly should only be attempted if it could be done with dignity. She shook as she cried. He placed a hand on her back and felt the seismic tremors overpowering her body.

Jamie tried. "Can I get someone? Can I call a neighbour?"

But Lynne could not hear.

He took her hand, trying to get her to at least sit up straight. Her other clammy hand slapped at the grimy concrete. Now kneeling, she began to rock back and forth, from her knees to all fours, still trying to force herself forward. The arm he supported was steady, but the other shook so violently under her weight he expected it to snap. He made more of an effort to steer her to sitting up. It made no difference.

He tried instead to guide her to standing but he knew, even as he tried to support her, that it wouldn't work. He glanced up and saw a light on in Blithe's room.

"Blithe's awake. Look, Blithe's awake!"

Lynne's hand went to her mouth, she gasped, looked up and nodded towards the sky, through all of this she didn't look at him. He might as well have been a spirit.

Then she sat still, with her eyes closed. The tremor of her breathing was all he could hear. And then she dropped his hand and stood up by herself. She hid her face in her hands and walked blindly towards the door. Jamie tore ahead to hold it open. All the while she cried, he had nothing to say. He followed after her to call the lift. Only then, did Lynne look at him. As the doors opened, she put out her hand to stop him going any further.

"I'm going up to my daughter now. You stay inside here, till yer mum comes. You stay here till then, you stay inside till ye see her waiting, you promise me."

He nodded.

"Yer a good lad, I see that."

Shock had locked Jamie into restraint, but when he saw her face about to crumple, he had to look away. With a twist, his face craned down to his shoulder and he threw his arms around her.

"I'm so sorry...'

She stiffened and gave him a gentle pat on the back. She was glad that he was no longer trying to look after her. He was just a frightened boy.

"I'm going up to my daughter now."

He stepped back from the lift as the doors closed.

* * *

It was an easy drive for Suzannah. She was tempted to speed down the streets, through red lights. Nothing was waiting. She was so angry; angry with her son, angry with her husband for letting him go. She'd raised the alert on social media and nearly called the police. To then hear his voice sounding so distant and strange, before being snatched away by some drunken self-righteous woman.

He wasn't so old that she couldn't drag him out by the ear. So much had been done to support and encourage him, to do this now, this week of all weeks it had to be some kind of rebellion. It didn't matter if the drunk woman was there, she would drag him into the car and then the verbal arsenal would launch, the like of which he had never heard. Stephen had just accepted a call centre job that he did not want, in order to support the little bastard. Well, he would see his mother in the grip of a spectacular rage. She'd never smacked him or struck him but tonight might be the night.

Jamie sat on the step where he had first kissed Blithe, one hand pressed up against the side of his face. His phone lay beside him, the screen shattered from where Lynne had dropped it. He heard the screech of a car, the rumble as it rolled into the car park, the click of the handbrake and the slam of the car door. He wasn't frightened anymore.

He needed a tissue for his nose. He was now cold in short sleeves, boxed in by dingy tiles. He gave a heavy sigh and stood up. He got as far as the doors, but instead of leaving, he pressed his face against them. He hated leaving her, but still he walked through them. Having done so, he looked up and saw that the light remained on in her room. He could hear footsteps walking round the building. He doubted he had the strength to explain. He was frightened that Blithe was witnessing grief as he had seen and heard it. He turned back to face the door. His mum's anger was irrelevant to him now. He slowly turned his head at the sound of her footsteps.

Suzannah saw him lit up under the awning. His head against the door as though he had recently headbutted it, shaking his head in what seemed to be a drunken nuzzling. Suzannah marched towards him. He would be dragged, hauled in by one arm and an ear. She stopped suddenly, as though she didn't trust herself not to throttle him. He slowly turned to look at her. Even from ten yards away, his face glowed pale and his red eyes showed a shattered hurt that was too sober. An emotional exhaustion, devoid of theatrics and as old as the hills.

"Mum..."

He said her name as though he wanted her but remained still against the door.

"I'm sorry."

She walked slowly towards him but he turned again from her, resting his face once more against the door.

Suzannah spoke gently. "Mon now."

* * *

Blithe had seen her mum drop to her knees, watched and even heard until she turned from the window. She had no desire to rush down to her. The sight should have cut cruelly but she remained paralysed in her room, waiting for it all to begin.

She wanted to return to the window but couldn't move to do that either. She couldn't bring her brother's name into her mind, couldn't picture him, couldn't mourn him, or miss him.

When she tried, her stomach clenched, constrained, and coiled. It seemed to hold her breath back, refusing to let the truth penetrate. Not yet, not just yet.

She sat down on her bed and noticed a scrap of paper, placed deliberately on her pillow. It was torn and used from hanging around the place, but her name was written in large capital letters.

Her brother's hazy half-life was still in evidence all over the flat; his dirty razors, his smelly shoes behind the door, his old pirate DVDs, his shaving foam splattered on the bathroom mirror. It was not fair to leave so little and for it all to be so stale.

She wished she had loved him more but as Jamie had said, she was no angel, and an angel she would have to have been.

She turned the envelope over. Her eyes filled as she read the unfamiliar writing. The note had been written before the writer knew that the worst had indeed happened. Whatever power it might have had to comfort her, however sincere and kind, was insignificant now, like a paper fan to a burning man.

Her brother would reform from years of memories and in the end, he would not be that goblin lying on the carpet – he would be complete, without scars. Once again, she wished she had loved her brother more, loved him openly. She let out a sigh that nudged tears down her face. She dropped the envelope. She could hear the lift rising and she hurried to the door, where she would be waiting when the lift opened.

BLITHE

I didn't want to tell you this. If you wanted the same then I would have to tell Robbie. If you didn't then I would have to stop seeing you, so I said nothing. But I love you so much.

J

ABOUT THE AUTHOR

Jen Gale was born in Ayrshire and grew up in Stirling. She always wanted her writing to be free of agenda and possess a high level of realism.

Writing since primary school, Jen notes that she didn't write stories to receive praise. Presenting stories provided an opportunity to highlight shortcomings in spelling and grammar, therefore it was best hidden. A recurring theme in her work is disadvantage featuring strong dialogue and familiar characters who tend to slip beneath the radar.

She says, "In fiction, it's not possible to love a character simply for being beautiful. True to life, it is the subtleties, flaws and insecurities that make characters loveable. That message makes this book more important than ever. Young people have always needed the freedom to make mistakes. Cupid's a Psycho is about those mistakes, letting go of them and perhaps also understanding that some mistakes might be worth making."